Also available from Caitlin McKenna

No Such Luck
Super Natalie
Manifesting Mr. Right
My Big Fake Irish Life
Logging Off

COLORADO CHRISTMAS MAGIC

CAITLIN MCKENNA

carina press

ISBN-13: 978-1-335-42583-6

Colorado Christmas Magic

First published in 2021. This edition published in 2021.

This edition published by arrangement with Harlequin Books S.A.

For questions and comments about the quality of this book, please contact us at CustomerService@Harlequin.com.

Carina Press
22 Adelaide St. West, 40th Floor
Toronto, Ontario M5H 4E3, Canada
www.CarinaPress.com

Printed in U.S.A.

To Mom and Dad,
who always gave us a magical Christmas.

To Lynn,
who has carried on our great family traditions.

To Jay,
who keeps the laughter coming.

What I enjoy so much about Christmas is being surrounded by family and friends. The memories we make each holiday season help to sustain us in difficult times, which is why I wanted to share *Colorado Christmas Magic* with you. May this help to illuminate the magic in your own life that is always there—even during the difficult times.

COLORADO CHRISTMAS MAGIC

Chapter One

Hearing insistent meowing, Charley Dawson glanced up from her laptop to find her three-year-old cat perched on top of his treehouse, staring out the window of her one-bedroom apartment.

"What is it, Clarence?" She rose from the kitchen table to see what held his interest—the house directly across the street was lit up like a Christmas tree with big bright bulbs of red, blue, green, orange, and yellow. She ran her fingers through his short white fur and had him purring instantly. "I know you like the lights, bud, but we're not decorating this year. We're through with Christmas."

Clarence gave a short meow of disappointment before jumping down and running off, leaving Charley mesmerized by the lights. She used to love Christmas—how it ushered in that warm, comforting feeling of home where nothing seemed impossible. The Christmas season sprinkled happiness in the air, ordained love to reign supreme over everything, and made the world feel like it was a better place.

But for her, the magic of Christmas was gone. Over the past several years, the season only managed to bring her heartache. Last year's sorrow came from her then-fiancé, Hunter, who coldheartedly dumped her on Christmas

Eve. After he left her, she'd cried on the couch with Clarence, staring at her Christmas tree, believing no Christmas would ever be joyful again.

With a sigh, she turned away from the window, gathering her long blond hair into a ponytail, then slid into the chair in front of her computer. She took one last bite of the sweet and sour pork before pushing it aside. The cold Chinese takeout reminded her of her love life—every relationship started sweet but ended sour.

She couldn't believe she was twenty-nine and still single—not that being single was a bad thing—but she had envisioned herself as a happily married career woman by twenty-five and a new mom by thirty. She was nowhere near meeting her goals, and she couldn't understand how true love kept eluding her—especially at Christmas.

She frowned at the blank page on her computer screen. For an hour's worth of work, she'd only come up with the title of her next blog post: "The Truth About Christmas." Did her readers sincerely want to know? Her popular blog, *The Cold Hard Facts,* was a real hit with *Authentic Lifestyles* readers. She debunked myths, urban legends, and uncovered the accurate but sometimes unpleasant truths behind long-held beliefs and traditions. She also exposed too-good-to-be-true business opportunities, shameful vacation getaways, and other consumer scams. Because of this, her boss suggested she break tradition and write something nice about the happiest time of year.

Bah, humbug. For Charley, Christmas was the most miserable time of year. Without having anyone to share things with, what was the point? Holiday parties became obligations; cooking ended up being a chore. She'd have to spend too much time baking for people who didn't appreciate it, and endure too much shopping chaos to buy gifts no one really wanted. "The truth about Christmas? Skip it!"

Abandoning her blog, she got up to pour herself a glass of wine and moved her pity party to the couch. Turning on the TV, she searched for anything that didn't involve love or hopeless romantics or jovial couples enjoying Christmas together. Even the commercials needled her with actors appearing so darn cheerful. No, she was definitely done with Christmas *and* love, once and for all.

But when channel surfing brought her to *It's A Wonderful Life*, her favorite Christmas movie of all time, she was immediately sucked in. "Clarence!" she called, putting her feet up on the coffee table. "Your show's on."

Clarence appeared from behind the couch and jumped into Charley's lap, as if he sensed she needed some affection. She snuggled in with her beautiful white angel and found herself weeping not twenty minutes into the movie. Then when George Bailey bitterly wished he'd never been born, puffy-eyed Charley found herself making a different kind of wish—a last attempt before she gave up for good. She wished—and out loud, mind you—for her soulmate to come find her since she wasn't getting the job done herself. The second this heartfelt wish passed her lips, the electricity in her apartment cut out.

"Just perfect. Exactly what I need. Oh, I get it. Are you trying to tell me that another one of my wishes will never see the light of day?" She cast her eyes upward into the darkness, assuming the power would snap on at any moment. But it didn't. "I figured as much."

With a loud meow, Clarence jumped off her lap. The tiny bell on his collar jingled as he ran down the hallway toward her bedroom.

Wiping off her tear-streaked face with the bottom of

her sleeve, she rose and fumbled around in the dark, attempting to locate a flashlight. She finally managed to find one in the junk drawer right as the power popped back on and her favorite Christmas movie was playing once again.

As she started to close the drawer, she caught sight of an old photo strip buried under takeout menus. She and her high school sweetheart, Jack, had spent the day at the Santa Monica Pier, eating cotton candy, riding the Ferris wheel, and taking silly pictures of themselves in a photo booth.

With a bittersweet sigh, she caressed the strip of photos. How happy her sixteen-year-old self looked. Why hadn't she been able to find that kind of deep connection with anyone since Jack? *Because Love lost my address.* She shoved the photo strip back in the drawer and slammed it shut.

"Chocolate. I seriously need some chocolate." *Anything to get my mind off Jack.*

On the hunt, she scrounged around in the pantry, surprised she couldn't find one little morsel. She moved on to her handbag, her workbag, yes, even her gym bag. When she came up empty-handed, she checked the freezer for bits of chocolate in the form of ice cream, but to her dismay, she was cleaned out. She had no choice but to settle for the two complimentary fortune cookies she'd received with her takeout. She never cared for fortune cookies. The fortunes never applied to her and the cookies tasted dull and boring—much like her love life.

Charley snagged them off the kitchen table anyway, slumped on the couch, and popped opened the plastic wrapping on the first one. She snapped the cookie in half,

crumbling it everywhere, then yanked out the fortune.
YOU WILL REUNITE WITH THE ONE THAT GOT AWAY.

"Yeah, right." She crumpled it up, tossed it on the coffee table, then opened up the second cookie for a redo.
YOU WILL REUNITE WITH THE ONE THAT GOT AWAY.

She sat up straight. It was a little weird to get the exact same fortune in two different cookies, and even more strange to get them right after she found pictures of Jack. "Ridiculous."

Jack had stolen her heart from the moment he'd spoken to her only to trample it to dust a little over a year later. She had tried to forget about him, she really had, but couldn't. She often wondered what had happened to him. She'd attempted to find him on Facebook but eventually gave up. Jack hadn't cared much for social media when it became popular, so she suspected he'd never changed his viewpoint on the subject. That made her even more curious as to where he lived and how he was doing. Did he ever think of her, or was he happily married? Maybe he had a gorgeous girlfriend and they were one of those couples she had recently passed by on the street, so happy and jolly that Christmastime had finally arrived.

Stupid fortune cookies.

Irritated at herself for thinking about him, she took to her blog and told the world *exactly* what she thought of Christmas. She was so certain her writing on the subject was sheer perfection that she posted it without waiting to reread it when she was in a better frame of mind.

The following morning, while shoving down smashed avocado on toast before darting out the door for work, she wondered if her life would ever change. It felt like every time she moved forward, she ended up right back in the same place.

As she drove to work, she couldn't stop thinking about Jack. Even though they'd met in high school, their relationship ended up being more than just infatuation or young love. The spark between them had been incredibly honest and deep. They had shared so much with each other that she truly felt she'd found her soulmate. She hadn't been able to see herself with anyone other than Jack. *Why did his parents have to move him so far away?*

Charley pulled into an underground parking lot off Sunset Boulevard and discovered she'd forgotten to turn on her phone. As she headed into the lobby and straight into an elevator, her cell began blowing up. She smiled, feeling downright confident her readers were, at that very moment, agreeing wholeheartedly with her sentiments about Christmas.

Yet when she stepped off the elevator and opened the onslaught of messages, that wasn't the case at all. She remained glued to her cell screen, reading negative comment after negative comment. Heart pounding, she weaved her way through the hallways of *Authentic Lifestyles Magazine* without ever looking up.

"Miss Scrooge?" she uttered in shock, abruptly halting in place. She bristled as she kept reading, frozen to her phone.

Bright, peppy Olivia Lancaster came bounding up from behind Charley and glanced over her shoulder. "You bashed Christmas?" her best friend asked incredulously before she snatched the phone and scrolled through the barrage of insults left on the blog.

"I didn't bash Christmas, Liv. I merely suggested skipping it."

"You did more than that." Liv's eyes widened with every comment she devoured. "'Despicable,' says Devoted Fan, 'Unforgivable' comes from Fact Junky, and 'You've lost me forever,' cries Quirky Girl."

"That seems a little extreme." Charley plucked her phone out of Liv's tight grip. "I'm *not* going to apologize for telling it like it is."

"No, of course not," Liv said with a big snort of a laugh. "No one would ever accuse you of holding back."

"It's my job." Charley raised her chin. In truth, she actually *enjoyed* squashing people's over-joyous perceptions of long-held beliefs. (Wrong-held beliefs, according to her.)

"I'm just glad I get to write about fashion. Lunch later?" Liv asked, walking back down the corridor.

"Sure." Charley headed to her desk where she fired up her computer, anxious to defend her position to her readers. She took a determined breath, let it out, then pulled up her blog. The comments continued to pour in, an additional fifty-four in a matter of minutes. She skimmed through the newest ones, trying to find anyone who would agree with her. Finally, her eyes fell on:

I despised Christmas—

At last, a like-minded reader.

Until I fell in love.

"Bah, humbug." She slammed back in her chair.

"Here ya go!" An overly enthusiastic guy held out her morning mail, and she could only assume he was a new intern.

"Thanks." She rifled through a half dozen letters and stopped on a silver envelope embossed with gold script.

She took note of the return address. *1 Kringle Lane, St. Nicholas, Colorado.*

Intrigued, she opened it.

Dear Charlotte Dawson,
You're invited to spend a complimentary week at The Carroll Inn, a five-star bed-and-breakfast in St. Nicholas, Colorado: Home of the famous Scrooge Legend.

Scrunching up her face, she flipped over the letter, expecting to see additional information, but the back of it was blank. *Pretty expensive solicitation for a gimmick.* Without another thought, she crumpled up the paper and pitched it in the trash.

Now, where was I? She returned to her keyboard and began typing:

Dear Devoted Fan,
While I understand—

"Charley?" the familiar voice of her boss rang out. Paul was standing in the doorway of his office, twirling his glasses in his hand. "Can I see you for a moment?"

She rose and followed him. Paul was a cool boss. Being called into his office was usually a good thing. He advanced his employees faster than any editor in chief around. She'd already reaped the benefits from working for him. When she'd come to him as an intern, he noticed her hard work and promoted her to fact-checker only one month later. Then, when he learned how successful she was as a blogger, he allowed her to become a permanent guest blogger with the magazine. Hopefully, Paul's request to see her meant another promotion.

He waved her in. "Great initiative, Charley. Yes, you can go and investigate the legend. I'm sure you'll want to debunk it."

She gave him a puzzled look. "What exactly are we talking about?"

"The invitation you received to St. Nicholas, Colorado." Paul held up the crumpled letter she'd thrown away minutes earlier.

She widened her eyes in astonishment. "How did you get that?"

"Didn't you leave it on my desk?"

"No. I *just* threw it away. As in minutes ago."

"Doesn't matter." He rocked back in his chair. "The important thing is you're going."

"To Colorado?" Charley asked with more disdain in her voice than she'd intended. "In the dead of winter? People can actually die in the dead of winter. That's a cold hard fact."

"Here's another cold hard fact—you leave first thing tomorrow."

She refused to budge. Her level-headed boss obviously wasn't thinking clearly. "But, Paul, it's freezing there."

She had lived in Los Angeles her entire life, and rarely had she ever ventured into the land of snow and freezing temperatures.

He pushed out a loud sigh, crossing his arms on top of his desk. "Charley, your blog is a great moneymaker for our magazine. Separating fact from fiction has driven your readership and our subscriptions to an all-time high. But you might have crossed the line this time."

"My blog is titled *The Cold Hard Facts* for a reason."

Paul reached over piles of paper on his desk and snagged a printed version of her latest post. He cleared his throat before reading it aloud. "'Face it. The holidays are a chore—the decorating, the shopping, the never-ending line at the post office, not to mention the hours of cooking, baking, and cleaning. Why torture yourself? No time to make Christmas cookies? That's what store-bought is for. Tired of spending hours wrapping presents? Send an eGift card instead. No time to trim a tree? Do yourself a favor and just skip Christmas altogether. It's not worth the hassle.'" He tossed the printout back on his desk and eyed Charley over the rims of his reading glasses. "You keep writing like this and you can rename your blog *The Cold Heartless Facts*."

She ran her hands over the arms of the chair, trying to feel justified for her comments even though, deep down, she knew she'd been off the mark. "I'm doing everyone a favor. I'm only voicing what everyone's thinking."

"Is that so? Then why does this *one* post of yours have more negative comments than all of your previous posts combined? Care to explain, *Miss Scrooge*?"

Shoot. He had seen the comment, the very comment that still gnawed at her. "Fine." She let out a defeated sigh. "I'll go." If she could debunk a legend *and* put the screws to Christmas, then subjecting herself to miserably cold temperatures would be well worth it.

"That's the *spirit*." Paul had a playful smirk on his face, so she knew the pun was intended.

"You know, the legend has to be a hoax because I've never heard of it."

He took off his reading glasses and leveled his gaze on her. "I thought that's why you put the letter on my desk."

"I didn't put—" She stopped herself. How the letter

got to his desk was truly a mystery, but one she'd have to tackle later. "Have *you* ever heard anything about this famous Scrooge Legend?"

Paul put his glasses back on and pulled up the town's website. "It's right here. 'Welcome to St. Nicholas, Colorado, home of the famous Scrooge Legend, where any Scrooge who enters the town will end up loving Christmas as much as Santa.'"

Charley exploded with a laugh. "Ridiculous."

Paul arched a brow. "Prove it."

Chapter Two

In downtown Denver, Detective Jack Brody sat at his desk in front of his computer, staring at a twenty-year-old photo of his uncle Bill. The man looked very similar to how Jack looked now—a solid build, thick dark hair, and sharp blue-gray eyes. The picture had been taken when Bill Brody was thirty-five, right before he disappeared without a trace.

Jack, an only child, had been extremely close to his uncle. He had just turned ten at the time of his uncle's disappearance. Back then, his parents clocked long hours at the office. Since his uncle worked in construction, he was able to pick Jack up from school and look after him until his parents got off work. They often passed the time by building model trains together or carving sailboats out of wood. His uncle had become like a big brother. When he vanished that Christmas Eve, it had devastated Jack.

The authorities had presumed Bill Brody dead, but Jack did not. He knew his uncle was out there somewhere, but when he was a kid, he couldn't get anyone to listen to him. After college, he sought out a career in law enforcement. Now he was a police detective with all the state-of-the art investigative tools at his fingertips, and yet he still couldn't find him. Uncle Bill was alive. Jack felt it in his bones; he knew it in his heart, and one day he would find him.

Jack's fingers flew over the keyboard, then hit Enter. He leaned back in his chair, waiting for his uncle's image to go through a twenty-year age progression. When the new photo emerged, he stared at the aged image as if he were burning it into his brain. "Where are you, Uncle Bill?" Would he ever get a solid lead on his whereabouts? "Please, help me find you." He hit Print and while he waited for the printer to spit out a copy of the aged photo, he noticed that none of the other detectives were in the bullpen. He rose to see what was going on.

Walter, one of the older detectives, called to him from the doorway. "Hey, Jack, can you help me with that darn coffeemaker? I'm at my wits' end."

Walter might have been pushing past retirement age, but the man knew how to work every coffeemaker known to man. Why would he be asking for help? And then it dawned on him.

"Sure." Jack suppressed a smile. "I'll be right there."

He seized his empty coffee cup and proceeded toward the break room, where Walter abruptly darted inside. Carla, a vice detective, was peering out the break room window, obviously the designated lookout. Jack pretended not to see her, and when he got a little closer, she sounded the alarm. The lights flicked off and he had to squelch a laugh as he listened to ten of Denver's finest trying to hide while being quiet. *They'll never make the SWAT team with their lack of stealth.*

Jack walked in, feigned confusion that the lights were off, then acted surprised as everyone popped up from underneath the tables and yelled, "Happy Birthday!"

He cracked a smile, shaking his head. "I don't believe you guys."

Carla stepped forward, holding a cake in the shape of a police badge. The top was ablaze with thirty lit candles. "Happy thirtieth, Jack. Make a wish and make it count."

"Hmm." He rubbed his hand over his chin. "Let's see."

"Need some help there, buddy?" Adam brought over paper plates and plastic forks. "Wish for a raise, and make it for the entire department!"

Everyone cheered. Jack loved having Adam as his partner. Whenever he started taking life too seriously, he could count on him to liven things up.

"Forget these guys." Carla waved them off. "Make it a good one. From the heart."

The rest of the detectives ridiculed her "from the heart" comment, but Jack took her advice. Thinking about his uncle and praying he'd find him someday soon, he closed his eyes and blew out the candles.

"Now *that* was a real wish," she whispered to him as a round of cheers broke out in the room.

"Cut him a real big piece," Adam instructed. "He's making the rest of us look bad with that gladiator body of his." He laughed like a chipmunk, patting his growing belly.

Captain Wollin maneuvered around Adam, staying out of the limelight. "Happy birthday, Detective Brody."

"Thank you, sir."

Carla handed the first piece to Jack before she offered a slice to Captain Wollin.

"I better pass if I want to get into my tuxedo next month."

"Fair enough," Carla said and gave the slice to Adam.

Wollin threw out his stale morning coffee, then refilled his mug with fresh brew. "So, Jack, are you still itching to get out of Denver for a few days?"

He nodded, swallowing a bite of cake. "I already put in for a week off at Christmas."

"What about working out of town right now?" he asked, taking a cautious sip of the hot coffee. "I've got something that needs looking into."

"Oh, yeah?" Jack set down the cake, his interest piqued.

"You remember Tony Braca?"

"How can I forget The Leech?"

"Well, it seems Tony managed to get himself a free vacation—one week in this town up in the mountains called St. Nicholas. You ever heard of it?"

He pondered the name. "That's the town that celebrates Christmas all year round. Don't tell me Braca traveled up there and swindled a bunch of nice folks out of their money."

"Not that I know of, but I suspect something else is going on there." Wollin looked around, then lowered his voice. "When Braca came back…well, he's not the same guy."

Jack pushed his brows together. "What do you mean?"

Wollin scratched the back of his head, then set his gaze directly on Jack. "Mr. Leech is now Mr. Boy Scout."

"You sure you're talking about the right Tony?"

"Yeah. Get this, he's now volunteering at a *church*, and he's holding down two jobs to make good on his debts. He's even back with his wife."

Jack blew out a breath, remembering the violent fights Tony and his wife used to have. "That's hard to believe."

"When I first heard about his attitude adjustment, I didn't believe it, either." The captain paused, seeming to consider his words. “But now the same thing has happened to my own brother.”

“You mean he got a free week or that he came back a changed man?”

“Both. When he came home after a free week at some B&B up there, I almost didn’t recognize him.”

Jack eyed the captain with concern. “How so?”

“Luke used to be angry all the time and pessimistic about everything. Now he’s Mr. Sunshine.”

“And that’s a bad thing?”

“No, but what concerns me is that Luke came into some money, and then boom, he gets invited to a town that instantly changes his way of thinking?” Wollin shook his head. “Something shady is going on there—a cult or a con game. I don’t know. Seems too good to be true.”

The captain never jumped to conclusions, and it bothered Jack to see how worried he was. “You want me to check it out quietly since we don’t have jurisdiction up there?”

“I’d really appreciate it if you could.”

“Yeah, no problem. I closed a case this morning, so I can go as soon as you say the word.”

“Thanks, Jack.” Relief washed over Wollin’s features. “I’ll get you set up at the same B&B where my brother stayed. That might be a good place to start. If anything feels off, even a little, I want you to remain in St. Nicholas and take all the time you need.”

“Will do, Cap. I’ll get to the bottom of whatever is going on there.”

Chapter Three

Joe Carroll teetered into the kitchen with an armload of firewood, shutting the back door with his foot. His wife, Mary, was humming along to "Good King Wenceslas" playing on her iPad while she decorated another batch of sugar cookies for their bed-and-breakfast guests.

Joe sniffed the air. "Something smells good." After passing through the kitchen to drop off the wood in the living room, he returned, looking for any handouts his wife would allow him.

"You may have *one*," she said. "The rest are for our guests."

He eyed all the cookies cooling on the rack and his mouth began to water. Even though he was nearly sixty, stepping foot in Mary's kitchen made him feel like a kid again and, like a kid, he chose the biggest cookie of all—a sugar cookie in the shape of a fat snowman.

He bit into it, savoring the familiar buttery, sugary taste that always brought on good memories of every Christmas past. His wife's sugar cookies were superior to all others because she added nutmeg and vanilla to her recipe. "Mmm. I think you've outdone yourself this time."

She bubbled with a small laugh. "Oh, Joe, you say that every day."

"And every day I'm right." He gave his wife of thirty-five years a quick kiss before he shoved half of the cookie into his mouth.

"For that, you can have two." Without hesitation, he reached for another before she changed her mind.

"Any details on our special guest?" he asked around a mouthful of snowman cookie.

"Our boss is sending us a young woman who has lost the Christmas spirit because she's given up on love. Her name is Charley Dawson and you can read all about her." Mary motioned to an ornate silver-and-gold metallic tube sitting at the end of the counter.

He popped off the end of the tube and dumped out a small ivory scroll. Uncurling it, he started reading as he reflexively reached for a third cookie. He bit into it, then let out a short chuckle. "Miss Scrooge. Her nickname is Miss Scrooge! When's she due to arrive?"

"Tomorrow, but we've got other guests coming in tonight."

Joe grabbed the milk out of the refrigerator and poured himself a small glass. "Guess I better get to fixing that towel bar in room two and the shower leak in six."

"*Or* you could call Mike and have him do the fixing," she suggested with a raise of her brow.

"Are you saying I'm not a good handyman?"

"I'm saying Mike is the professional." Her mouth twitched with amusement.

"I can fix both with my eyes closed. You'll see."

"Uh-huh." Mary turned her back on him to slide another tray of cookie dough into the oven, and he took that as an opportunity to steal another one from the cooling rack.

"Well, I better get crackin'," he announced, thinking he got away with it.

"I saw that." Mary pressed her lips together, holding back a smile.

Joe offered a sheepish grin. "I guess women really do have eyes in the back of their head."

His wife's eyes twinkled. "Yes, we do."

Jack sat opposite the woman he'd been dating for the past few months and wondered why they were fighting so much. Lisa was a friend of a friend he'd met at a football game, and his first impression of her had been that she was smart, pretty, and very outgoing. She was so outgoing that she'd been the one to ask him out.

At first, he hadn't bit. There was something about her he couldn't put his finger on—something that wouldn't work long term. His friend Owen complained that it was his jaded detective sense getting in the way of a possibly great relationship. Owen not only pointed out how pretty Lisa was, but that her bubbly, friendly, assertive manner meant she'd pick up the slack at social functions when Jack didn't feel like making small talk with complete strangers. Jack knew Owen was right, so when Lisa suggested coffee for the third time, he finally took her up on it.

To his surprise, their first few dates were great. They laughed a lot, discovered local bands together, tried new restaurants. But he frequently got called into work, which ruined some of Lisa's plans. She'd take it so personally that he'd feel obligated to make it up to her. Being guilted into buying her flowers or some small gift for every missed date had sent the wrong message. She thought he was much more serious about their relationship than he'd intended.

"I don't understand why I can't go with you," Lisa argued, "especially if you're going to a romantic B&B."

"I have no idea if it's romantic or not," he said. "I'm staying there to do an investigation. More than likely it's a run-down home off the interstate that's calling itself a B&B." He took a swallow of his wine, certain the image he painted for her would end their present topic of conversation.

Lisa pushed the vegetables around on her plate, then set her gaze back on him with renewed vigor. "But it's your birthday. You wouldn't let me throw you a big party, so let's celebrate it with a week away."

He released a weary sigh, realizing just how little she knew him. The only reason he had agreed to dinner at a stuffy suit-and-tie restaurant was so she would promise not to cram his condo with a bunch of people he barely knew. "You know I'm not big on celebrating my birthday, and even if I were, this investigation isn't a vacation. The department's paying for my stay, which means I'm not allowed to bring guests."

"So don't tell them." She shrugged. "I know you have to work, and I'm fine with that. I just want to see more of you, Jack. Not less."

He wished he felt the same way, but the divide between them was getting to be too great. She loved being the center of attention, going to parties, living on social media, and he did not. He was methodical and cautious while she was uninhibited and spontaneous. She wanted to be on the go all the time, while he preferred to take a night off, stay home and relax. Truth be told, he was surprised she hadn't dumped him already.

"I'm sorry I can't take you." He reached for her hand. "But there's nothing I can do." Only there was something he could do. He could do them both a favor and call it quits.

"Okay," she finally said with a constrained smile, brushing off her disappointment. "But when you get back, I think we need to have a serious talk about our relationship."

"Aren't we having a serious talk?"

"Hardly." She laughed. "We're having a talk that's serious, not a serious talk."

Jack worked in fraud and financial crimes. As a detective, it was his job to get inside a scam artist's head to figure out his or her motivation. When he first began dating Lisa, he'd been intrigued by her thought process. She knew how to get someone to agree to something without them knowing it. She knew how to put someone on the defensive. She knew how to phrase questions to corner someone a heck of a lot better than he did. Now, nearly three months later, he was exhausted by it.

"Besides, I don't want to ruin your birthday," she added.

"You won't." Every year, he'd start off his birthday by updating his missing uncle's photo, so there wasn't anything she could say or do that would make his day worse.

She sat back and eyed Jack. "I feel like our relationship has…stalled, and we need to address that."

Finally, they were on the same page. "I couldn't agree more."

"You do?" She gave him a surprised look. "You think we should move on?"

He nodded. "I want you to be happy."

"Oh, Jack." She leaned forward, smiling, almost giddy with excitement. "I can't believe this is happening. If we had moved on a month ago, we could have avoided weeks of disagreements." She beamed a bright smile. "I don't want to ruin anything you have planned for the big ring reveal, but I only ask that you invite—"

"Wait a minute." He put his hand up. "What are you talking about?"

"Getting engaged," she said as if it was obvious. "Moving our relationship on to the next level."

Jack's eyes popped wide. "What?"

"Isn't that what you were talking about?"

"No. Not even close."

She let out an exasperated sigh. "Jack, if your car stalls, you give it your full attention. You put everything you've got into it, and when it starts up again, you drive down the road together, happily ever after."

"Or you push it to the side of the street because it's completely dead."

Confusion filtered through her eyes, followed by an understanding of the misinterpretation. "Oh. I see." She slumped back in her chair. "For the record, I interpret the phrase *moving on* as moving on together because, after all, we're still together. If we were broken up, then it would mean moving on separately as in, 'Yeah, we broke up, but I'm not ready to move on.' Got it?"

"Noted." How did they not have the same vocabulary? He was five years her senior but sometimes it felt like fifteen.

"Moving on." She intently focused on him. "Are you saying you don't want to get married now?"

"Correct. We've only been dating for a few months.

I don't see how marriage could be considered the next level."

"What else would it be? You know I'm against living together."

"Actually, I didn't know that because we've never discussed it."

"It's on my Facebook page. *Everybody* knows that."

Jack closed his eyes and took a deep breath. He'd never understand why so many chose to post intimate details about themselves on a worldwide bulletin board.

"I'm sensing you're not ready to move on to the next level," she voiced with disappointment.

"I'm sorry."

She looked dejected, and after a long moment of silence she said, "It's not ideal, but I can wait. How long do you think you'll need?"

Jack frowned. Their miscommunication was far more serious than he realized. "Lisa." He sighed, shaking his head. "We're so different on just about every level."

"Which is a good thing. It wouldn't be a saying if it weren't true. Opposites attract."

"Until they realize they're completely wrong for each other."

"You honestly think that?" Her voice climbed an octave higher as her mouth set in a grim line. "I thought we were good together. I had no idea you've been so miserable with me all these months."

Less than three months, he wanted to correct. "I never said I was miserable."

"I would certainly hope not." She crossed her arms and stared out the window for several moments of uncomfortable silence. "I suggest we take things slow so we can figure it out." But when he didn't answer, her chin began to quiver. “You do want to get married *eventually*, don’t you?”

He couldn’t give her the it’s-not-you-it’s-me speech, even though it was the truth. “I’m nowhere near thinking about marriage.”

“So…what? That’s it?” Her big brown eyes welled with tears.

Why did she have to cry? She made him feel like he was a callous, heartless jerk. He wasn’t and he didn’t want to be thought of in that way, even by a soon-to-be ex-girlfriend. “I’m not trying to upset you. We’re just too different. You need to be with someone who loves adventure and your friends and hanging out on social media. I’m not that guy.”

She dabbed at the corners of her eyes with her napkin. “You don’t have to be.”

“But you want me to be, and that’s the problem. I just don’t see us compatible enough to make it work.”

“You don’t give yourself enough credit. I think all you need to—” Lisa’s phone buzzed. She glared at it and frowned. “It’s my boss. I have to take this.” She walked outside with her call.

He’d never had a girlfriend argue against a breakup. Maybe she *could* make his birthday worse after all.

Chapter Four

Early Tuesday morning, Charley dropped Clarence off at Liv's, then dragged herself to LAX. She normally couldn't live without checking her phone every five seconds, but after reading the steady stream of negative comments regarding her Christmas post, she welcomed the two-hour, no-phone flight to Denver. At least she'd managed to post a quick follow-up on her blog before she left. She explained to her readers that perhaps she'd been a little hasty in suggesting such a dramatic move as to skip Christmas, and in honor of her devoted fans, she was on her way to St. Nicholas, Colorado, where she hoped to find the Christmas spirit. She actually hoped to kill the Christmas spirit by debunking the Scrooge Legend, but she decided to keep that little bit of information to herself.

Once Charley arrived in Denver, an affable man in his late forties greeted her at baggage claim.

"Welcome, Ms. Dawson. I'm Fred, and I'll be your driver today." Fred had a genuine smile and his silver-tipped hair stuck out from under a wool cap.

"Nice to meet you, Fred." She gestured to carousel five. "I think that's where we'll find my bags."

He snagged a luggage cart and closely followed after

her. "Are you planning on skiing or doing a little snow-boarding while you're here?"

"Not this time." *Or ever, if I can help it.*

"That's too bad." He frowned. "We have the best resorts around."

"I imagine you do." She pleasantly smiled, knowing she'd never step foot in one.

"I see you came from Los Angeles. How do you like living out there?"

"I love it. I just left seventy-degree weather." She sighed.

"That hot, huh?" Fred let out a slow whistle. "I bet it's hard to get into the Christmas season when it's beach weather."

That's why I love it, she wanted to say. "We make the best of it," she replied, and he nodded sympathetically.

"Oh, that one's mine." Charley pointed to a cluster of black bags. "With the red and green ribbons attached to the handle."

Fred grabbed it before the bag traveled around again. "Smart to put ribbon on your luggage for easy identification." He touched the Christmas-themed ribbon. "I see you're getting into the Christmas spirit."

"I am," she fibbed. She had plenty of ribbon on hand because eGift cards never required wrapping. "There's the last bag." She motioned to a black garment bag flying her decorative ribbons.

He plucked it from the carousel and placed it on the cart. "Good to go, Ms. Dawson?"

"Lead the way."

She immediately regretted coming to Colorado when she stepped out the airport doors and was hit with freezing temperatures. "Oh!" She threw on the parka she'd bought the night before and zipped it up to her ears. She wrapped a scarf around her throat and was in the process of slipping on her gloves when Fred stopped in front of a red SUV and popped the trunk.

"Here we are." He opened the back door to let her in before loading her luggage. "There's water in the cup holders and snacks back there as well. Help yourself."

She got settled in and promptly turned on her phone. It pinged so many times with all the incoming messages that it sounded like an old-fashioned pinball machine. She hastily scanned the comments, relieved to see that her Christmas post addendum had smoothed at least some of her readers' ruffled feathers. The first dozen comments were good-hearted and sweet in nature, but as she continued to read, she came across a lot of snarky ones. One woman wrote that Charley shouldn't return until she found the Christmas spirit. Another said she hoped her time away would put her in a better mood.

Don't hold your breath.

Fred opened the door and climbed into the driver's seat. He buckled up, then glanced at Charley in the rearview mirror. "Got everything you need?"

A ticket to Tahiti would be good. "Yes, thank you." She flicked him a glance before immersing herself in her blog. She couldn't leave it in its present condition.

"We have a two-hour drive to St. Nicholas, but the scenery is a must-see."

"Great," she halfheartedly mumbled, already diving into work.

After Jack spent a few hours online researching St. Nicholas, his gut told him Captain Wollin was making too much of his brother's new outlook on life. The town was a tourist destination that promoted the Christmas spirit all year long. Their very livelihood depended on folks having a great experience. Luke's cheery disposition was probably nothing more than the result of a relaxing vacation.

Jack grabbed his jacket, then did a quick check around his condo before heading out the door. He had mixed feelings about going to St. Nicholas. He wanted to get out of town now that he had broken up with Lisa, but going to a place that was nothing but Christmas would only remind him of his uncle. After all the years that had passed, it still pained him to enjoy the season without him.

As he threw his bag into the back of his SUV, his cell rang. "Hey, Cap. What's up?"

"Got a call from the B&B," he said. "Someone double-booked your room, but I managed to get you into the one where Tony Braca stayed."

"Two different B&Bs are giving away free nights?" Jack's voice raised in surprise.

"Looks that way. I didn't realize that until I talked to Braca's wife last night. The scam appears bigger than I suspected."

Jack eyed his one bag, wondering if a week's worth of clothing would be enough. "No problem. I'll check them all out if I have to. Text me the new address, and I'll keep you posted."

Jack disconnected, now second-guessing his initial feeling about St. Nicholas. How could small-town B&Bs afford to be giving away free weeks to anyone? He could understand hotels doing it by targeting people as potential timeshare holders, but these were independently owned and operated B&Bs. And why would they want to give a free week to the likes of Luke and Braca? He was missing something.

Jack hopped in his SUV and got on the road. Not five

minutes later, his cell rang again. When he saw that it was Lisa, he ignored it. Their breakup had taken three hours last night. He'd never experienced anything like it. She spent most of the time telling him how great a guy he was, followed by her opinion on how opposites work better long term than those who are similar. Not convinced, he was finally able to end it by promising to remain friends, but he was already regretting that decision. After two more rings, she hung up.

He settled back, cracked open a bottled water, and took a swig. He never imagined turning thirty would make him feel so unsatisfied with his life. Worse, it felt empty. No girlfriend, no cat, no dog. Not even a fish in a bowl. Would he be one of those guys who remained single because he never fell in love?

That wasn't entirely true. He'd fallen in love once, way back in high school. Now, years later, he hadn't experienced anything close to what he had shared with Charley, and he didn't know why. He'd had years to figure it out and failed. He couldn't even pretend to enjoy being in a relationship, as evidenced by ending yet another one.

He felt bad about hurting Lisa and wondered if his buried feelings for Charley had affected him more than he realized. He hadn't meant to, but he'd given Lisa mixed signals, so every time he pushed her away, she'd try harder. He should have broken up with her a month ago when he knew it wasn't going to work. Did this mean that no relationship was ever going to work because he couldn't let go of screwing up the only love relationship that had meaning? How he wished for a redo with Charley, but too much time had passed for that to ever be a reality.

Chapter Five

During the long drive to St. Nicholas, Charley hadn't taken in the scenic view once. She was so annoyed by all the harsh comments left on her blog, she felt she needed to explain her position, her *correct* position, addressing each and every one of them. Only when the car began to slow had she finally afforded a glance out the window.

Fred was turning off the main highway and onto a heavily forested winding road. Thinking she was getting close to her final destination, she set her phone aside. She needed to pay attention to the town she'd be investigating. Being from Los Angeles, she knew a thing or two about the movie industry and its movie magic. It wouldn't be the first time she discovered that a legend was a manufactured hoax.

Fred drove past a road sign that read:

WELCOME TO ST. NICHOLAS
BELIEVERS: 12,123

Charley laughed.

He glanced at her in the rearview mirror. "First time to St. Nicholas?"

"And last," she said with conviction, catching his eye. "I'm not a fan of cold weather."

"Well, this place will keep you warm, mark my words."

Fred put his focus back on the road, and Charley's thoughts wandered on to the Scrooge Legend. When and how had it begun, and why was it named after Ebenezer Scrooge? She hadn't been able to find much about the legend's origins online, which was fine. The most reliable information would come from the town of St. Nicholas itself. She'd start by conducting interviews with the townspeople. She'd also go to their historical society or library to comb through any articles related to the legend, and then she'd draw the line between fact and fiction for her readers—facts always winning—and the ridiculous Scrooge Legend would be debunked.

It seemed like a fairly easy, straightforward job—especially when the legend's assertion happened to be a wild one. To claim that any Scrooge entering the town would have a change of heart was truly laughable. Most likely the townspeople put on a good show for strangers in order to keep the money flowing in. It was a jaded theory, but it was the most realistic.

Charley studied Fred through the rearview mirror. He came across as a jovial, carefree man, the type who would know a thing or two about the legend. "I take it you've been to St. Nicholas a few times."

"I bring people here all year round. It's a popular destination."

"Have you heard about their Scrooge Legend?"

"Oh, sure." He nodded. "Who hasn't?"

"Any truth to it?"

"All truth. That's why it's legendary."

She squelched a laugh and averted her gaze out the window. She couldn't wait to debunk it.

Fred slowly turned onto Main Street, and Charley, slack-jawed, could only stare in astonishment. Before her lay a winter wonderland of beauty. Blanketing the entire town was a layer of freshly fallen snow sparkling like tiny diamonds in the late afternoon sun. Quaint decorated storefronts lined equally festive streets. Wreaths, garland, and silver bells hung from every door, awning, and lamppost. There was a huge town square with meandering paths, park benches, stunning snow-covered pines, and in the center of the square stood a breathtaking sixty-foot Christmas tree.

"Wow. It's like a picture postcard."

"Yes, it is," Fred said with satisfaction.

She remained glued to the window, unable to peel her eyes away. Everywhere she looked, there appeared to be such a strong sense of family. She felt like they had driven into a nostalgic Christmas card or a Norman Rockwell painting. A little girl on her daddy's shoulders hung a Christmas ornament on the town tree. Farther down, three little kids lay on the ground, making snow angels, with their golden retriever wagging his tail and barking at them. Beside the kids, a family of four was building a lopsided snowman.

On the other side of the street, two women smiled and pointed at items on display in a shop window. College kids wearing University of Denver sweatshirts loaded ski equipment into their SUV. A middle-aged couple held hands while strolling down the sidewalk, and a group of friends laughed as they entered a tiny café.

Her gaze bounced from one side of the street to the other, and then back again. Teenagers were throwing snowballs by the clock tower. In the distance, a horse-drawn carriage was going over a snow-covered bridge, and below that were ice skaters on a frozen pond.

"This is so beautiful," she said, her voice breathy, taking in all the cute stores, the inviting cafés and not one chain or brand name among them. She saw more smiles and greetings in a minute than she'd seen in a month back home. No one was on a phone or seemed to be in a hurry. No car honked, nobody yelled, nothing intruded on the peace that imbued St. Nicholas. The town was so charming and picturesque it didn't seem real.

At the end of Main Street, Fred turned right and drove over the little covered bridge. A bubble of delight rose inside Charley. On the pond below, a few of the ice skaters were wobbly and holding hands while others skated with grace and ease. A small hut situated near the pond had a line of people in front of it. A sign above the door read Hot Cocoa.

Once over the bridge, Fred drove her through a heavily wooded residential neighborhood where every house and every yard displayed massive amounts of Christmas decorations. Charley couldn't wait to see it all lit up at night.

Two more turns, and Fred pulled the car up to a beautiful two-story home nestled in a circle of grand snow-covered pines. A Santa and his sleigh sat off to one side with reindeer, elves, and a big sack of presents. Illuminated oversize candy canes lined the walkway. Poinsettias adorned the front stoop. Garland and fairy lights wrapped the porch railing, and wreaths and candles sat in every window of the Carroll Inn.

Charley zipped up her coat, then threw on her hat, scarf, and gloves while Fred retrieved her bags from the trunk. When she finally stepped out of the car, only her eyes remained exposed.

The front door opened and an older couple emerged. Her first impression was that they truly looked like they belonged together. They both had salt-and-pepper hair and the same healthy roundness that came from great home-cooked meals. They wore matching red-and-green Christmas sweaters and had an easy air about them. The man placed a hand on his wife's back and whispered a few words, making her laugh, which revealed cute dimples in her cheeks. The strong bond they shared was clearly visible.

"You must be Charley," the woman exclaimed, all smiles, hurrying down the front steps to greet her, as if she were her own daughter coming home for Christmas. "Welcome."

Charley lowered her scarf, revealing a big smile that had taken over her face. "Thank you."

"Good to see you folks again," Fred said, setting down Charley's bags.

"Afternoon, Fred," the woman replied. "Thanks for delivering our guest safely."

"Until next time." He tipped his hat to her, then peered at Charley. "I hope you enjoy St. Nicholas, Ms. Dawson."

"Thank you, Fred." She paid him a generous tip before she turned back to her hosts.

"I'm Mary Carroll, and this is my husband, Joe." The bright-eyed woman gestured to the man standing next to her.

"Nice to meet you both." Charley peered up at the house. "It's so beautiful here." She reached for her bags but Joe beat her to them.

"Don't you dare lift those. I'll get them." Joe had a

lovable grandpa quality about him that made her want to hug him.

"Come on in," Mary said, and led the way.

Once inside, Charley couldn't seem to take it all in as she stood in the foyer. Christmas was everywhere. To the left was a long sideboard decorated with several sparkling Christmas cards, a crystal bowl filled with Christmas candy, and two tall vases full of colorfully stacked Christmas balls. To the right was an exquisite handmade eighteen-piece nativity set including the Three Wise Men's jeweled camels, a shepherd's sheep, and the shining Star of Bethlehem hanging above the manger. Straight ahead was the home's showpiece, a gorgeous ten-foot Christmas tree trimmed so impeccably that it could have been on the cover of a magazine.

Charley deeply inhaled the pleasant fragrance of pine. "You have a lovely home." She slipped off her gloves and began unwinding the long scarf wrapped around her neck.

Mary watched with amusement tickling her lips. "I see you're not used to cold weather."

"Born and raised in Los Angeles," Charley stated proudly. "Cold to me is sixty degrees."

Mary let out a hearty laugh as Joe entered with Charley's bags. "Joe will show you to your room while I make us some hot cocoa."

"That sounds wonderful." Charley followed Joe up the staircase.

At the top of the landing, she took note of the small colorful fiber-optic Christmas trees sitting next to each door of every room down the second-floor hallway, while trumpeting angels hung from above. She couldn't help but feel like they were announcing the arrival of a Christmas Scrooge. "I've never seen so many decorations."

"It's all Mary," Joe said, pride filling his voice. "She's got an interior decorator's eye, especially when it comes to Christmas." He stopped in front of the first door on the right, and even the doorknobs were decorated with Christmas ribbon. "Here you are. The Nutcracker suite."

She stepped into the room, her home for the next week, and was filled with amazement. There was a four-poster bed with garland wrapped around each post, and a rich forest-green down comforter topped with red-and-white reindeer shams. Opposite the bed stood three-foot nutcrackers on each side of a wood-burning fireplace.

On the mantel were a snow globe, a couple of elves, and a jolly old Santa Claus sitting in a rocking chair with perfectly wrapped presents at his feet. Then her eyes landed on something she hadn't seen in a very long time—an Island of Misfit Toys Charlie-in-the-Box.

Charley gasped. "A Charlie-in-the-Box!" She walked over to the mantel and stood by her favorite Christmas toy. "May I?"

Joe nodded, and she carefully removed it from the mantel to get a closer look. "Mary's had that for years."

"I used to have one when I was a little girl." She studied every detail, remembering how her mother would play the toy's sayings for her when she went to bed. "I don't know what happened to it." She gently touched Charlie's cheek before putting him back in his place.

"Please make yourself at home," Joe said. "The bathroom's right through there. Just holler if you need anything."

"Thank you, Joe."

After he left, she sat on the bed in order to fully appreciate all the fantastic decorations surrounding her. She felt the corners of her mouth involuntarily rise into a big grin. "Nope." She swiftly hopped off the bed before she got too comfortable. A few decorations were not going to sway her. She was there for one reason only—to debunk the famous Scrooge Legend.

Jack blew past St. Nicholas's welcome sign and wondered if he'd read it correctly. *Number of believers?* Did the scam involve the entire town?

The navigation voice blurted out another command, and Jack followed it blindly. He drove slowly down a long private road, sensing the system was wrong. He honestly didn't know why he still listened to the thing. Ahead of him sat a one-story house dwarfed by a large red barn. As he approached, a heavyset middle-aged man wearing a red baseball cap and coveralls sauntered out of the barn to greet him.

Jack rolled down his window.

"Hi, there," the man said, wiping grease from his face and hands with a rag. "Are you looking for a bed-and-breakfast?"

"Seems I'm not the first."

The man cracked a smile. "Those navigation systems are dumber than a tree stump."

Jack laughed. "I couldn't agree more."

"Okay, well, what you're going to want to do is take a left at the end of my drive." He gestured toward the road. "Keep going for about a quarter of a mile, and then you'll see it on the right. A quiet, peaceful, two-story inn. You can't miss it."

"Much appreciated, Mike," Jack replied, and the man gave him an inquisitive look. "On your coverall."

"Oh, right." Mike chuckled, running his hand over the embroidered name tag. "Well, have a nice time in St. Nicholas."

"Thank you."

As Jack drove back down the driveway, he laughed again at the man's dumber-than-a-tree-stump comment. It was his grandmother's favorite saying.

Chapter Six

Mary placed a bowl of nuts on a serving tray with cheese, crackers, and Christmas cookies, while Joe pulled down three mugs from the cabinet and lined them up next to the stove.

"She seems like a very sweet girl," he remarked. "Hard to believe she's a Scrooge."

"You say that about all of them." Mary gave the hot cocoa another stir, then poured it equally into the three mugs. "Remember Brooke, the terror in heels?" She topped off the cocoas with whipped cream and a sprinkle of shaved chocolate before setting them on a second tray.

"Brooke was definitely a handful."

"She sure was." The high-powered attorney had arrived demanding everything but left asking for nothing, due to her dramatic turnaround. "It's not for us to question—only to move them in the right direction." She eyed her husband, who seemed like he had something else on his mind. "What's troubling you?"

"I guess I worry about the day we can't do this anymore," he admitted, leaning against the counter. "They're like our kids, you know? Every last one of them."

"I feel the same way." She came over next to him and took his hand. "And when the time comes, we'll pass the torch to the next innkeepers, and the Scrooges of the world will continue to be helped for years, decades, and centuries to come."

He nodded, but she could still see doubt filtering through his eyes.

"I think our retirement is far down the road," she said. "Don't you?"

A tiny smile crossed his face. "I'd like to think so."

"All right, then." She patted his hand. "Let's go help Charley."

Charley descended the stairs right as her in-sync hosts set down two trays of goodies in a sitting area.

"Perfect timing," Mary announced, motioning her to a cozy-looking chair by the fire.

Charley joined them, scoping out the goodies. "I hope all of this isn't just for me," she said hesitantly as she sat, noticing there wasn't anyone else present. "Am I your only guest?"

"Goodness, no." Mary handed her a mug of hot cocoa. "We had a lot of couples come in late last night, so they're all out exploring the town."

The whipped cream atop the cocoa was so thick, it had to be homemade. It sure beat the canned whipped cream Charley had in her refrigerator back home. She took a sip and got some of it on the tip of her nose. "Oh!" She chuckled from embarrassment and wiped it away. "This cocoa is incredible."

"I'm glad you like it." Mary smiled, sitting back. "How do you like your room?"

"It's beautiful and comfortable, but I don't..." Charley trailed off, averting her eyes, trying to figure out how to phrase her next question without offending her hosts.

"No need to be shy," Joe spoke up. "If there's a problem, we want to know about it."

"Oh, no, nothing like that." Charley wasn't sure how to delicately put it, so she'd just have to come out and say it. "What's the catch?" She leveled her gaze on the couple. "Is this some kind of new timeshare pitch where you rent one of your rooms once a year?"

Both Mary and Joe burst with a laugh. "Goodness, no," Mary replied. "You were invited to be a guest of our town."

"For free?" she questioned with uncertainty. "With no strings attached?"

"For free. That's what complimentary means," Mary assured her in such a sweet voice that it sounded too sincere to be patronizing.

Perhaps her perfect hosts were being paid by someone else who'd expect something in return. "Who invited me?" she asked, determined to find out.

"Well, Santa, of course." Mary took a steady sip of her cocoa.

This time Charley laughed. When Mary didn't laugh with her, she eyed Joe, who was stone-faced.

"Santa," she repeated, thinking she obviously hadn't heard correctly.

"The one and only," Mary said, taking a cookie for herself.

Charley kept throwing quick glances between the two, scrutinizing them, certain she'd catch them looking uneasy about the lie they were feeding her. But the Carrolls didn't appear uneasy or nervous in the least. *Santa?* She honestly couldn't believe they were talking about *the* Santa Claus. "Can I meet… Santa, to thank him in person?"

"Oh, that's impossible." Mary roared with a laugh. "You know how busy he is right now."

"You bring up a good point," Charley said. "He *is* very busy, so how does he have time to single me out and invite me up here for a week?"

The Carrolls glanced at one another, then back at her without answering. The silence became thorny and strained, but she wasn't going to let them off the hook. She'd wait to hear the truth; she'd wait all night if she had to.

Finally, Mary leaned in and, barely above a whisper, said, "*You* know."

Charley looked at her blankly. "Know what?"

"You *know.*" Mary stared at her intently as if that was supposed to help her decode the cryptic message.

"No. I don't."

Mary fussed with the back of her hair, looking very uncomfortable. "I believe it was spelled out in the letter."

Charley shook her head. "No. It wasn't."

Joe cleared his throat. "What Mary's trying to say is Santa thinks you're a Scrooge."

"Joe!" Mary chided her husband, her face aghast.

"She's a straight shooter, Mary. Why tiptoe?"

"Thank you, Joe, for your candor," Charley said. "I didn't realize Santa was so sensitive that he had to call out his critics."

"Goodness. He isn't doing any such thing." Mary seemed clearly agitated now. She took a few rapid breaths, letting them out with distressed sighs, before fixing her gaze back on Charley. "You've been brought here for a specific reason."

"Which is what?"

Mary shrugged. "How would I know?"

How would she not *know?* Charley looked to Joe for an answer.

"No idea."

"None whatsoever?" She stared at the couple, totally baffled by their answers—or lack thereof.

"Well…my guess is you've lost your faith in something or someone, and Santa wants to help you find it again," Mary surmised.

Charley shook her head in exasperation. "I don't know what you're referring to. I really don't."

"Then you will," Mary said calmly.

"When?"

"Don't know."

"That's up to you," Joe chimed in.

"Uh-huh." Charley sat back, hoping to make sense of what they were attempting to tell her, but she couldn't figure it out. Trying one more time, she leaned forward, putting her elbows on her knees, and asked them directly, "What exactly do you get out of all this?"

Mary clasped her hands together. "It's not always about getting something, Charley."

"No, it's not." Joe helped himself to some cheese and crackers.

"But we're here to help," Mary reassured her with a cheery smile pasted on her face. "And to answer any questions you might have. Any at all." She shoved the tray of goodies under Charley's nose. "Cookie?"

Jack followed Mike's instructions and found the B&B right where he said it would be, only it didn't look quiet or peaceful. The front door was wide open with large hoses running down the front steps to two flood restoration trucks.

"This doesn't look good." He parked in an area marked for guests and hopped out. He walked up to the front, weaving around workers carrying in dehumidifiers, and knocked on the door. "Hello?"

A moment later, a young woman no more than twenty-five appeared a bit frazzled. "Yes?"

"I'm Jack Brody. I think I'm supposed to be staying here, but—"

"Mr. Brody. I'm so sorry," she said, smoothing down her messy hair. "We had a situation, as you can see. Come in."

He hesitated, catching a glimpse of the flood experts walking upstairs with their equipment. "You know, I can find a motel or—"

"They're all booked," she told him, exhaustion coloring her voice. "I know because I had to find lodging for my other guests."

"Oh." Jack shoved his hands inside his coat, running options in his head.

"The good news is I can offer you a very comfortable foldout couch. At no charge, of course."

"I couldn't," he replied. "You've got your hands full."

"We insist," a young guy said, coming into the house with plastic tarps and empty cardboard boxes. He set them down and extended his hand. "I'm Nolan and I see you've met my wife, Felicity."

"Jack." He shook Nolan's hand. "What happened, if you don't mind my asking?"

"A twelve-year-old boy decided to get his father's attention in a big way."

"Wow."

"Yeah. Luckily, we have insurance."

"Which we might not even need," Felicity reminded

her husband. "The boy's father said he'd pay for all the damages."

From what Jack had seen on the job, few responsible parties lived up to their word. "You might want to document everything, just in case."

"We are," she said, "but I have a good feeling it will all work out, especially since the incident finally got father and son talking again."

Jack instantly thought about Luke and Braca. "Glad to hear something good came out of it."

"Won't you stay?" Felicity pressed. "Unexpected things happen a lot here in St. Nicholas. I bet if I call around tomorrow, I'll find someone who received a last-minute cancellation."

Unexpected things? As in scamming people out of their hard-earned money? Jack realized the flood situation was a golden opportunity for him. He could casually inquire about the town and the other B&Bs while he helped them get their place back in order. "I'll stay if you allow me to help you clean up."

Felicity hesitated, then looked to her husband.

"Thank you, Jack," Nolan said, picking up the plastic tarps. "We could use it."

Jack grabbed a handful of boxes. "Lead the way." He followed the young couple into the dining room where papers, books, and office supplies were piled high on all the tables.

"With water pouring down the walls of our office, we had to quickly throw everything in here," Nolan explained.

Several ornate silver-and-gold metallic tubes were scattered on one of the tables. "These are cool." He picked one of them up and inspected it. "What are they for?"

"Uh..." Nolan was suddenly tongue-tied.

"Oh!" Felicity hurried over and snatched it out of Jack's hand. "It's just a little thing I do for the guests on Christmas. Let me get them out of the way." She scooped them off the table, threw them in a box, and hurried out of the room.

An uncomfortable silence fell between him and Nolan, which only made Jack suspect they were hiding something. But what? As the two began moving stacked-up chairs away from the walls, Felicity popped back in.

"Great news, Jack. Another B&B not far from here can take you first thing tomorrow morning," she said. "They just had a one-week cancellation. I told the proprietor what's going on over here, and she's happy to accommodate you. We all work together when unexpected things happen."

I bet you do. "Are you sure you don't want me to stay and help you out for a few days? It's no problem."

"Thank you, but we'll be fine," she insisted. "Now, I better go check on the workmen."

Felicity hurried out, leaving Jack wondering how he was going to interrogate the couple in a few short hours without raising suspicion.

Chapter Seven

With her hat and gloves firmly in place and her coat zipped up to her ears, Charley stood on Main Street, staring at the town map, trying to locate Kringle Lane.

"Morning," a woman said as she passed by with a smile.

"Morning," Charley called after her, having been taken off guard. The town's friendliness felt foreign, and she didn't quite know what to make of it. She reached for her phone and called her friend on FaceTime. "Morning, Liv."

"Wow, I was expecting a dire plea of 'Get me out of here!'" Liv joked. "Hold on. I'm going to prop you up against a stack of magazines so I can keep working."

The picture on Liv's phone jostled around before it finally settled, allowing Charley a full view of her friend at a design table. Liv's assistant passed three fashion photos over to her. She took two seconds to study them before she shook her head and motioned for more.

"Go ahead, Charley. I'm listening."

"You've got to see this place." Charley turned her phone camera around and slowly panned the beautiful town in front of her. "Isn't it gorgeous?" She reversed the view, setting it back on herself, and noticed Liv wasn't looking at her cell screen at all. Not allowing that to deter her, Charley tried to engage her again. "Liv, you won't believe how friendly the people are here. It almost doesn't seem real."

"I'm sure it's fake," Liv threw out with a flick of a glance before she was handed more photos. "But why am I telling you that? You always find that nugget of ugly in paradise. What's St. Nicholas's blemish?"

Charley found the nearest bench and sat down. "No outward blemish that I can see, but I do feel like they aren't telling me the whole truth as to why I was invited." She raised her eyes and offered a smile at a couple passing by.

"Then I guess Miss Scrooge will also need to be Miss Sleuth," Liv remarked, scrutinizing two more fashion photos before handing them back.

"I'm already on it. I'm tracking down the return address on the invitation I received."

"Good."

Charley didn't know if Liv was talking to her, or her assistant. She watched the FaceTime camera jerk around again before Liv's face filled the screen.

"I hate to cut this short, but I've got to go," Liv said, focusing on something off camera.

Only then did Charley remember their weekly marketing meeting. *How could I forget?* "Call me when you catch your breath."

Liv let out an ironic laugh. "And when will that be exactly?"

"Bye, Liv." Charley disconnected the call and sat there for a minute. Watching Liv work while she was trying to carry on a conversation with her left Charley with an unsettled feeling. She suddenly didn't miss being in that environment. She never realized the stress of it until she saw it on camera. At the same time, she'd never be able to live in a town like St. Nicholas that was so darn cheery—not unless she were in love, and that was never going to happen.

The sun broke through the morning clouds, bathing Charley in light. She found herself unzipping her coat as she studied the map again. She rose and walked to the next corner where she found Noel Lane instead of Kringle Lane.

"Huh?" Thinking she had the map upside down, she went in the opposite direction only to find Reindeer Road. Completely confused, she knew she needed to ask for directions.

Charley stepped inside a nearby coffeehouse and was instantly immersed in its warm atmosphere of overstuffed chairs, nooks filled with cute coffee items, and a light instrumental rendition of "The First Noel" playing overhead. She drew in a deep breath, relishing the rich aroma of freshly ground coffee beans. She had to try one of their coffees. She got in line and checked out the hot drink menu written on a chalkboard above her.

An efficient barista in her late thirties kept moving the orders along nicely, so it wasn't long before Charley heard, "Hi, there. How can I help you?"

Getting on board with the small-town friendliness, Charley promptly glanced at her name tag. "Morning, Piper. I'd like to try your gingerbread latte. Regular, please."

"Sure thing." Piper got to work behind the counter while Charley took out her map.

"Can I ask you where Kringle Lane is?" She unfolded the map on top of the counter. "I can't seem to find it."

Piper tilted her head to get a better view. "That's because it's not a street but a location."

Charley gave her a puzzled look.

"You're looking for 1 Kringle Lane, correct?"

"Yes."

Piper handed over Charley's latte. "There's a red mailbox on the north end of the town square. That's 1 Kringle Lane."

"A mailbox?" It dawned on her. "Of course. Kris Kringle." Charley laughed. "That's Santa's mailbox?"

"As long as I can remember, and I've lived here for fifteen years."

"Do you believe in the Scrooge Legend?"

"Absolutely." The barista wiped down the counter. "You won't find anyone around here who doesn't." Piper sounded like her driver, Fred.

Charley took out her wallet. "How much do I owe you?"

"It's on me," she said. "I'm assuming you're a guest of our town?"

Charley gave her a curious look. "How did you know?"

"No one asks about the address unless they've received a Scrooge letter. I did the exact same thing."

Her mouth fell open. "You were a Scrooge?"

Piper chuckled at her reaction. "A lot of us were."

There were previous Scrooges in town that she could interview? "What do you mean by *a lot*?"

"I don't know." Piper shrugged. "If I were to guess, probably a quarter of the town."

"That many?" *Just what kind of weird cult is operating in St. Nicholas, Colorado?* "How does it work?"

"Hmm." Piper chewed on her lower lip. "In short, my life was a mess, then I came here, everyone was so welcoming, and suddenly I started seeing things differently. Before I knew it, everything turned around for me."

Yep, it's a cult all right. "Just like that?"

"Yeah. Just like that."

Charley couldn't miss the sincerity in Piper's voice, which only meant one thing—she was still brainwashed. Charley wanted to arrange a sit-down interview with her but a line of customers was growing behind her. "Thank you for your time and for the latte," she said, stuffing a five in the tip jar.

"My pleasure. Enjoy your stay in St. Nicholas."

Charley exited the coffeehouse and immediately crossed the street to the town square. This was crazy. A quarter of the residents were former Scrooges? She'd easily be able to find more than one person who could tell her the ugly truth behind the so-called legend.

Charley followed the meandering path, passing the Christmas tree in the center of the town square and continuing to the north end where the mailbox was supposed to be located. When she came around an old-fashioned lamppost and a cluster of large pine trees, she saw it, standing alone, right in front of her. *Where's the spotlight snapping on and the chorus of singing angels?*

The mailbox was indeed red. Bright red. Santa red. The shape and height appeared similar to a typical USPS mailbox, but it had a flat top, ornate gilded legs, and a large flag shaped like a candy cane attached to the right side. On the front of the mailbox, and in bright gold letters, it read 1 KRINGLE LANE.

"It exists." Charley grabbed her phone. "It really exists." She snapped a bunch of pictures, then backed up and took some more.

She stared at the mailbox, willing it to spill all of its secrets. She wasn't sure what she expected. Would it light up and suddenly spit out letters to potential Scrooges? How exactly did the whole thing work? Who was generating the letters to get so many people to come to St. Nicholas? Was the town hurting for money? It didn't appear that way, yet the townspeople seemed deliriously happy. Were they putting on a show for her? If so, what was their end game?

She thought about what Piper said. *Everything changed... just like that.*

"Just like that?" Nothing changed *just like that.* "Bah, humbug," Charley spat, turning on her heel. She'd locate the post office and find out exactly who owned the mailbox.

Charley was maybe fifty feet down the path when she heard metallic hinges squeaking with a low hollowed groan. It was a similar sound she heard every time she dropped a letter into the mailbox outside her apartment building back home. She whipped around, expecting to see someone dropping off mail, but no one was near the mailbox.

"Okay, that was a little weird." She walked back over and inspected it. She pulled on the handle, but it wouldn't open. She yanked harder, thinking the door was hung up on something inside, but it actually didn't feel stuck. It felt locked. She fixed her eyes on the enigma. There had to be a logical explanation for why it wouldn't open.

She spied a park bench a few feet away, walked over to it, and sat down, waiting for someone to use it. Charley closed her coat up over her ears and took a small taste of the gingerbread latte. In an instant, memories of her childhood filled her head.

Every December her father would kick off the Christmas season by bringing home a box of the most amazing gingerbread cookies she ever tasted. They weren't the usual thick, hearty gingerbread cookies—these were thin and delicate with a smooth, rich flavor of ginger, cinnamon and nutmeg. She and her dad would enjoy two each, every night after supper, until they were gone. While they dipped their cookies in a glass of milk, they'd talk about her dreams and future aspirations, and Charley realized how blessed she was to have a father like him.

She'd been nine when her dad brought home the first batch of cookies, and it became a tradition that lasted for ten years. Now he lived in London where his work and new wife had taken him. She missed those moments with him as much as she missed her mother, who had passed away five days after Charley's twenty-second birthday.

Charley was suddenly startled out of her thoughts by a studious-looking twenty-something guy walking up to the mailbox. He pulled open the Velcro flap on the front pocket of his computer bag and retrieved a blank piece of paper and pen. He wrote something down on the paper, contemplated it for a moment before folding it in half. He then opened the mailbox door with ease. The hinges squeaked with a low groan, and she was certain that exact sound was what she had heard a few minutes earlier. The guy dropped in the piece of paper, flipped up the striped candy-cane flag, and walked away.

"Excuse me?" She jumped to her feet, hurrying after him.

The guy turned around, tossing his sandy brown hair out of his eyes. "Yes?"

"Um...sorry to be nosy, but did you throw a piece of paper into that mailbox?"

"I did," he answered cautiously, as if he were waiting for Charley to tell him the reason for her inquiry.

"But it's a mailbox. Don't you need an envelope and a stamp?"

An amused smile tugged at his lips. "You're not from around here, are you?"

"No."

"That's Santa's mailbox for Scrooge requests. No postage needed." He turned to go.

"Scrooge requests?" she asked breathlessly, not wanting him to leave.

"Yes." He faced her. "The famous Scrooge Legend?"

She gave him a blank stare, pretending not to know about the legend because she wanted to hear his interpretation of it.

"Tell me you at least know of the legend," he implored.

"I heard something about it but not any of the details."

The guy readjusted his shoulder strap, walking back to her. "Every week, Santa invites a real Scrooge, or Scrooges, to stay in St. Nicholas. During that time—"

She held up her hand. "What do you mean by a real Scrooge?"

"Generally, it's anyone who hates Christmas or is stingy."

That's clearly not me.

"Scrooges are also defined as people who ruin things for everyone else because they're unhappy."

Okay, maybe that's me, a little. "That describes a lot of people I know," she said with a chuckle. She thought it was funny; however, he barely cracked a smile, and Charley imagined him wondering what kind of horrible people she had as friends. Embarrassed, she cleared her throat, then got the conversation back on track. "Um… so, Santa brings Scrooges here. And then what?"

"The Scrooges are filled with the true meaning of Christmas, which changes their lives for the better. And on a grander scale, their new outlook on life changes the world for the better."

She nodded, considering his words. *I could use a little of that.* "So, the mailbox is like a suggestion box?"

"That's a good way of putting it, yes. Anyone can suggest someone, but only Santa knows who's really a Scrooge."

Santa. Ha! Right. "It's a noble idea. If only it were true…"

"Who's to say it isn't?"

"Me. I'm apparently a Scrooge, and I don't feel any different."

He cocked his head. "When did you arrive?"

"Yesterday."

The guy laughed. "You're at the very beginning. Find me in a week and try telling me you're not changed." He started to walk away.

"I'm at the beginning of what?" she asked quickly.

"Your adventure."

"You wholeheartedly believe in this, don't you?"

He smiled. "I wouldn't have suggested my ex-girlfriend if I didn't."

An ex-girlfriend who's a Scrooge, and he wants her to be happy? Now that *is a noble gesture.*

"See ya around, Miss Scrooge," he said over his shoulder.

"I wish people would stop calling me that," she muttered under her breath as she walked back over to the mailbox. She wrapped her hand around the handle and pulled, expecting to hear the metallic hinges sing. But they didn't. The door wouldn't open for her. "What the heck?" She yanked on it with all her might and the darn thing remained shut. It didn't make any sense. She'd just witnessed a guy dropping in—

She dug around in her handbag for a pen, then threw her bag back over her shoulder. "A Scrooge, a Scrooge.

Who is a Scrooge?" She was joking when she told the guy she knew a lot of Scrooges. Truth was, she was the only one. *Think.* There were a couple of old bosses and a landlady who could be considered Scrooges, but none of those people were in her life now, and she definitely didn't want them to be again. The guy wanted to help his ex. Hers were jerks. *Think, think*—she gasped.

Jack. He could be considered a Scrooge. She furiously scribbled his name on her coffee sleeve. "All right, *Santa.* You think I have a problem with Christmas? Wait until you get a load of this guy." She tried the handle again, and with the sound of squeaking hinges, she tossed the coffee sleeve into the mailbox with sheer abandon.

"Let's see if you can find my high school sweetheart. Facebook couldn't, so I'm fairly certain you won't be able to, either." Charley raised her chin proudly, as if she had just bested a world champion chess player. "Oh, what was that, Santa?" She put a hand to her ear. "Is that a challenge, you ask?" She smiled with total satisfaction. "You bet it is."

A couple came out of nowhere, walking along the path. She knew they'd seen her talking to the mailbox because they wouldn't stop gawking at her.

Charley awkwardly waved at them before she turned and hurried away. "I knew something was wrong with this town. It's already got me talking to inanimate objects."

Chapter Eight

Unable to come up with a logical explanation as to why the mailbox only accepted Scrooge suggestions, Charley needed to talk to someone at the post office, but on her way over there, she decided to interview some of the locals about the Scrooge Legend instead. Each story sounded more spectacular and, dare she say, more far-fetched than the last.

One woman discovered she had a twin sister who miraculously showed up in St. Nicholas the same time she did. Another woman literally ran into a man she met in France who she *knew* was her soulmate. They were now happily married with children. A true Scrooge of a man tried to actually buy the town, just so he could stop their year-round Christmas celebration. He was now the current mayor, and he approved of all things Christmas. As much as Charley wanted to believe these stories, too many stars would need to align for any of it to have actually happened.

She checked the time. The interviews had taken longer than expected, so she'd have to skip the post office for now and get back to the inn. Mary was serving afternoon snacks for the guests at three, and she didn't want to miss it. The relaxed atmosphere would make it easier for her to interrogate guests without their knowledge.

When she opened the inn's front door and entered the foyer, she was happy to see several couples hanging out in the living room.

"Charley!" Mary came out of the kitchen with two trays of appetizers. "Come meet our other guests."

She followed her host into the living room where Mary set down the trays to make the introductions.

"Charley, I'd like you to meet Rebecca and Tom Byrnes. They've been coming to St. Nicholas for the past eight years. Selena and Dominic are here for their third year, and this is Kim and Matt Foster, who are celebrating their anniversary with us."

"Congratulations," Charley said to Kim and Matt before greeting the whole group. "It's very nice to meet all of you. This is my first time here."

"Hot cider?" Mary offered, holding a heavy tray of filled mugs as the group eagerly helped themselves.

"Oh, and here's our latest guest." Mary gestured to a man descending the stairs. "His name is Jack Brody."

Charley gasped, whipping around, and when she saw him, she was frozen from shock. Her heart was drumming so loudly, she couldn't hear anything else. She couldn't fathom how she was actually staring at Jack Brody, *the* Jack Brody—the one who stole her heart and locked it away. The Jack Brody she swore she'd get over but never did. The Jack Brody who was no longer a cute, lanky, sixteen-year-old with boyish charm, but a gorgeous thirty-year-old man who was approaching her that very moment.

Her eyes drank him in. His thick black hair was cut short which only accentuated his high cheekbones and rugged square jaw. His toned, muscular body nicely filled out his button-down shirt and dark denim jeans, and the way he carried himself down the stairs told Charley he was confident and in control of any situation.

Jack's gaze locked on to her with instant recognition, and she swore time stood still.

"Do you know Jack?" Mary asked.

"Yes," Charley heard herself say breathlessly, but she wasn't sure if she had answered Mary or some unspoken question Jack was asking her from afar.

"Well, isn't that nice?"

"How is he here?" Her mouth barely worked as she grappled at the plausibility of a mailbox bringing a person to town. "I put his name in the box only a few hours ago."

"What was that?" Mary turned an ear toward Charley. "Did you say something?"

Charley couldn't tear her eyes away. She unexpectedly gasped for air, not realizing she'd been holding her breath.

"Are you all right, dear?" Mary asked with concern.

No, she was not. She had spent years fortifying thick, impenetrable walls that she put up against Jack Brody, and in an instant, they had crumbled to dust. All of those explosive, damning words she swore she'd throw at him one day had suddenly left her brain. She had a whole speech prepared, an abridged version of it, and even a four-word sentence—depending on the time she would have to deliver it. But the second she laid eyes on him, for the life of her, she couldn't remember one negative thing to say.

"Charley, are you okay?" Mary asked again.

"Simply placing a name inside a mailbox works?" she uttered faintly.

Mary furrowed her brows, tilting her head to one side.

"Mailbox?" And then she nodded with understanding. "Not any mailbox, dear. But to answer your question, yes, it does work."

"No." Charley swiftly cast a glance at Mary. "That was impossibly fast."

"Well, Santa can deliver toys all over the world in one night, so one little name in a mailbox…" Mary shrugged. "Looks like you have some catching up to do." She nudged Charley toward Jack before she attended to her other guests.

Charley gulped, still hearing her heart hammering.

"Charley Dawson." Jack shook his head in disbelief. "How the heck have you been?"

A rush of heat flooded her cheeks. She couldn't get over how Jack's sixteen-year-old round baby face had matured into strong, chiseled angles. And though his blue-gray eyes were framed with laugh lines, they were still very distinct and intense. "Good. Uh…"

Her mind was spinning. Pushing aside how gorgeous her ex-boyfriend was, she couldn't figure out how he was standing in front of her. The Scrooge Legend wasn't real. Challenging Santa to find him for her couldn't be real, either. She was a grown woman. She knew that. It had to be something else. It was too much of a coincidence for both of them to be staying at the same bed-and-breakfast in the middle of nowhere. Another tiny gasp escaped her lips as she suddenly remembered the fortune cookie saying YOU WILL REUNITE WITH THE ONE THAT GOT AWAY. No. Not possible. Was it?

Nerves took control of her. Not knowing what to do with herself, she grabbed two mugs of hot cider off the table and thrust one at Jack. "Have some cider." She tried to take a gulp but discovered it was still very hot. "Oh! It's hot. Be careful."

"I figured it would be." He looked at her curiously before blowing on the cider. He took a tiny taste, not taking his eyes off her. "I can't believe we're both staying here."

"I was thinking the same thing." She flashed him an insecure smile. "What are the odds?"

"Seventy-six million, two hundred thirty thousand, eighty-nine to one."

Charley gawked at him.

"Kidding!" He grinned. "I have no idea, but I'd bet it's a high number, especially since I was booked at another B&B until they had a flood."

"A flood?"

"A mischievous kid left the water running."

"Oh!" She immediately took a drink of cider, covering the fact that she had absolutely no idea what to say to him.

He jammed his hand in the front pocket of his jeans. "Do you still live in LA?" he asked, checking out a plate of appetizers.

She hated how he appeared to be so incredibly relaxed, and she was ready to jump out of her skin. He was acting like he'd seen her a few weeks ago. *Calm down. Just breathe.*

"Yeah." She forced herself to sound casual. "I work at the magazine *Authentic Lifestyles*. I'm sure you've heard of it."

The crease between his brows deepened. "I don't know that one," he said, and she wondered if he was happy to see her or if he was just making conversation. "Not much time to read magazines with my job."

Play it cool. "What do you do?" she asked nonchalantly.

"I'm a police detective in Denver."

"A detective? That must be exciting," she replied enthusiastically, attempting to hide her surprise. She always thought he'd be an attorney like his dad.

"It's not as glamorous as Hollywood portrays it to be. There's a lot of paperwork and hours digging for answers. I probably spend seventy percent of my day doing research on anyone and everyone connected to a case."

Did you ever think of doing research on me? She felt herself blushing at the thought. *Change the subject.* "So, do you come here often?"

Jack laughed and she instantly closed her eyes in dread, totally embarrassed by her stupid question.

"What I meant was why are you in St. Nicholas?"

He took a slow sip of cider, then spoke in a warm, buttery tone. "I'm here on a case."

She shut the sound of his sexy voice from her mind, determined to stay on topic. "Really?" She raised her brows. "Ya got trouble, right here in St. Nick's City?" she joked.

"With a capital T."

She blasted him with a big grin. "You remember."

"How could I forget? Our school put on the worst production of *The Music Man* ever." He cringed. "And you made me sit through it."

"Our friends were in it. We had to support them."

"Yeah, I'll never forget what you told them when they asked your opinion. You said their performances were 'so incredibly original.'"

"I said that?" Charley laughed. "I can't believe you remembered that." She couldn't stop smiling, thinking back. She and Jack had been considered the perfect couple. They had so many of the same interests. They loved baseball, volleyball, and surfing. They spent hours at the beach together. They rarely disagreed with one another because they thought alike, often sharing the same viewpoints. Their taste in music was even the same. Their favorite bands were Coldplay and Green Day. All of their friends told them they would end up married to each other, and Charley believed them. She thought Jack had believed them too. Maybe he did at one time, but that was long ago.

They fell into an awkward silence. It felt like they could simply pick up where they left off, but she knew that sort of thing only happened in movies. He had crushed her years ago and she needed to keep that in mind. “You were saying you were on a case?”

“A potential one,” Jack answered vaguely.

“Can you give me a hint?”

“Yes.” He leaned into her, lowering his voice. “But later.”

It was then that Charley understood magnetic attraction. Without warning, she felt her body being pulled to his, and he must have felt it, too, because he pinned her with his gaze. Her pulse raced and her cheeks flushed as he brushed his arm against hers.

Jack cleared his throat, breaking eye contact as he stepped away from her. “What about you? Are you here on vacation with your husband?” He checked out her hand.

If he was asking her, there was a good chance he was still single. Charley indirectly eyed his left hand. No ring—though he could have left it at home. “No, Detective.” She held up her left hand, finally feeling like she was on equal footing with him. “I’m as free as a bird.”

He offered a crooked smile, and she couldn’t tell if

he was embarrassed that she caught his less-than-subtle question or if he was pleased with her answer.

"If you're not on vacation, what's brought *you* to St. Nicholas?" he asked.

"I'm kind of on a case myself. I received a complimentary week here, so I thought I'd check it out."

Jack's face registered surprise. "At this B&B specifically, or could you have used your free week at any of the B&Bs?"

"No, just here. Why?"

"A friend of mine stayed at another B&B for free." He scanned the room, as if he were trying to find a criminal lurking within the bed-and-breakfast guests. "Is this B&B one of those timeshare deals?"

"That's what I thought!" She couldn't believe how, after fourteen years, they still thought alike. "But, no. It isn't." She moved closer, speaking in conspiratorial tones. "I took the free week because I'm determined to get to the truth behind the Scrooge Legend." Recognition flickered across his face. "I take it you know what I'm talking about."

Jack nodded. "Any Scrooge who enters the town will end up loving Christmas as much as Santa."

"That's the one, though my understanding is that the legend's purpose is to get to the root of why someone doesn't like Christmas. It focuses on why a Scrooge is so unhappy."

"Interesting. You know, I think your invitation is connected to what I'm investigating."

"Are you serious?" Could the legend be a front for criminal activity? Talk about debunking a story. It would be her biggest reveal of fact over fiction ever.

"Do you want to have dinner with me tonight?" His intense gaze instantly held her captive.

"Oh…uh…" she stammered. He sure knew how to take her off guard.

"What I mean is, we can share information," he clarified.

"Oh. Right. Yes." She waved away the embarrassing thought that he had actually asked her out on a date. "That's a good idea. To share notes." She nodded enthusiastically for good measure.

"Great." He glanced at his phone. "I've got to take care of something for work, but why don't we meet back here around six? We can grab a bite in town and talk about it."

"Sure," she said casually, feeling ridiculous at how she had jumped to conclusions. "See you then."

Charley's thoughts were spinning as he walked away. He glanced back at her, and she felt mortified that he'd caught her staring at him. She flashed him an awkward, fractured smile. Adding to her embarrassment, she then gave him a hesitant wave before he turned and climbed the stairs.

What was wrong with her? It was absurd to think he could be interested after fourteen years. Then again, he *had* turned around to look at her. Was it possible? No, she was an old friend helping him out on an investigation—she was sure that's what he thought of her.

Charley bit her lip. What was she doing? He broke her heart when they were kids. He could easily do it again. *Stop! Stop thinking about him. You have no idea if he's married or has a fiancée or is even interested. Most importantly, you shouldn't care.*

"Jack's a handsome one," Mary said, cozying up next to her. "How do you two know each other?"

"We were high school sweethearts."

"Oh, how wonderful." Mary didn't move, still looking toward the stairs where Jack was only moments ago. "And here you are, together again."

"Not together."

"Not yet," Mary sang, arching a brow, then left her alone with that thought.

Chapter Nine

"Charley Dawson," Jack whispered as he strode down the hallway with his room key in hand. She looked amazing. How they managed to be in the same place at the same time, he'd probably never know, but he wasn't going to question it. Maybe the Big Man upstairs was looking out for him after all.

He opened the door to his room, threw his key on the table, and stared out the window. How was she still single? She was smart, funny—oh, man, if she wasn't beautiful. Those luminous forest-green eyes of hers still sparkled when she smiled, and her gorgeous sun-kissed hair brought back so many memories of them spending summer days on the beach together. He remembered what Felicity had said about unexpected things happening in St. Nicholas. What an understatement. How incredibly lucky he was to see Charley again.

He unzipped his bag and began unpacking. It was hard to believe how only yesterday he had resigned himself to a single, solitary life. Over the years, he'd never wanted to get too involved, never wanted to commit past tomorrow with anyone he'd dated—except Charley. With her, he had been all in—at least, until he and his family moved out of state.

Weeks after the move, he'd handled things poorly with her and that was on him. Thinking back, his teenage self had figured it would all work out. But one month went by, and then two. He'd known they'd be going to separate colleges. How could any long-distance relationship survive that? Seeing no future for them, he let the relationship fall apart.

But he never stopped thinking about her. He kept tabs on her throughout the years. It was easy to do as a detective. He'd probably never admit it to her, but he'd known she worked at the magazine before she told him. He even knew where she lived—though that was it. He wouldn't dig into her personal life. It wasn't right. Besides, if he had learned she was happily married with children, it would have crushed him.

Jack hung his shirts in the closet, thinking about how nervous she looked when they made eye contact. He'd been fairly nervous himself. His heart had been going a mile a minute. He thought he'd covered better than she did, but still, if she had known what a wreck he'd been, she would have laughed.

How many times he had picked up the phone to call her… He'd wanted to explain what happened so that maybe she would give him a second chance. But he always talked himself out of dialing her number. Believing he would never find someone like Charley again, he buried himself in his work and learned how to become emotionally detached. He thought remaining indifferent would help him deal with his lost love, but it didn't. Sometimes it was all he could do to just get to the end of the day.

Of course, something stirred inside him the second he'd laid eyes on her. His buried emotions shot through him and surfaced within seconds. That scared him enough to have him retreating back to his room to regroup. He needed a game plan. He had to figure out if it was at all possible…the two of them…together again? Could he explore the possibility without either of them getting emotionally hurt in the process?

Jack finished emptying his suitcase, zipped it up, and set it in the corner of the room. What was he thinking? Charley might not even want to go down that same road with him again. She didn't exactly jump at the chance to have dinner with him. When she didn't reply, he immediately felt stupid for asking. At least he was able to think fast and cover his fumble by highlighting the work angle. Unfortunately, now it would *have* to be about work. He shook his head, disappointed.

Jack's cell abruptly rang, startling him out of his thoughts. "Captain Wollin. I was just about to call you."

"How's it looking up there?"

Charley immediately came to mind. It was strange enough for him to run into his high school girlfriend, but then to discover she'd received one of those mysterious complimentary weeks at a B&B—well, that was a little too coincidental. He was sure Captain Wollin would agree.

"There was a flood at the B&B Braca stayed in, but the good news is I'm at the one where your brother stayed."

"I thought they were booked." Wollin sounded surprised.

"They didn't have a room available until today, but something seems off about these B&Bs."

"I knew it! Do you want me to send Adam or Kenny up there to help you?"

Jack thought about it. He was already distracted by

Charley and needed to stay focused on his job. Yet how could he ignore the gift he'd been given to reconnect with her again? He'd been so lonely over the past decade. While all his buddies were getting married or having their first child, he couldn't commit to any woman long enough to have a serious relationship. As his friends began to move on without him, he began to feel a deep void overtaking his life that pushed out love and commitment and his ability to build a lifelong partnership with someone he truly loved. If he was being given a second chance with Charley, he couldn't squander it. "No need to send them. It might draw too much attention. Let me get to digging and if I find it's too much, I'll let you know."

"All right, Jack. Keep me posted, and be safe out there."

He hung up wondering if he was being foolish. He wasn't in high school anymore. He lived in the real world where dreams were dashed and fairy-tale relationships were just that—a fantasy that rarely existed outside the mind of the dreamer.

Jack stared out the window, watching the late afternoon sun retreat behind a thicket of trees. The Christmas lights outside turned on, illuminating the bed-and-breakfast property. It was beautiful, he had to admit, even though Christmastime wasn't very merry for him anymore. It hadn't been for a long time.

The massive number of lights reminded him of his early childhood when decorating his house was a whole thing—a tradition that lasted for days. That was before his uncle disappeared. Then a cloud fell over the season. He'd been miserable during the holidays for years—until he met Charley. Though they had shared only one Christmas together, she'd helped him to enjoy it again. Once he had moved away from her, he went back to dreading the season. Was it a coincidence he'd run into her three weeks before Christmas? For years he'd hoped he'd see her again, and now it had finally happened. Maybe the realist could have faith in the dreamer once again.

After assessing that none of the other B&B guests were considered Scrooges, Charley politely excused herself. She needed to get to the post office for some answers before it closed. She was a woman grounded in facts and science, not fortune cookie sayings and magical mailboxes. For all she knew, whoever invited her had also managed to get Jack up to St. Nicholas under false pretenses. But why?

The post office was located on Holly Street, another beautiful area of St. Nicholas. It reminded her of the architecture in the Swiss Alps—white stone buildings framed with steep, black roofs. Enormous clock hands adorned the entrance to the town hall, and next to the town hall was an equally impressive post office.

When she opened the door, she assumed she'd see one or two mail service windows sharing space with a copy center and an office supply store, but that wasn't the case. The massive building was for the post office only. It had ten service windows and not one was closed. She'd never been inside a post office where all the windows were open. It seemed overkill for such a small town. Then again, maybe not. The line was out the door, spilling into the lobby and weaving around the area near the box rentals.

Knowing it would take forever to get up to the counter, she turned to leave when a woman standing in line said, "It moves fairly quickly, especially when all the windows are open."

The woman scooted a box forward with her foot since her arms were loaded down with other packages. "And if you have to wait in line for more than ten minutes, they give you a voucher for a free hot chocolate, redeemable at any St. Nicholas café."

"Seriously?" She'd never heard of such a thing.

"That's St. Nicholas."

"You just saved me a trip back here. Thank you." Charley found the end of the line and checked her watch. Not that she was going to insist on a free voucher, but there was no way she'd be standing in front of a clerk in less than ten minutes.

Two women in front of her were exchanging gift ideas for their husbands, and a couple ahead of the women were laughing at something funny. Charley couldn't believe how many customers were talking to each other, as if they were at a cocktail party. How could everyone be in such a good mood, standing in line at the post office?

An instrumental version of "Deck the Halls" faintly filled the lobby. She'd never heard music in post offices before. Was this a new thing or did it apply only to St. Nicholas?

The line continued to move, and eight minutes later, she was summoned to an open window where a jolly clerk with curly blond hair and a welcoming smile drummed his hands on the counter, keeping the beat to "We Wish You a Merry Christmas." He immediately noticed her empty hands. "What can I do for you, out-of-towner?" he asked in a cheery voice.

"Is it that obvious?" Charley dipped her chin to inspect her own clothing.

"Not at all. I know practically everyone who comes in here. When I see an unfamiliar face, I just assume."

"Well, you assumed right. In fact, because I'm an out-of-towner, I'm curious to know when you pick up the mail from Santa's mailbox."

"Oh, gosh, we don't handle anything from that location."

She cocked her head to one side. "But don't you collect *all* mail?"

"That we do. That's our job. But not from Santa's mailbox." He threw his hands in the air with a hands-off gesture.

"Don't tell me Santa collects it himself," she said with an easygoing smile.

"No, no." He rolled with a laugh, then got serious. "One of Santa's helpers retrieves all correspondence left at that location."

One of Santa's helpers? "And that's allowed?"

"Why wouldn't it be? He owns the box." The clerk was still drumming his hands on the counter, not at all upset or uncomfortable with her questions, which didn't make sense if the town was hiding something.

"He doesn't rent the box from you?"

"No, he owns it outright."

Charley was getting nowhere. She had to change her line of questioning. "Does it bother you that he doesn't ask for postage?"

"Why would it?" He looked at her curiously. "We're not providing a service. We're not delivering the mail."

He had her on that one. "Have you ever seen anyone pick it up?"

"No, but we know it's one of Santa's helpers."

Not exactly the answer she was looking for. "How do you know it's one of Santa's helpers?"

"It's not one of us, so who else could it be?" He beamed a broad smile.

She glanced at the line behind her, expecting to see everyone glaring back at her, but they weren't. They were happily conversing with each other while waiting for an open window. She put her attention back on the clerk. "Have you ever seen a Scrooge letter?"

"Of course." He quit drumming and leaned in. "We send them out every week."

"Oh!" Her eyes widened, excited. Finally, she was getting somewhere.

"I know, right?" he said, conspiratorially, as if he were sharing a juicy piece of gossip. "Who knew there were so many Scrooges in the world?"

Charley frowned. "No, wait, I think I misunderstood you. Are *you* the guys generating the letters?"

"Golly, no!" He exploded with a big belly laugh, then instantly turned professional again. "They're dropped off in the lobby here, and we mail them out—because they have stamps," he added with a chuckle. "In case that was your next question."

"Funny." She smiled. "Who drops them off?"

"I imagine one of Santa's helpers."

And they were back to the same circle of canned answers. She refused to let that deter her. "Have you ever caught one of Santa's helpers on camera?"

"Nope. Never have," he said, sounding a little disappointed. "But I assure you we get those letters delivered."

"I know you do. I got one myself."

"Oh," he said in a singsong way. His face reddened, no doubt from what he had said earlier about Scrooges.

"Well, why didn't you say that in the first place?" He grinned, quickly recovering. "Welcome to St. Nicholas!"

"Thank you—" she glanced at his name tag "—Wyatt."

"Is there anything else I can help you with?" Wyatt was back to drumming his hands on the counter, this time to "Jingle Bells."

"Not at the moment, but thank you for your time."

"Oh!" Wyatt held out a slip of paper, a voucher for a free drink. "Here ya go."

"That's very sweet of you, but I wasn't in line for ten minutes, and I didn't buy anything."

"Doesn't matter." He wiggled the voucher in front of her to take it. "It's on me."

"Thank you, Wyatt." She turned to go. "I love the Christmas music, by the way. They don't play it in my post office back home."

"Well, it is Christmas in *St. Nicholas*, after all."

"Yes, it is," Charley said. *Yes, it is.*

Chapter Ten

Charley had wanted concrete evidence that her seeing Jack had been manufactured, not magical, before she met him for dinner. She felt safe in reality but too vulnerable in potentiality—which was where her emotions were taking her. This assignment of debunking the legend was supposed to have been fast and easy, yet the more she experienced in St. Nicholas, the less likely she saw that happening. Now she had an unexpected obstacle in her path, a very handsome obstacle that was clouding her rational mind with every minute she spent with him.

She sat facing Jack in a booth by a window in the town's only twenty-four-hour diner. Sitting on her hands, she stared at the menu, just as she had done in high school. Jack looked to be studying the menu, too, only she suspected neither one was. She glanced at him when he wasn't looking, and though she couldn't be certain, she thought he'd been doing the same. They were definitely uncomfortable around each other, as if they'd somehow been thrust back in time with no escape from teenage awkwardness, and the silence was getting more unbearable by the minute.

"Evening, folks," chirped a welcoming waitress, coming to their rescue. "I'm Angel, and I'll be taking care of you this evening."

Charley smiled at the woman who had such shiny black hair, it almost glistened. It was neatly pulled back in a bun, and her chocolate-brown eyes were deep and soulful. She had no idea how much of an angel she really was at that moment.

"Evening, Angel," Jack said, studying her. "I have to ask. Is Angel your real name, or are you assigned a Christmas-themed name?"

Her eyes smiled. "It's been my name ever since I received my wings." She winked and Charley laughed. "Do you two need more time, or do you know what you want?"

Both is what Charley thought.

"Ladies first." He motioned to Charley.

When Charley was nervous, she ate, and right then, she could have eaten a burger and a whole pie by herself. She took one look at muscular Jack and opted not to order either. "I think I'll have the Cobb salad with the dressing on the side. And an iced tea, please."

Angel jotted down Charley's order, then looked to Jack. "And for you?"

"I'll take the cheeseburger, no onions, fries, and a root beer."

Charley couldn't believe what she just heard. Her gaze immediately fell onto his broad shoulders and muscular arms. She inspected the outline of his body through his shirt. Yes, he still appeared to be a solid mass of muscle.

"Easy-peasy," Angel said before she gathered the menus and flitted away.

This dinner feels surreal. If she closed her eyes, she'd swear they were back at their favorite diner in Studio

City, grabbing a bite to eat before going to the football game. Yet fourteen years had gone by. There was so much to ask him she didn't know where to begin. Never did she think she'd be at a loss for words because there was too much to say.

Jack's body was quivering, which she traced to his foot nervously tapping on the floor under the table. Apparently, he was also having difficulties finding the words, and the awkward silence threatened to swallow them whole if she didn't say something.

"How can you possibly eat burgers and fries and still look like…that?" she asked with tinges of envy in her voice.

His mouth curved into an easy smile. "High metabolism."

A high metabolism that resulted in a great body she couldn't stop staring at, and now he hit her with a disarming smile that wouldn't quit. Just what she needed to remain clearheaded.

"That's not fair," she protested, clicking back into the conversation.

"Look who's talking," he threw back. His eyes lingered on her face—probably studying every line and every imperfection—she was sure of it. "Wow, Charley, you haven't aged a day since high school."

She felt heat splash across her cheeks. *What was he doing to her?* "Oh, I don't know about that."

His lightheartedness waned as a fiery intensity in his eyes suddenly snatched hold of her, luring her in. "I didn't think it was possible, but you're even more beautiful today."

Her breath caught in her throat as his gaze remained

steady, quickening her pulse, and for a moment she had no sense of where she was.

"Here are your drinks," Angel announced, startling Charley so much that she jerked back, instantly breaking the connection with Jack.

Only then did she take a deep breath. She cast her eyes downward, embarrassed that a few words and a single look from Jack had yielded her powerless.

Angel threw glances between them. Charley could only assume the waitress felt the charged air because she disappeared without saying another word.

Charley released a small single-note laugh before she fixed her eyes on Jack again. "So…"

He smiled. "So…"

Where to begin. Should she tell him how he never really left her thoughts? She opened her mouth, hoping whatever came out would be right, but instead, her hair was pulled by a little boy sitting in the booth behind her.

"Atley, get down!" a woman chastised her son. "I'm so sorry," she said to Charley.

"No worries," she replied as the woman made her son sit on the opposite side. She then shared a look and a laugh with Jack, realizing they were in the wrong place to navigate whatever was happening between them.

"So…uh…work…" he trailed off, rubbing his forehead, as if the thought of work was already giving him a headache.

"Yeah…work," she mirrored, but with an added layer of disgust.

He dipped his head, smiling, before he shifted in the booth, as if physical movement would push him into work mode. He traced the line of his jaw with his fingers, which only made her want to do the same. "Regarding the free week you received…"

"Right." She forced herself back to the matter at hand. "I got a letter in the mail, probably the same letter your friend received."

"I never saw it. What did it say?" He stared at her, never blinking, never wavering.

His dazzling eyes weren't letting up in the intense department. *Focus.* She unwrapped the paper straw and dropped it in her tea. "It said I was invited to St. Nicholas for a complimentary week."

"And what was your obligation to receive the free week?"

"There wasn't one."

"Did you read the fine print?"

"There wasn't any." She retrieved the letter from her handbag and attempted to smooth the wrinkles before handing it over.

He noted the crumpled-up condition and gave her an inquisitive look. She just smiled at him and shrugged. He read it, flipped it over. "Did the Carrolls explain why you were invited?"

She swiftly broke eye contact. "Who knows?"

"What aren't you telling me?" His tone was teasing in a suspicious kind of way.

"Nothing." She tried to sound as nonchalant as possible.

"I'm a detective. I know you're holding something back."

She offered a dismissive grin, slumping down in the booth. "I'm sure that's what all you detectives say."

"Only when it's the truth." His eyes bored into her again. He was good, and she was certain no criminal ever lasted more than thirty seconds under his scrutiny.

"Fine," she said on a sigh. "Apparently, Santa thinks I'm a… Scrooge."

Jack exploded with a laugh, which only annoyed her. "You? But you love Christmas."

She was impressed he even remembered. "I used to, but not anymore."

"Why not? What happened?"

"Doesn't matter. What I want to know is who sent me here. I first thought the letter was in response to my blog, but I—"

"You have a blog?"

"Yes, but it can't—"

"What's it called?" Jack pulled out a notepad and clicked his pen.

"The Cold Hard Facts."

"Great title." He jotted it down, then set his gaze back on her. "Let me guess. You said something negative about Santa."

"Nooo," she said as though she were running musical scales with the one word. "I said Christmas was too chaotic, and everyone should just skip it." She crossed her arms with a single nod of her head, still feeling her suggestion was a sound one.

He grinned, then took a drink. "I'd say that's motive for your invitation."

"I hate to tell you this, Detective, but you're wrong. My take on how to handle Christmas had only been posted less than an hour before I received the letter, so it can't be tied to my blog. What about your friend? Is he a Scrooge?"

"I don't know him that well, but yes, he could have been considered one. I'll be checking into it later." Jack tapped his pen on the table. "Okay, so it has to be somebody you know who thinks you're a Scrooge. A coworker, a friend, a family member who didn't like what you gave them last year for Christmas."

"I'll have you know, I gave out really expensive gift cards."

"Gift cards?" He said it in a sad way, like he felt sorry for her that she couldn't think of anything better.

"And what did you give as gifts, *Santa*?"

"Doesn't matter." He brushed it away. "If you can't think of a potential suspect in your work or personal life, then we'll need to track down whoever sent the letter."

"I tried. The return address is a mailbox."

"That's great." He opened his hands like he had just solved the mystery. "Tomorrow we'll stop by the post office and find out who owns the box."

"It's not a PO Box," she clarified. "I'm talking about a private, free-standing mailbox on public property."

He pushed his brows together. "Are you sure?"

"I already stopped by the post office and that's what they told me."

"Where's the mailbox located?"

"Out there, in the town square." She indicated with a tip of her head. "I'll take you over there after we eat."

He leaned closer to the window but couldn't see much due to the glare on the glass. He clicked his pen. "Walk me through the process."

She sat forward, excited to share her information. She could get used to having a partner on her investigations, especially if it were Jack. "The mailbox is for Scrooge suggestions. Anyone who knows a Scrooge can place his or her name inside the mailbox, but only Santa decides who gets invited to town."

He raised a brow in disbelief. "Santa?"

"It *is* Santa's mailbox," she said with a tongue-in-cheek grin. Even though she was quite willing to rule out the possibility of Christmas magic at play, there was something very odd about that mailbox, and that was a cold hard fact. "I know what you're thinking. I thought it was ridiculous too. I was so confident in my assumption that I decided to prove it by suggesting you."

"Me!" He seemed truly insulted. "Why me?"

"Oh, come on. You know why. When we were in high school, you couldn't get through Christmas fast enough. Your house was one of four on the entire block without any decorations."

He gave a slight nod, knowing she was right. "Well, I didn't get a letter or a free week."

"But you're here."

"Because I'm on a case. Like you, I want to know who's sending out these invitations and why."

She took a sip of her tea. "According to the locals, this town, or something in this town, *magically* turns people's lives around for the better."

Jack scribbled in his notepad, then leaned back, taking her in. "Now I want to focus on you."

She inhaled sharply, trying not to get lost in his eyes. "What about me?"

"Is your life being turned around?"

More like being played with. Never did she think she'd see him again. "I've been here for a whopping twenty-four hours."

"Which means the clock is ticking. The legend has only six more days to make the magic happen for you." Only after she laughed did he get the double entendre. "Sorry." He shook his head in embarrassment. "I didn't mean to derail our conversation."

"Do you see me complaining?" She smiled at him.

He chuckled and glanced at his notes, getting back to business. "Has anyone contacted you about the letter?"

"No." She sat up, refocusing. "If I was invited here because someone thinks I'm a Scrooge, why hasn't anyone asked me to come to a Scrooge group therapy session or sit with a hypnotist who will change my feelings about Christmas?"

Angel brought over their dinner and set the plates before them. "One Cobb salad and one cheeseburger and fries."

"Thanks, Angel." Jack looked over his food. "Hey, do you happen to know when the mail gets picked up at that mailbox out there?"

Her forehead wrinkled. "You mean Santa's mailbox?"

His lips tightened, as if he were restraining a grin from taking over his face. "Yes."

"If the candy cane flag is raised, it gets picked up the same night."

"Who picks it up?" he asked.

"One of Santa's elves," she answered in all seriousness.

Jack caught Charley's eye. She was also trying not to laugh. "Of course," he replied, staying professional.

"Anything else?" she asked him with a pleasant smile.

"No. Thank you."

Charley waited for Angel to be out of earshot before she said, "Bet you weren't expecting that answer."

"Trust me." He squirted ketchup on his burger. "I've heard it all."

He shoved a handful of fries into his mouth while staring at his plate, and she sensed he had slipped into his own little investigative world. Even though they'd been apart fourteen years, she knew he hadn't been satisfied with the odd answers that Angel had given him. Jack looked to be working out the problem in his head. "What's the plan, Detective?"

He glanced up at her as if she had instantly appeared out of thin air. He sat back, wiping the grease from his fingers with a paper napkin. "We're going to conduct a stakeout."

Her mouth fell open. "A stakeout?" He nodded. "Cool." She was totally on board with that. At first she hadn't been able to understand what drew him to detective work, but now she was beginning to understand. There was something sexy and dangerous in being a voyeur, not to mention unraveling a real-life mystery. Now *that* was exciting.

He dove into his food. "Eat up, Charley. It could be a long night."

She picked at her salad, cursing herself for not ordering the burger. She eyed Jack's, which looked so much tastier than lunch meat on lettuce.

He cut his burger in half and plopped it on her plate without saying a word. *Just like old times.*

Chapter Eleven

By the time they left the diner, it was well past eight. Jack had to admit the town looked impressive at night with all the Christmas lights outlining every store, every lamppost, every tree branch. Even Miss Scrooge was finding it difficult to ignore. And he was finding it difficult to ignore *her*. She still had that lively, effervescent quality he remembered so well, but it had greatly diminished. He wondered what had stifled her endless optimism.

"Do you want to walk around the town before we get to work?" he asked.

"Sure," she said, moving closer, and he barely stopped himself from grabbing her hand.

Back in high school, they would always hold hands. He couldn't believe how, after so many years, it was still such a natural response. Not trusting himself not to do it again, he shoved his hands in his pockets. "So, what have you been doing the last fourteen years?"

"Uh, well, let's see. I went to UCLA for journalism, and after I graduated, I couldn't find a job in my field, so I bounced around until I got an internship at *Authentic Lifestyles,* where I've been ever since," she said in one breath. "I guess that doesn't sound like a whole lot for fourteen years." With wide eyes and hands to her cheeks, she presented her best expression of horror, which made him laugh. "What about you?"

"I studied criminal justice at the University of Colorado, Denver. After that, I went to the police academy, was a police officer for a year, helped out a sheriff in a small town for another year, and now I'm a detective where I focus mainly on fraud and other white-collar crimes."

She looked at him thoughtfully. "That's impressive, Detective Brody."

"No more than your story," he replied, attempting to put the focus back on her. He wanted to know what made her tick. "What's your blog about?"

"Gosh." She sighed loudly. "I guess the best way to describe it is I reveal the facts behind a romanticized story, legend, or myth."

"Oh, yeah?" He nodded with interest. "Like what?"

"Well." She shrugged. "For instance, why do we enjoy stories taking place in medieval times? Why are little girls taught to dream of living in a castle with Prince Charming? The most common answer is 'because it's romantic.' But was it really? Of course not. I point out that life in medieval times was just that. Medieval. It was tough. No antibiotics, no sanitation. They slowly poisoned themselves by using mercury in medicine and lead in kitchenware. People didn't bathe for months. There were rampant fleas and—"

"Seriously, Charley?" He frowned.

"Oh, yeah. Those are the cold hard facts about life back then."

"No, I mean, you're seriously writing about this?" The question tumbled out of his mouth before he had a chance to rephrase it. It sounded way too harsh, even to his own ears, and he had to fix it fast. "You, Charley Dawson, Queen of Light and Optimism, are out there crushing little girls' dreams?" *Oh, no. That was worse.* He added a laugh, hoping she wouldn't take offense. *Too late.*

"Little girls aren't my readership," she replied icily. "Besides, my blog covers a wide variety of subjects. I have articles that talk about which hotels are the cleanest, which cities are the safest. I'd think you, being a detective, would appreciate that there was someone out there, like me, who tells it like it is."

"I do and I am." He put his hands up in defense. "Sorry. Will you ever forgive me, milady?" he asked in jest, and she poked him in the ribs with her elbow.

She had a sour expression on her face. He couldn't tell if she was pretending to be mad, or if she really was. *Best not to guess wrong.*

"I really am sorry. That came out all wrong because you actually crushed me. I mean, here I honestly thought castle life was all about slaying dragons and winning the heart of a noble lady such as yourself with your ethereal flaxen hair and your beguiling forest-green eyes."

Charley shook her head, truly laughing this time. "You're impossible."

Not to love. He finished their high school saying in his head. When he glanced at her, she was staring at him with a pensive look on her face, and he thought that maybe she had remembered their saying too.

"Apology accepted," she finally said as she moved closer to him again.

"How are your parents?" he quickly threw out, choosing a neutral topic of conversation.

"My mom passed away from cancer when I was twenty-two."

"Oh, Charley, I'm so sorry. I remember how close you were as a family."

"Thanks. It came as quite a shock," she said, walking slowly with her head down and her hands tucked deep in her pockets. "My dad had a very tough time, as you can imagine, so he threw himself into work. He's with an investment firm that has him traveling a lot. Two years ago, he met someone in London where he now lives."

Jack was beginning to understand the change in her. It would be hard enough to lose one parent, but then to have the other move halfway across the globe had to be tough. "Do you at least see him when he travels back to LA?"

"He was promoted to the London office. I haven't seen him since he moved."

"Then you'll have to visit him." he said, trying to sound cheerful.

"Maybe," she replied, though Jack sensed there was more to the story. "How are your parents?" She flicked him a glance.

"Good," he told her, but held back that his mom had continued to ask about her long after they broke up. "They live five minutes from me, so I see them often—probably too often because I'm a lousy cook."

Charley laughed. He wanted to ask her more about her life but was afraid he'd step in it again, so they fell into a comfortable silence.

As they walked along a path in the town square, they accidentally bumped shoulders. He thought she did it on purpose since she'd poked him with her elbow, but then they bumped into each other again, and then again.

"I'm seriously not trying to run into you," Charley said, a little flustered.

"It's not you," he said, realizing what was happening.

"Did you know that humans can't walk a straight line without a focal point?"

"Is that true?"

He nodded. "But we're probably bumping into each other because you're left-handed and I'm right-handed. Those are our dominant sides, which means we're walking a little off center of a straight line."

"Okay, Mr. Brainiac, let's test your theory and switch sides."

They did and walked toward the Christmas tree without running into each other once.

"You're right!" she exclaimed, overflowing with that bubbly charm he'd missed for so long.

"Just one of the weird facts I've picked up being a detective."

"Permission to put that under the Weird Facts section on my blog?"

"Be my guest."

She stared up at the sixty-foot Christmas tree, and he heard her take in a satisfied breath. "What a beautiful tree."

He was impressed himself. The tree was expertly decorated with just the right number of lights, shiny bulbs, and bows. A bright silver star adorned the top, and for a moment, he remembered the good Christmases of years gone by. "It really is."

They stayed there for a few more minutes, listening to Christmas carolers and observing families taking pictures in front of the tree. Jack kept giving her sidelong glances. Her eyes lit up when she watched children, and she laughed at goofy dads being silly. He wondered if she wanted to have children. He had wanted the whole package at one time, but gave up on that dream a few years ago.

As they continued their stroll, he became aware of all the couples walking arm in arm. Charley seemed to notice them as well. Had she been apathetic about being in a relationship like he had? It didn't seem possible. She was too much of a people person, whereas he could go days without social interaction. He knew losing her mom and missing her dad were sure to dampen her spirits, but he sensed there was something else that had made her lose her spark. She might not want to tell him, but he would know soon enough. He was a detective, after all, and he was very good at his job.

Shortly after nine, they were back on the Scrooge case and in full stakeout mode. Jack thought it best they didn't inspect the mailbox before the stakeout, so instead, he parked his SUV on the side of Main Street, far enough away to avoid detection but close enough to monitor the situation.

"Do you go on a lot of stakeouts?" she asked as she sipped hot coffee, keeping an eye on Santa's mailbox.

"It depends on the case, but I've had my share."

"I'm guessing you don't have a nine-to-five job."

"Does anyone anymore?"

She laughed. "Good point."

Jack stayed focused, scanning the area around the mailbox. Not that he wanted to show off for Charley, but he was determined to catch and question whoever was collecting the mail. And maybe he did want to show off a little.

"All those long hours must be tough on your wife." She fixed her eyes on him.

Jack raised his bare hand, minus any wedding ring—

just like she'd done for him earlier. "I'm not married, either."

"Good," she said with satisfaction. "I mean, it's good we got that out of the way."

He looked at her curiously. "Are you saying that you wouldn't have come along on this stakeout if I'd been married?"

"No, I was just wondering." She shrugged. "And now I can concentrate on the task at hand." She let out a loud determined breath and zeroed in on the mailbox.

He smiled, amused by her behavior. He peered through the binoculars, then passed them to her.

"Flag's still up," she said, sounding disappointed, before she handed them back.

"We've been at it for less than an hour," he reminded her. "You're not already bored, are you?"

"Me? No. It's exciting to stare at a mailbox. Best Wednesday night I've had in a long time."

He laughed. "You remind me of my partner, Adam. He's funny, like you. Makes the stakeouts more interesting."

"Well, someone needs to be your sidekick," she teased. "But I'm glad to see you're not so serious, like you were as a teenager."

"Oh, I'm still serious. Ask anyone in the department. You just seem to be making me laugh." He thought about that for a moment. It had been a long time since he laughed so much on a date—not that it was a date, but if it were...

Her mouth hitched up into a half smile, and he found that very attractive. "How come your partner's not with you now?"

"It's better I'm alone—to keep my investigation on the down low, so to speak."

"Ah. I'm guessing Mary and Joe don't know you're a detective."

"Nope. I'm just a guy taking some time off."

"Copy that. I'll keep your true intentions on the DL," she said in an affected voice, then suddenly sat up straight. "Who's that?"

He swiveled his head to see a conspicuous-looking man wearing a hat and a long dark coat walking toward the mailbox. Jack raised the binoculars to his eyes. "One of Santa's elves?"

The man slowed, stopped several feet short of the mailbox, and scoped out his surroundings.

Charley gasped. "Oh, my gosh. This could be it."

The man retrieved a ringing phone from his pocket and answered it. He kept looking around as he talked, then abruptly disconnected the call.

"That's weird." She frowned.

Jack continued to study the man through the binoculars. "He's waiting for someone."

A minute later, a woman came running up. They hugged, exchanged words, then rushed off toward the diner.

He lowered the binoculars. "False alarm."

"Shoot," she grumbled.

He glanced at the time on the dashboard: 10:03. "I hope Angel's right."

"She said it's always collected when the flag is up."

He peered through the binoculars again. "The flag's still up." He handed them over to Charley so she could see for herself.

She set them to her eyes. "We could still get a lead tonight."

"Spoken like a true detective."

As Charley remained focused on the mailbox, he found himself studying her face—her pretty lips, her determined chin, her slender but slightly turned up nose.

She lowered the binoculars and he quickly averted his gaze, feeling guilty he'd been staring at her without her knowledge.

"I know we're working here, Jack, but do you mind if I ask you something personal?"

"Not at all." He gave her his undivided attention. "Fire away."

She paused for a moment and took a deep breath before she raised her eyes to meet his. "I've been wanting to know why you—"

A cackle from a teenage boy had Jack and Charley turning to see a group of high school kids wandering down the sidewalk, joking around. One of the boys scooped up snow from the side of the street, threw it toward his friend, but hit the car window by Charley instead.

She let out a startled scream.

Jack jumped out of the car. "Hey! Get over here."

The boy who threw the snowball seemed shocked to see six-foot-two Jack get out of the SUV. "I'm sorry, sir." He cowered. "I was aiming for my friend."

Jack couldn't miss the look of terror on the kid's face, so he dialed it back. "You need to work on your aim."

The boy froze as though he wasn't sure what to think until Jack cracked a smile. "Yes, sir!"

"Jack, look!" Charley bolted from the car, pointing to the mailbox.

He whipped around to see that the flag was down.

They raced to the mailbox, certain they'd find someone hiding behind it, only no one was there. Nobody was even near it. Jack cast his flashlight down the walkway in both directions, expecting to see someone running away, yet there wasn't a soul in sight. He combed the nearby bushes and also came up empty-handed. "I can't believe we missed the pickup."

"We looked away for what, a minute?" she asked. "How could someone have collected it and disappeared so quickly?"

"I don't know." He inspected the packed snow around the mailbox, trampled by people's boots, and worked his way around to the back side of the mailbox. Though the snow had seen less traffic, no single set of footprints stood out to him. He shined his light on the collection door and noticed a vintage, ornate, heart-shaped padlock. The detailed design reminded him of the metallic tubes he'd seen at Felicity and Nolan's B&B. "Check this out."

She came around and stood next to him. "Whoa." She bent down for a closer look. "How old do you think that is?"

"Hard to tell, but I'd guess early 1900s. Can you hold this for me?" He gave her the flashlight and began manipulating the lock. "Interesting." He ran his hand over the gold facing.

"What?"

"It's a combination lock and key."

"So?"

"It's not an either/or combination. It's both. Look here. Four numbers open this facing, which exposes the keyhole. It's a two-lock system."

"That's pretty cool." She studied the intricacy of it. "How long do you think it would take to get it open?"

"To enter a code and then use a key… I don't know, maybe ten, fifteen seconds."

"Then the guy must have been a magician to get out of here in under thirty."

"Agreed," Jack said, standing. "I want to check it out again in the daylight."

"What time is it?"

He checked his watch. "Quarter after ten."

"Maybe it'll be picked up at the same time tomorrow night."

He took one more look around, then eyed Charley with determination. "If it is, we'll be ready."

Chapter Twelve

It was midnight before Charley crawled into bed. She was bone tired but couldn't sleep. Seeing Jack again brought back so many good memories. She remembered how they had passed love notes to each other in history class and went bike riding around the neighborhood after school. They spent many Friday nights on her couch with pizza and a scary movie. One of her favorite memories was that of the homecoming dance where they shared their first kiss. She remembered the long summer at the beach, the great talks, the constant laughter. And then it abruptly ended.

She punched her pillow, trying to get comfortable. Why had she let him in again, especially after she swore that she never would? She needed to know why he broke up with her. She'd been about to ask him that very question when snowball-wielding teens barged in on the moment. Now she was powerless against his charm. Being with him again made it feel like a single weekend had passed, not fourteen years. She closed her eyes, focusing on the peace that had enveloped her while she was sitting by his side and, at last, she fell asleep.

A few hours later, Charley was dreaming of Jack painting a house, their house. He was on a ladder with paintbrush in hand, whistling "Deck the Halls." In the distance, she heard bells. Church bells? No, that wasn't right. They were jingling like tiny bells on Clarence's collar. In the dream, Clarence was wearing a different collar, but then Clarence turned into a mouse, and the mouse was wearing a costume covered with jingle bells. She didn't know why Christmas bells were in a summer scene of Jack painting their house. The house was a pale yellow, only when he dipped the paintbrush in the can, the paint turned to red and green stripes. And there went those bells again—jingling incessantly. They were getting louder, right by her ear and—

"Oh!" She sat bolt upright in bed. Those bells were not in her dream but in her room. She scrambled to turn on the light. No one was there. *Maybe someone is in the bathroom.* Heart pounding, she silently slid out of bed and tiptoed to the bathroom, swiftly flipping on the light, only to find herself staring at her own reflection in the mirror. She let out the breath she'd been holding and rubbed her eyes. "I'm losing it."

She turned off the bathroom light, ready to return to bed, when she spotted a Christmas decoration—a small stuffed mouse standing on the fireplace mantel. She walked over to it and picked it up. She didn't remember seeing it before—then again, she *must* have seen it because her subconscious stuck it into her dream.

The stuffed mouse was wearing a red-and-green vest with a matching hat. There was a jingle bell attached to the tip of his hat and several tiny bells attached to the bottom of his vest. He wore thin gold-framed glasses and had a sweet expression on his face.

"You are adorable. I don't remember you being here

yesterday." She continued to study the mouse. "You fit right in, but I swear you weren't here when I went to bed."

Charley suddenly felt a little spooked. She strode to her door and wiggled the doorknob. It was still locked. She sat on the end of the bed with the mouse and inspected his back, turning him upside down, searching for any hidden cameras. Finding none, she set him on the mantel and got back into bed, wondering if everything was connected—the letter, seeing Jack, being called a Scrooge (which actually hurt her feelings, even though she pretended it didn't).

The mouse fell over and jingled. She got out of bed again, picked him up, and this time she placed him farther back on the mantel.

"I'm not a Scrooge," she felt inclined to tell the mouse. "Obviously. A Scrooge wouldn't talk to a Christmas mouse."

She sat on the end of the bed and stared at him. "So… what's your name, where are you from?" She chuckled, and then leaned back on her hands. "You look like an Arthur. Do you like Arthur?" The mouse didn't move. "I'll take that as a yes. Arthur it is. Okay, Arthur, are you here to spy on me to report back to Santa like your little elf friends? If you are, you can tell him that he should know the reason I'm not a fan of Christmas anymore."

She got up and got a drink of water. "Last year, my fiancé called off our engagement on Christmas Eve. The year before that, I found my previous boyfriend kissing someone else at a Christmas party. And the year before that, the guy I'd been dating for six whole months chose Christmas Day to call it quits. Three failed relationships in three years, all ending at my favorite time of year." She shook her head. "You can see why I'm done with

Christmas, so if Santa wants me to stop being a Scrooge, he will need to put my soulmate in my stocking this year, instead of a lump of coal! Think that could happen for me?" She eyed Arthur, who remained motionless. "I didn't think so."

She ran a hand through her disheveled hair and glanced at the alarm clock by her bed. It was five in the morning. "So much for going back to sleep."

She opened a drawer, retrieved a sweatshirt and leggings, then threw them on. She grabbed her book off the nightstand, quietly closed the door behind her, and tiptoed downstairs. Right as she was about to settle in the living room to read, she heard clanking noises coming from the kitchen. Charley had to investigate.

"Mind if I come in?" she asked at the entrance to the kitchen where Mary was hard at work baking cinnamon rolls.

Mary looked up, startled. "Oh, my goodness, Charley. What are you doing up so early? Grab some coffee. Did you not sleep well?"

She poured herself a cup, slid out one of the barstools, and sat down. "I managed to get in a few hours before I was awakened by the sound of...jingle bells." She watched her host intently, waiting for an amused reaction, only Mary didn't have one.

"Yes, that happens here," she said matter-of-factly.

Charley let out a tiny laugh. "Oh, okay, good to know. Glad you don't think I sound crazy."

"Why would I think that, dear?" She afforded a brief glance at Charley before she set her attention back to rolling up dough coated with butter, raisins, cinnamon, and sugar.

"If you'd seen me twenty minutes ago, I was telling my woes to that Christmas mouse on the mantel."

Mary frowned. "I don't remember a Christmas mouse in your room."

"You know the one. He's got a red-and-green vest on, with a matching hat, and he wears gold-framed glasses."

"Oh, Arthur," Mary remarked casually. "Yes, he's a very good listener."

"Arthur?" Charley couldn't believe her ears.

"Yes, well, that's what I call him, anyway."

"I named him Arthur too!"

"How funny. Well, he does look like an Arthur." Mary cut the dough into equal sections, then placed them on the baking pan.

"I'm beginning to understand your town's welcome sign." She sipped her coffee.

"Our sign?"

"The one at your town's border. Most signs state the population, but yours states the number of believers, as if everyone living here believes in the magic of Christmas."

"I guess we don't have a reason not to." Mary shrugged as she pulled out a hot tray of cinnamon rolls before sliding another into the oven. She then transferred the baked rolls to a cooling rack.

Charley loved how the locals appeared to have blind faith that their lives would always run as smoothly as a freshly paved road. Unfortunately, her life was full of potholes. "You believe in the magic of Christmas, even when things go in the wrong direction?"

"*Especially* when they go in the wrong direction. That's the time to have faith that it's all going to turn out for the best." Mary reached for another mixing bowl and threw in two cups of powdered sugar, a couple tablespoons of softened butter, and a splash of vanilla.

"You'd think differently if you were me."

"How so?" Mary began stirring, slowing adding milk to her glaze for the cinnamon rolls.

"I seem to suffer from love loss around the holidays."

"I'm sorry to hear that."

"No more than me." Charley sighed. "Christmas is supposed to be about love and joy. Just once in my adult life, I'd like to know how that feels."

"Just once?" Mary challenged. "Why not all the time?"

"I'll take what I can get."

"Don't sell yourself short, Charley. I can see that you're a beautiful woman inside and out, and I'll bet a basket of my best cookies that Jack would agree with me."

The mention of Jack brought a smile to Charley's lips. "I still can't believe we found each other after all these years."

"And at Christmas." Mary winked at her.

"I hadn't thought of that." She took a big breath and let it out. "Back in high school, Jack and I had only one Christmas together. After my family opened presents, he came over for the afternoon. My next-door neighbors rented a snow machine for their two kids, and since I was their favorite babysitter, they asked us to join them. We made snow angels, and built a pathetic-looking snowman with an undersized head. We even had a snowball fight, pitting the girls against the boys." She smiled, thinking back. "Us girls won, of course."

"Sounds like it was a good Christmas." Mary gave her glaze one last stir before she poured it over the slightly cooled rolls.

"It was. But that was years ago."

"Doesn't mean good Christmases are all in the past," Mary said. "Embrace the spirit of Christmas while you're here. I promise it'll heal your heart, and it might even bring you a little Christmas magic."

Charley stared at the perfectly cooked, perfectly shaped cinnamon rolls covered in white glaze and thought they were a work of art. "I think you're the one with the magic. I can't remember the last time I had one, but those cinnamon rolls smell heavenly."

"It's time to break your cinnamon roll drought." Mary placed a roll on a plate and handed it over with a fork. "Careful now. It's still hot."

Charley cut off a small bite, blew on it, then slipped it into her mouth. "Oh, wow," she said with her mouth full. "Incredible."

"There's plenty more, so help yourself. I've got to go roust Joe."

As Mary left with a couple of cinnamon rolls and coffee for her husband, Charley wondered what the catch was to the Scrooge Legend. *There's always a catch when something's not true.* She picked up the delicious cinnamon roll and studied it. "And aren't you quite a lure."

Jack finished getting dressed for the day and eyed the clock. It was ten after seven. If he were still in Denver, he'd be leaving for work, but today, he was dragging. He had stayed up half the night reading every post Charley had written. It was fascinating to see how her mind worked, especially when it came to debunking legends. She pulled everything apart, paid attention to the details, then slowly rebuilt her theory with facts to support her point of view. It wasn't unlike what he did with every case. He remembered how much they thought alike in high school, and it apparently still held true.

He closed his computer and put it away. For the first time in his career, he was finding it difficult to keep his mind on a case. All he wanted to do was get to know Charley again. Of course, it would have been helpful if he'd made another date with her before they'd parted the previous night. He'd neglected to ask for her cell number, which was why he hauled himself out of bed on four hours sleep to hopefully run into her at breakfast.

Jack grabbed his coat off the back of his chair, glanced out the window, and spotted Charley climbing into Joe's truck. He frowned, watching them leave, knowing he might not see her all day. With a disappointed sigh, he picked up his wallet off the dresser and headed downstairs for breakfast.

Mary was pouring coffee for some of her other guests when he entered and sat down at the nearest empty table. "Good morning, Jack." Mary came over. "Coffee?"

"Please." He snapped open his cloth napkin, setting it in his lap.

"How did you sleep?" She poured coffee into his cup.

"Best night I've had in a long time," he replied, not wanting to lie. He did have the best night, discovering Charley's blog. "Though I might have done something to your shower. It started dripping this morning."

"That darn thing," she groaned. "Joe said he fixed that. I'm so sorry. This time I'll call a real plumber. Now, how about some homemade cinnamon rolls, scrambled eggs, and hickory smoked bacon?"

"Sounds fantastic," he said, rubbing his hands together in anticipation.

"I'll get that started for you." She checked the creamer to make sure it was full.

"Do you happen to know where Charley went with Joe?"

"He gave her a lift into town. Charley said she's spending the day there. Something about helping out a detective."

He smiled. "That's great, really great." And he couldn't stop smiling.

Chapter Thirteen

Charley conducted more interviews that morning, hoping to find someone who would tell her that the Scrooge Legend was all a hoax, but to her great disappointment, no one did. She finally realized that if she interviewed every resident of St. Nicholas, she'd hear nothing new. Many residents came to town as a Scrooge or arrived because they knew a Scrooge, and the ending was always the same. Happy with a capital H.

"Bah, humbug!" If whoever invited her now thought they could change her into a believer, they were sadly mistaken. She came here to debunk the Scrooge Legend and that's what she was going to do. She just needed to figure out how the mailbox was rigged and who was behind the invitations.

She stood in front of the metallic enigma. She had no idea why she was drawn to the thing. It was a silly piece of metal. *A piece of metal that apparently changes lives.* She had difficulty believing Christmas magic was part of the equation. Yet after hearing all the Scrooge stories and testing the theory herself, it made her wonder. Jack was already in town before she dropped his name in the mailbox, but would they have run into each other if she hadn't?

That's it! She'd suggest someone else. *But who?* She had to come up with another Scrooge… *Or do I?*

She took out a pen from her handbag and scribbled Liv's name on the back of an old receipt. She went to open the door but it wouldn't budge. *What?* She tried again. Nothing. Was the door remaining closed because Liv wasn't a Scrooge, or was there some rule that stated one name per customer?

Frustrated, she walked behind the mailbox to see if she could get into it another way. She bent down to examine the vintage padlock. She yanked hard on it, but it was firmly locked, as expected.

"Four numbers. What would they be?" She thought for a moment, then dialed in 1-2-3-4 and pushed the tiny latch on the facing. It didn't spring open. "Hmm. Santa, elves, Christmas." She dialed in 1-2-2-5, pushed on the tiny latch, and the facing popped open. "Yes!"

"You started without me?"

She shot up with a squeaky gasp to find gorgeous Jack standing inches from her. "Jack!" She put her hand to her chest as she took him in. He had a rugged look to him today—a perfect five o'clock shadow accentuated his strong jaw and brought attention to his blue-gray eyes. He wore a chestnut-colored barn coat that fit nicely over his broad shoulders, and his well-worn cowboy boots weren't just for show. "You scared me half to death," she said, attempting to hide the true reason for ogling him.

"Sorry, Miss Sleuth." He dazzled her with a lopsided grin, and she could almost hear a Southern accent as he spoke. "I figured I'd find you here."

He was looking for me? She smiled, lifting a brow. "Good instincts, Detective."

"What were you all excited about?" He broke the hold

he had over her by shifting his gaze to the mailbox. "Did you find something interesting?"

"Better. I figured out the combination."

"What was it? Christmas day?"

"Show-off."

Jack came around to the back of the mailbox and as he stood next to her, she felt weak in the knees. He exuded strength, confidence, security—and it was intoxicating. He took a picture of the lock with his phone. "That's a pretty cool lock."

"Yeah," she said, still gazing at him. *Focus.* She stepped away from him in order to concentrate on debunking the Scrooge Legend. "I wonder why the access door is in the back. I thought mail was collected from the front?"

"Depends on the mailbox. But federal mailboxes use keys these days." He stood up to inspect the rest of the mailbox. "This definitely does not belong to the government." He attempted to flip up the flag, but it wouldn't move. "That's weird." He examined the side of the flag.

"The flag won't raise until a name is deposited," an elderly woman's voice rang out behind them. A tiny woman, appearing to be in her late seventies, approached with a piece of paper in her hand.

"Watch." As the woman slowly shuffled over, Charley nudged Jack and motioned to the name LYDIA typed in big black letters on a blank sheet of paper.

"Excuse me, but don't you need an address and a stamp on that?" Jack asked.

"Oh, no. Santa knows where my daughter lives." She effortlessly opened the door, dropped the piece of paper inside, then easily raised the flag. "I should have done that a long time ago," she said in a steady yet somewhat frail voice.

"Why didn't you?" Charley asked.

"I was hoping my daughter would *want* to come and see me, but she hasn't, and I've waited years. Now she's changed so much that even her husband doesn't know who she is anymore."

"I'm sorry," Charley said sympathetically.

"No need." She smiled. "It's all fixed now."

"How can you be so sure?" Jack asked.

"Because I live in St. Nicholas. If you ask me, the Legend of Scrooge needs to be changed to the Legend of Miracles."

Miracles? Charley thought that was an interesting choice of words.

"Ma'am?" Jack called as the elderly woman was making her way back down the walkway. "Do you know who collects the mail here?"

She pivoted around. "I imagine it's one of Santa's helpers."

"Have you ever seen anyone pick it up—with your own eyes?" he asked.

"No, but it's always collected late at night. Now, if you'll excuse me, I need to get the house ready for my daughter's visit."

Charley watched her hobble away. "What a sweet lady."

"I hope she won't be too disappointed when her daughter doesn't show."

"Maybe she will." Charley eyed Jack. "I think it's time we admit that something unusual is going on here. The Scrooge stories, this fickle-working mailbox, the fact that you and I are investigating the same story—the number of unexplained things is stacking up rapidly."

"Not unexplained. Yet to be answered. Take the mailbox, for instance. I bet the flag is triggered when the door opens." He tried the handle, but it remained shut. "What the heck?"

"The door doesn't open without a suggestion."

"Absurd." With all his might, he yanked on the handle to no avail. "Someone is messing with us." He studied the trees above him.

Charley cast her eyes upward. "What are you looking for?"

"Hidden cameras."

She scanned the area with him. "See any?"

"No." He blew out a frustrated sigh and stared at the mailbox.

"Try putting a name in there."

"What?" He gave her an odd look.

"I want to see if it will open for you. I tried to deposit another name earlier, and I couldn't."

Jack rubbed his chin. "I can't think of anyone who has a problem with Christmas."

"It's a wide net. Anyone who's cheap or selfish or simply makes others miserable can be Scrooges. Surely in your line of work, you've met someone like that."

"Unfortunately, yes." He took out his pen and notepad, flipping to a blank page. "Wait. Will this person suddenly appear in town?"

"Like you did?" Charley challenged, arching a brow. Even though she doubted the existence of Christmas magic, deep down she wanted it to be real. She wanted to believe Santa brought Jack to her. She wanted to believe that the world hadn't singled her out for a lonely, loveless existence. If Jack's Scrooge showed up, she'd be one step closer to believing in Christmas magic and a happy ending. "Yes, if this is real, your Scrooge will come to town."

"Forget it." He put away his pen.

"Why? Were you about to suggest a drug dealer or a bank robber?"

"Drug dealers and bank robbers aren't on Santa's list."

"True. But they're clearly Scrooges."

"Do you think I'd unleash a drug dealer or bank robber on the good people of St. Nicholas?"

"I thought you didn't believe in Christmas magic," she reminded him, crossing her arms.

"I don't. This whole thing is a hoax."

"Agreed, but we need to prove it."

"Right." Jack jotted down a name. Curious, she leaned closer to him, attempting to see what he wrote, but he tore off the paper and folded it in half before she could make out one letter.

"Ready?" He reached for the mailbox handle.

"You bet."

He pulled on the door, and it opened with ease. "This is illogical."

"You'll get no argument from me."

He shoved the paper in his pocket and struggled to move the flag while the door was still open, but it wouldn't budge. He retrieved a small flashlight from inside his jacket and shined the light inside.

"See anything?" She jockeyed for a better position over his shoulder, wanting to see inside the mailbox for herself.

"The flag appears to be completely independent from the door," he said, sounding disappointed.

"Let go of it."

He released the handle and it banged shut. She attempted to open it for herself, but nothing happened.

Jack shook his head. "How is this possible?" He yanked on the handle and it remained shut. He then withdrew the Scrooge name from his pocket, placed his other hand on the door, and it opened with ease. "I have no words for what's happening here."

"Check the flag."

He made an effort to move the flag again, but it wouldn't budge.

"Maybe the flag won't move until a name is deposited."

"There's only one way to find out." He tossed the name inside the mailbox and let go of the handle. He touched the flag again, and it suddenly moved up and down easily.

She gasped.

"This defies all logic." Jack kept the flag in the raised position.

"What now?"

"We've got to find whoever is picking up this mail. He or she is the link to this whole operation."

"And who is that exactly?"

Jack studied the buildings closest to the mailbox. "Do you see that?" He pointed to the bank building across the street.

Charley shielded her eyes as she turned in the direction of the sun. "What am I looking for?"

"Security cameras. C'mon."

Chapter Fourteen

Charley trailed Jack through the park, trying to keep up as he hurried across the street and into the bank. Once inside, he assessed each employee before he homed in on a distinguished-looking man talking to a younger employee in the loan department.

"I bet that's the bank manager." Jack motioned to the older gentleman. "Time to get some answers."

As they approached, the man glanced up. "Can I help you?"

"I'm Detective Brody." Jack flashed his badge. "Are you the manager?"

"I am." The man skimmed Jack's credentials. "Is there a problem, Detective?"

"I'm not here on official business, but I was hoping you could tell me if your security cameras capture any area of the town square?"

"Our high-angle cameras cover the street and roughly a quarter of the square closest to our building."

Charley locked eyes with Jack. "That's where the mailbox is."

"Santa's mailbox?" the bank manager asked.

"Yes," she replied.

A small smile crossed the man's face. "You must be a guest of our town."

"That's a polite way of calling me a Scrooge," Charley said, "but, yes, I am."

He placed his hands behind his back. "I prefer guest. Welcome, Ms...."

"Dawson," Charley finished for him.

"Ms. Dawson," he acknowledged with a nod, "would you follow me, please?" The manager buzzed them into the back and led them down a long hallway. "You impress me, Ms. Dawson."

She peered up at him. "How so?"

"You're the first guest I know of who's brought her own detective."

"Oh, he's not *my* detective," she said with a laugh.

The manager scrutinized Jack over the rims of his glasses. "Are you sure about that?" He raised a brow to Charley, unlocked a door, and the three walked inside.

There was a surveillance console with eight monitors recording various parts of the bank, including the outside.

"Let's see. You want camera five." The manager sat down at the console and pulled up the digital files for camera five. "What time are you looking for?"

Jack leaned in. "A few minutes after ten last night."

The manager selected the time and date, then opened the video file. "Here you go." He hit Play, then moved aside so they could get a closer look.

On the monitor, the playback showed the teenagers walking along the sidewalk with the mailbox clearly visible in the background. One of the kids threw a snowball and hit Charley's window. When Jack got out of his car to yell at him, the video went black.

Jack jerked back. "What happened?"

"I'm afraid we lose picture every time the mail is collected." The manager sounded almost bored with the question.

"You don't expect me to believe that," Jack said.

The manager remained calm, as if he had been through this exact scenario several times before. "Please continue watching." He motioned to the screen.

On the monitor, the video resumed at the point when they ran over to the mailbox.

Jack frowned. "I find it convenient that the very footage we need to see is corrupted. Did you tamper with this?"

"No, Detective, I did not, nor have any of my employees."

"Have you thought about replacing the camera?" she asked.

"Yes, we've replaced the camera at least three times now."

Jack kept looking over the video file, no doubt trying to figure out if the missing material had been deliberately deleted.

"It's a shame the video is corrupted," Charley said. "We wanted to identify the person who's collecting the mail there. Have you ever seen anyone picking it up?"

"Unfortunately, no."

Jack stood and leveled his gaze on the manager. "Isn't anyone in this town curious?"

"Very much so, Detective." The man pushed his glasses up on his nose. "Our town has very discreet cameras covering that square in every angle imaginable."

"That's great," she said. "Where can we find the footage?"

"Police department."

* * *

Jack seemed fired up as they made their way to the police department. "Do you think the manager's hiding something?" she asked, hoping he'd let her in on whatever was going on in his head.

"Absolutely. He acted as if he already knew the video would be missing before we viewed it."

"But why would he destroy it? He didn't even know we were coming."

Jack stopped, took a breath. "This town makes money because of the Scrooge Legend. If someone obtains evidence proving it isn't real, tourism would fall dramatically."

"I thought the same thing, but look around." She swept her hand over the town. "It's all about Christmas here, all year round. They make plenty of money on that alone. We're missing something."

"Maybe, but whatever it is, most of the town is in on it." They reached the doors of the police department. "Our only lead is that ridiculous mailbox. It's imperative we find whoever is connected to it."

"Then the local police should be able to help us, especially since you're a detective."

"Only this town isn't in my jurisdiction."

"Oh, right. You're on the down low," she teased. "Then I guess we won't be shaking down anyone in there for answers."

Jack held back a smile as he opened the door for her. "I guess we won't."

Fifteen minutes later, they were sitting with a police officer in a CCTV room, searching for the requested time from the previous night.

"We've had so many skeptical guests over the years

that we decided to install cameras overhead in that particular area," the officer said.

"Overhead?" Jack perked up. "Where?"

"In the light fixtures along the pathway leading to and from the mailbox."

"Jack and I didn't notice any surveillance out there this morning."

"They're very well hidden," the officer explained, "unlike the cameras outside the bank."

She moved closer to the row of video screens as the officer uploaded the files. "Who was monitoring the cameras an hour ago?"

"No one. We continuously record the area but never play it back unless someone like you requests it."

"Have any of the cameras ever been hacked?" Jack asked.

"Never. Why do you ask?"

"The mailbox in the town square isn't...working properly." Jack swallowed his words, seeming reluctant to voice anything out of the ordinary.

The officer eyed Jack. "What do you mean?"

"It doesn't open automatically," she answered, stepping in.

"The mailbox is rigged." Jack cut to the chase.

"Impossible," the officer said. "That's Santa's mailbox. No one messes with it."

"What happens if someone does?" she had to ask.

"They'd probably get a lump of coal in their stocking," he joked. Charley laughed but Jack did not. The officer cleared his throat. "As Detective Brody can attest, all mailboxes are protected under federal law, so any form of tampering is considered a crime."

"Crime or no, I think whoever picks up the mail has

something to do with it," Jack said, "so if you can start last night's recordings a little after ten, we'd greatly appreciate it."

"You got it." The officer synched up twelve recordings which covered every angle of Santa's mailbox and hit Play.

Charley and Jack watched the events of the previous night unfold across all twelve monitors in twelve different angles. At the exact same time, all monitors went black, like camera five had done at the bank.

"What?" Charley's jaw dropped at the now-black screens.

"No!" Jack paced off a few angry steps. "That's impossible."

The officer remained unfazed. "This happens every night the mail is collected. I had the same reaction the first time I saw this, but now you know why the bank manager showed you their footage instead of immediately sending you here. You've now viewed recordings from two independent surveillance systems. If you go to the jewelry store down the block, they will show you the same thing. Everyone loses picture when the mail is removed from that mailbox."

"Every time?" Jack gave him a skeptical look.

"Without fail."

Jack scrubbed his face and let out a frustrated breath. "This is…unbelievable."

The officer shrugged. "So it goes in St. Nicholas."

Chapter Fifteen

When Charley and Jack left the police department, she could tell Jack was stewing. "Are you okay?"

"I've been better. I've come up against weird stuff on cases before, but this is infuriating."

"We'll figure it out," she said, confidently. "Maybe there's some kind of electrical interference that happens, or maybe the surveillance systems are actually all connected, but they refuse to disclose that information."

"Or maybe whoever is collecting the mail utilizes a jamming device to interfere with all the security cameras at the same time."

"Can someone do that?"

"Sure. It's highly illegal, but yes."

"Then why haven't the police taken the 'mailman' into custody?"

"You've got to be able to catch a criminal to charge him, and according to this town, there is no criminal. They'd be taking Santa or Santa's helper off the streets because he was picking up his own mail. Think of the bad optics."

"It wouldn't be the best PR move." She zipped up her coat, starting to feel the cold.

"Looks like my California girl needs something hot to drink." Jack stopped at a coffee vendor.

I'm his California girl? She suddenly felt a lump of emotion in her throat. *Did he really mean it?*

"Here you go." He handed her one of the drinks. "I got you a white chocolate latte."

"They're my favorite." She wondered how he knew. "Thank you."

They decided to wander through town for a little while and not talk about the Scrooge Legend. She was fine with taking a break from the investigation because her mind kept drifting toward Jack anyway. "Did Mary bring you a cup of hot cocoa last night to help you sleep?"

"She did. She sure knows how to take care of her guests. Only I didn't sleep. I stayed up and read your blog."

"Really?" She was shocked, excited, embarrassed, and terrified all at once. "And?" She bit her lower lip.

"I liked it." He looked at her directly. "I was wrong to judge it so quickly. You lay out the facts nicely. You shine a light on the details and why you see things differently. You'd be a good detective."

"Aww, thanks." She couldn't seem to stop smiling. "That's a huge compliment coming from a real Denver detective."

"It's the truth," he said, as if he wanted to make sure she really heard him.

And she did. Charley couldn't remember a time when any of her ex-boyfriends gave her such glowing praise on anything she did. She wondered if Jack knew how rare a quality that was these days. "What got you interested in police work?"

He hesitated for a moment before he said, "My uncle Bill went missing."

She came to an abrupt halt. "What? When?"

"On Christmas Eve when I was ten." A sense of heaviness flickered in his eyes before he cast his gaze to the ground. "He disappeared without a trace."

She could feel her heart breaking for him. "Oh, Jack. I'm so sorry. How come you never told me?"

For a moment he appeared dazed, his thoughts far away, as if he were reliving it all over again. He cleared his throat, then took her hand without the slightest hesitation. That one gesture touched her deeply. He reached for her as though he needed her support in order to discuss something so painful. When they started walking again, Charley didn't push him to talk about it, and they must have walked a good five minutes, in silence, before he spoke.

"I had a hard time dealing with it. My uncle was like a big brother to me. He disappeared when my family lived in Chicago. We searched for him nonstop for years, but it was like he vanished into thin air. My dad was eventually transferred to LA. It had taken such a toll on everyone that we decided, as a family, not to talk about it to our new friends and neighbors. I would have said something to you if I hadn't promised my parents."

"Of course. That's completely understandable. I'm sorry for what you've been dealing with all these years." Charley tried to imagine what that would have been like. Jack was an only child, as was she. Since his uncle had been like a brother to him, his disappearance had to have been even more devastating. "Have you come across any new leads since you became a detective?"

"Not any that amount to much. My uncle worked in construction, so he went where the work took him, but it was almost always in or near Chicago."

"Was he married?"

"No, which I never understood." Jack got that distant look in his eyes again. "He loved kids, loved family. That's why he always spent Christmas with us. He'd come over on the weekends, and he and my dad would map out a decoration design. They'd string lights together and we'd all trim the tree on the first night, but that was just the beginning. On Sunday, after church, they'd haul out the big stuff from the attic—five-foot nutcrackers, two train sets, flying angels, talking moose heads… It often took them a couple of weekends to complete, but after they finished, every inch of our house screamed Christmas. When we moved to LA, we couldn't bring ourselves to carry on the tradition without him."

"I imagine that would have been very difficult. I wouldn't have wanted to, either, but now I understand why you and your family never decorated your house for Christmas."

"You thought I was a Scrooge."

Charley gasped, throwing a hand to her cheek. "Oh, Jack, I'm so sorry. I feel awful that I teased you about it!"

"And every time you did, I almost told you."

"Will you forgive me?"

"Nothing to forgive. You didn't know." He inhaled a deep breath before shifting his focus to the Christmas scenes around them. A father and son were throwing snowballs at each other. A family of four walked by as the mom and dad were asking their kids what they wanted to get Grandpa for Christmas. In the distance, horses were pulling a sleigh across the town's snow-covered bridge. "My uncle Bill would really love St. Nicholas."

"I'm sorry if this is tough on you, being in a town that's nothing but Christmas."

"I'm fine." Jack caressed her hand, then wrapped it around his arm while they strolled along, linked together. "This place actually reminds me of the good times I had with him. He was always teaching me different skills of his trade. He'd say, 'A young man needs to have a plan.' He loved to build miniature towns for model trains, carve airplanes and sailboats out of wood, and construct dollhouses for sick kids at the hospital. I was terrible at all of it." He shook his head with an embarrassed laugh. "But Uncle Bill would say, 'Don't worry about it, young man. Being good at something takes time, and there's always tomorrow.'"

"He sounds like he was a wonderful uncle."

"He was, and still is." Jack heaved a long sigh. "My gut tells me he's out there somewhere."

"Then you'll find him." She gave his hand a squeeze. "You will."

"Thanks for your vote of confidence, not that I've earned it. I haven't come close to cracking the Scrooge Legend."

"I haven't exactly, either. Why don't we forget about that for a while longer and do something Christmassy?"

He lifted a brow. "What do you have in mind?"

She needed something that would completely distract him from the sad reminder of losing his uncle, something that would take his full concentration. "I got it!" She pressed her hands together. "Time to test your memory, Mr. Brody."

"You're talking to a detective. I think I got this."

"Oh, you think so? Tell me, what was the activity I wanted to try in high school?"

"That narrows it down to two or three dozen options."

"Ha-ha."

"I can probably rule out hang gliding and water-skiing. Mind giving me a hint?"

"Okay, Detective, here's your last clue. You said you wouldn't be caught dead doing it in a million years."

He scratched his head, seeming lost at finding an answer when his eyes suddenly fixed on her. "Oh, no." He groaned.

A huge grin spread across her face. "Oh, yes."

A half hour later, Jack appeared to be doing all he could to remain standing on tiny steel blades at the edge of the town's frozen pond. "I can't believe you talked me into this."

Charley's hands were flying in all directions, striving to maintain her balance as well. "Yeah, me neither," she said regretfully. "I'm not sure what I was thinking."

A rowdy group of kids came out of nowhere and swiftly raced by them, followed by a young girl practicing an advanced figure skating combination.

Charley and Jack looked in both directions before they hesitantly stepped onto the ice right as three future hockey players blew past them, joking around by trying to push one another to the ice.

For a split second, she saw a look of terror in Jack's eyes, and she held back a laugh.

"Shouldn't one of us know what we're doing?" He cautiously took one step forward.

"What's the fun in that?" she said, following him.

Within seconds, Jack's body jerked uncontrollably and Charley reached to steady him. As he regained control, she yelped, losing her balance. Jack, with his fast reflexes, grabbed hold of her before she fell.

"We must look like a comedy act."

"I hope no one's recording this because I'll never live it

down." He immediately scanned the area for any phones pointed at him.

She threw her arms out for balance and hit him in the face. "I'm so sorry."

She almost did it again, but he swiftly blocked her. "Maybe we should try this together."

"Good idea."

He took hold of her hand, and they stepped out on the frozen pond.

She tightened her grip on him. "Please don't let me go."

"Never." He flashed her that disarming smile of his.

She wobbled violently. He helped steady her, but wobbled a bit himself. They finally found their balance together, taking one step and then another. They were no longer flailing about recklessly because they were walking on the ice instead of skating.

"This isn't as bad as I thought it would be." He stared intently at the ice while everyone else was flying by them.

"Hate to break it to you, but I don't think we're actually skating. We need to glide more than walk." She gestured to the other skaters for examples.

"Got it. Right foot first?" She nodded, and they took off, gliding together, at last getting the hang of it.

Exhilaration rose up and spread across her cheeks. "We're doing it, Jack. We're skating!"

He laughed, loosening up. "We'll be speed skating before you know it."

They traveled a few more feet before Charley ran over a bump formed in the ice and lost control, taking Jack down with her. "Ow!" she cried out.

"I second that." He moaned through gritted teeth.

Staggering to his feet, he waited to get his balance before helping her up.

She brushed off the ice and her wounded pride. “Fun fact: over fifty thousand people sustain injures on the ice every year.”

“You’re telling me this now?” Jack gawked at her, and she shrugged. “I don’t think you understand the meaning of a fun fact.”

“Sure I do.” Her mouth twitched with a playful smile. “People don’t call me The Cold Hard Facts Queen for no reason.”

He chuckled. “Here’s a real fun fact. Ice-skating is great exercise.”

“Oh? And you know this from personal experience?”

“Heck, no.” He swatted the thought away. “I read it in a fitness magazine.”

She laughed. “One point to Jack Brody.”

Chapter Sixteen

Mary sat at her desk in the office with the phone cradled on her shoulder. “Yes, I have you booked for two weeks, leaving on the seventeenth of February.” She wrote the reservation down in her book. “Have a very Merry Christmas, and we’ll see you in the New Year.” She hung up and stared at the ever-growing pile of clutter she once called her office.

Joe came around the corner with a scroll in his hand. “Looks like we have a Christmas wish to help fulfill.”

She gasped. “Are you serious? It’s been years since we’ve had one.”

“At least five,” he said, leaning on the doorframe.

“What’s the wish?”

“A family reunion, and it’s for one of our own. Do you want to take a guess?”

“Hmm.” She leaned back, thinking. “It has to be someone who’s familiar with the original purpose of the mailbox.”

“Correct.”

“Is it someone older?”

“Correct, again.”

“Mrs. Murphy?”

“You’re getting colder.”

"Mr. Clarkson?"

"Even colder."

"I'm never going to guess. Who is it?"

"Our handyman."

Her jaw dropped in shock. "Mike?"

"Yup."

"It's about time." She let out a relieved breath. "I thought we were going to have to cast the wish for him."

Joe laughed. "I did too."

"Our sweet Mike." She played with the collar on her blouse. "Does this mean his family lives here?"

He skimmed the scroll. "Unknown."

She sighed. "I hate it when our boss doesn't tell us everything."

Her husband arched a brow at her. "Do you really?"

"I guess not. I would miss seeing the magic in action." She hoped Mike had a large family so she could plan a big blowout reunion. "Oh! I just realized something. The magic might have already started."

Joe tilted his head. "How so?"

"I've had Mike out here an awful lot lately. Already three times this week, and he just so happens to be working upstairs right now."

A big grin took over Joe's face. "You know what this means?"

Mary rubbed her hands together in excited anticipation. "We're going to have a front row seat."

Charley and Jack inched their way toward the bed-and-breakfast, clearly stiff and sore.

"I need a hot bath," she moaned with barely enough energy to be heard.

"Professional ice skaters we are not." He wasn't moving any better.

"Do you mind if we scratch ice-skating, or any form of skating, off our list?"

"Done," he said with lightning-fast speed, which made her laugh, but the laugh hurt her ribs, which made her groan.

She stopped in front of the porch stairs, cursing under her breath. "Did the number of steps double while we were gone?"

"C'mon, Grandma." He gingerly grabbed hold of her waist, easing her up to the front door.

She couldn't help but wonder if this was how they were going to move when they were in their eighties. Would they still be in each other's lives then? Would they be good friends or could she dare dream that they might be something more to each other? The chemistry between them was undeniable, but their time together was up when her free week ended. They lived separate lives in different states. She needed to keep that in mind if she didn't want to get hurt again. At the same time, she couldn't dismiss the fact that they had found each other after fourteen years. Wasn't that worth exploring?

Jack let out a big exhale as they finally reached the top step. "I'm guessing we should skip our planned stakeout," he said, pushing open the front door for her.

"Why?" She feigned a sudden burst of energy as they hobbled inside and tackled the stairs to the second floor. "We'll be sitting, not moving, not skating, with hot coffee. Sounds like a great way to spend the evening to me."

"When you say it that way, yes, it does." He stopped at Charley's door to drop her off. "You go take that hot bath. I've got some work to do, but how about we head out around seven for dinner, followed by a stakeout afterward?"

"Dinner and a stakeout." She nodded. "A perfect night out."

After Charley disappeared inside her room, Jack let out a groan and limped down the hallway, feeling the pain in his hip, his shoulder, his ankle. He'd definitely need to take some ibuprofen and a hot shower. He reached inside his jacket for his room key when he realized that his door was propped open. "Hello?" he called out.

A heavyset man appearing to be in his fifties came out of the bathroom with his toolbox in hand. "Afternoon." He huffed, slightly out of breath. He mopped his brow with a handkerchief before shoving it back in his pocket. "You shouldn't have any more trouble with your shower. The water leak is all fixed, young man."

Jack stilled at the handyman's choice of words. If Jack hadn't *just* been talking about his uncle, he probably wouldn't have noticed. How many times had he thought he'd seen or met his uncle when he had some random interaction with a middle-aged man? Too many to count—and he'd been wrong every time.

"Much appreciated," Jack said as the handyman lumbered past him toward the door. *It's not him. Let the guy go.* But he couldn't. He'd rather be wrong, yet again, than to always wonder. "You know, your voice sounds familiar. Have we met?"

The man turned around and studied Jack's face. "I… don't know." He squinted and cocked his head, as if he were trying to place him. "Have we?"

For a moment Jack could not speak. The handyman

had the same blue-gray eyes that both he and his uncle shared. "You remind me of my uncle Bill."

The man stood there, rooted in place, his eyes searching Jack's face. "Yeah? How so?"

"Uh..." Jack knew that if they ever met again, his uncle might not recognize him because he was no longer a ten-year-old kid. But if the man standing in front of him *were* his uncle, he apparently didn't recognize his own name, either. Jack rubbed a hand over his brows, feeling a little embarrassed. "It was just the way you said 'young man.'"

"Oh." He laughed. "I seem to say that to any male younger than me. For obvious reasons." He laughed again.

He's right. It's not him. Jack cracked a smile. "It's a common phrase."

"Yeah."

Yet, he's still standing here. Was there a glimmer of recognition, after all? "You know, we also have the same blue-gray eyes."

The handyman took a few steps closer to Jack and stared at the color of his eyes. "Hey, you're right." He blew out a surprised breath. "What do you know? I'm Mike, by the way." He extended his hand.

His name is Mike? "Jack."

"You know, you do look a little familiar. Did you stop by a barn a few days ago, trying to find the B&B out on Noble Fir Road?"

Jack dropped his head down. "Mike, yes. Of course. I should have recognized you. I'm so sorry."

"Don't be. I should hope I look different when my face isn't covered in grease," he said. "I take it you never found that B&B, since you're staying here."

"I did, but they had a flood, so I moved over here."

"And then you had a shower leak. Maybe it's you, Jack."

He laughed. "I see your point." Was he feeling like he knew Mike from briefly meeting him before or could he really be his uncle?

"Well, if you have any more problems, tell Mary to give me a holler."

"I will. Thanks, Mike."

Jack closed the door and threw his hands on his head. *Is that him?* He walked over to the window and waited for Mike to leave. If he really was Uncle Bill, why would he have changed his name to Mike? Jack often wondered if his uncle's disappearance had anything to do with the neighborhood where he had lived. Chicago was no stranger to organized crime, and his uncle's area had ties to the syndicate. It would, at least, explain the name change.

Jack spotted Mike in the driveway, getting into what appeared to be a ten-year-old pickup. He tried to make out the license plate as Mike drove away but too many Christmas decorations blocked his view. Jack expelled a big breath and turned from the window.

Was he reading too much into it? The man had blue-gray eyes and used his uncle's favorite term "young man." He'd also used one of his grandmother's phrases when Jack first met him at his barn.

He fired up his computer and launched the age progression app in order to add forty pounds to his uncle's photo. The program recalculated the image, widening his uncle's face, and making him appear heavyset. Jack stared in shock at the result. The man looked strikingly similar to handyman Mike.

Chapter Seventeen

Charley was lacing up her boots when a text pinged in on her phone. She retrieved her cell and opened it.

Hi Charley, it's Jack. Mary gave me your number. I'm sorry, but I can't make dinner. Something's come up with work. I hope you understand.

What? He couldn't tell her in person by walking down the hallway and knocking on her door? Why was he bailing on her? Everything was going so well. They'd been doing a pretty decent job reconnecting—opening up to one another, laughing together, skating together. They'd held hands—and he'd taken her hand, not the other way around. Was he having second thoughts? Why else couldn't he face her?

She went over to the window and stared out at the Christmas lights. They'd talked a lot about his missing uncle. Maybe it had put him in too much of a melancholy mood to see her tonight. But what if that wasn't the reason?

She could feel herself starting to spiral into her comfortable home of doubt and insecurity. What if he decided there was no point in moving forward when she was only there for a few more days? What if he simply didn't want to get involved again? Why had she allowed herself to feel something for him? She was such an idiot. And now she was stuck in a ridiculously happy town. *I should pack up and go.*

She grabbed her suitcase and threw it up the bed. *But I don't have my story. I can't leave now.* She clenched her hands and let out a frustrated shriek. She was there to debunk a stupid legend, and she wasn't going to leave until she did.

Reluctantly, she put her suitcase away. She thought about reaching out to her readers to let them know that love was a scam—something she was in the process of proving—but she knew that wasn't an option either, not if she wanted to keep her job. No, the thing she needed to do was throw herself into work.

She set up at the table in her room and retrieved her computer out of her bag. She would fact-check an article due in after Christmas. It was about tropical island getaways. She had almost forgotten about her favorite type of vacation. She loved going anyplace where warm weather, sparkling beaches, and delicious tropical drinks were on the menu. Diving into the article would be the perfect distraction.

She opened the document on her laptop and read the title: "Love in Paradise." She grumbled, pushing back in her chair. On impulse, she pulled up her blog and noticed a few more comments on her Christmas post. One was from a new reader named Reality Check and it had just been posted.

Dear Miss Scrooge,

I enjoy your blog, except for your last post disrespecting Christmas. Maybe it's not Christmas you're upset with but an unpleasant circumstance surrounding it. Might I suggest focusing on a past Christmas you loved when you were a child or a teenager. Rekindle the love you felt way back when, and you'll find the Christmas spirit once again.

"Oh, Jack. For someone who's a detective, you aren't very subtle."

But what was he doing? Charley scooped her hair up in a ponytail and reread the comment. It seemed familiar. Especially the rhyme. And then she gasped. She was suddenly reminded of a poem the entire student body created in high school. During her junior year, the school was having a real problem with graffiti, so the principal challenged his students to add to a poem he began. The only rule was there couldn't be any vulgarity. He wrote, "Open your eyes and you will see, everything that's meant to be."

Some students had thought that meant they were to write about things from the past, and some said it should be about the future. She'd thought it was a little bit of both. It was amazing how it developed into a beautiful, unifying work of art. When Charley contributed to it, she kept the flow of the poem, but she also put a secret message in it for Jack. She never said anything to him about it, but when it was his turn to contribute, he understood the message and replied with one of his own. No one knew except the two of them.

He remembers the poem? She couldn't believe it. *How very clever of you, Jack.* He actually took a little of what she'd originally written: "Remember that fire way back when, through the ashes, we live and love once again."

She assumed he hadn't remembered exactly what she'd written but he remembered what needed to rhyme. *Way back when* and *once again.* And, of course, mentioning love definitely got her attention.

Now it was her turn. Not only did she need to rhyme with what Jack had written, but she needed to answer the comment and give him a place to meet her. *Ugh.* His poem contribution had been "Love, come find me. I'm at the place on the hill. When life moves too fast, it's best to keep still." She scooted her chair up to the table. "What rhymes with hill and still?" *Uncle Bill.* No, she didn't want to make it about him.

"Oh!" She started typing.

Dear Reality Check,

Reading your comment gave me such a thrill.
Come find me at the diner, if that is your will.

She hit Post, grabbed her coat, handbag, and key, and hurried out the door. She debated whether or not to go directly to Jack's room, but then decided against it, thinking she might ruin whatever surprise he had planned. She ran down the stairs, needing to find Mary. She poked her head into the living room and found her sitting with coffee and a book.

"Evening, Mary," Charley called. "Is anyone going into town?"

Mary glanced up from her book. "Not that I know of, but you're welcome to use my car. The key's right there on the hook."

"Thank you so much." Charley snatched the key off the hook and flew out the door.

Five minutes later, she stepped into the diner and immediately searched for Jack in case he had somehow beat her there. Not seeing him, she asked to be seated at a booth by the window. She quickly ran through the menu, then glanced out the window, expecting to see him any minute.

"Hello again." Angel greeted her with a warm smile. "Just you tonight?"

She took another peek out the window. "Hopefully not. I'm Charley, by the way."

"Nice to formally meet you, Charley. Are you enjoying your stay in St. Nicholas?"

And if by that you mean coming here for work but reuniting with my high school sweetheart, then yes. "Best vacation I've had in years."

"I'm so happy to hear that," Angel said with a sigh, placing her hands over her heart. "It seems like people only want to go somewhere tropical nowadays. But there's something to be said for small towns, especially ones like St. Nicholas."

"I couldn't agree with you more."

"Well now, can I get you something to drink while you wait?"

"I'll take an iced tea when you have a chance."

"Be right back."

Charley continually switched her focus between the sidewalk outside and the entrance to the diner. A family of four came in, followed by an older man who looked so much like the classical picture of Santa that she almost asked him where he left his Santa suit. At least he was wearing a red flannel shirt, so she gave him credit for that. The man smiled at her, and she at him, as he sat at a table behind her.

Angel dropped off her tea, and Charley was beginning to wonder if she'd been wrong about the comment left on her blog. Maybe it wasn't from Jack. She pulled it up on her phone and reread it. Even if she hadn't been reminded about the collective high school poem, the comment was so specific. The moniker Reality Check also seemed like a perfect username for sensible Detective Jack Brody.

She stared out the window, feeling her high spirits slipping away. She'd been waiting for over twenty minutes. The bed-and-breakfast was only five minutes away. Had he not seen her reply?

Angel returned to the table. "Men," she groused. "They love wristwatches yet they never seem to know the time."

Charley mustered a small laugh. "You are so right. I think the problem has become an epidemic."

Angel squeaked as she laughed, which made Charley genuinely laugh.

"Looks like the party has started without me," Jack said, walking up to the table.

"Well, look who finally decided to show." Angel threw a hand on her hip.

Jack stiffened, shifting his gaze between the two. "I didn't know I was late."

"That's another good one." Angel winked at Charley before she shooed him into the booth. "What can I get you to drink?"

"I'll take an iced tea."

"I'd grab you a menu, but just take Charley's. Lord knows she's had enough time to memorize it." Angel left without waiting for a reply.

"What did I do?" He gawked at her with wide eyes.

"My fault." She put her hands up in defense. "I gave her the impression that someone was joining me twenty minutes ago."

He looked at her, confused. "I'm sorry if my text wasn't clear. I—"

"It was, but then I saw the comment you left on my blog, so I assumed you got my reply."

Angel came back with Jack's iced tea. "Ready to order?"

Charley had no desire for a diet plate now. "I'll try your grilled cheese and tomato soup combo."

"Good choice." Angel looked to Jack. "And for you?"

"The combo works for me."

"Easy-peasy." Angel picked up the menu and hurried off.

Jack immediately dove back into their conversation. "I didn't send you a message through your blog."

Was he serious? "Then how did you know I'd be here?"

"Mary told me you went into town, so I just assumed. I finished up my work early and had stopped by your room."

He was working after all? To think that she almost tumbled down the insecurity rabbit hole for nothing. If it hadn't been for that comment on her blog, she would have. "Seriously? You didn't leave a comment on my blog?"

He shook his head. "With my job, I try to keep a very small digital footprint."

Charley was deflated, and then embarrassed. "Reality Check is going to think I left a very strange reply." She pulled up the comment on her phone and handed it to Jack.

As he read it, his smile grew. "I love this last line, 'Rekindle the love you felt way back when, and you'll find the Christmas spirit once again.' I wish I'd written it, but I can't take credit."

"Now I feel really stupid. I thought you remembered the high school poem."

He gave her a puzzled look, then examined both the comment and her response. "The poem! I forgot all about that." He handed back her phone. "That poem turned out far better than I ever expected, and your contribution was so much better than mine. You talked about a fire—figuratively our romance, and literally the car on fire in the school parking lot."

She smiled, ecstatic he remembered. "The fire not only represented our sizzling high school romance, but it also referred to our initial spark. That was the first day we met."

"When I saw you through the smoldering ashes, I dramatically said to my buddy, 'I might live to love once again.'" He closed a fist and placed it on his chest, reenacting the moment.

She laughed. "You were charming with your over-the-top acting."

"I had to be because I wasn't very subtle, especially with my poem contribution." He shook his head in embarrassment. "I asked you to the new football field so I could kiss you."

"But you wrote it so eloquently. No one knew what you were really saying but me." That crisp November afternoon had been one of the best days of her life. "Those were good times."

"Yes, they were."

They sat in silence with identical lingering grins on their faces.

"Here you go." Angel set down their grilled cheese combo plates. "Can I get you anything else?"

"No, everything looks great. Thanks, Angel." Charley was even more curious as to why he broke up with her. She had always assumed that he never really loved her, but maybe she had misjudged him. "It's been ages since I've had a grilled cheese," she said, staring at beautifully grilled crispy sourdough bread with white cheese oozing out of its side. "It almost looks too good to eat."

"Almost." He picked up half of his sandwich and the gooey cheese strings parted. "That's awesome." He waited for her to do the same, and then together they took a bite. He moaned, as if he'd just tasted pure goodness, and gaveled his fisted hand on the table. "Dang!"

"Oh, wow," she said with her mouth full. "Best. Ever." She swallowed and pulled her sandwich apart, inspecting it. "I think there's at least three cheeses in here."

"Pretty upscale for a twenty-four-hour diner."

"I've got to ask Angel." She swiveled her head and spotted Angel talking to the guy who looked like Santa. The man suddenly bellowed with a big belly laugh that carried throughout the restaurant.

"Whoa. That guy should be making a living as Santa."

"That's what I thought when I saw him walk in."

The man pushed back from the table and got up. He said something to Angel, then handed her money for the bill. She gazed at it, appearing shocked, and hugged him. As he made his way toward the exit, she called out, "Drive safely, R.C. Merry Christmas."

Angel dried her eyes and began bussing his table when she noticed Charley and Jack watching her. "How are you two doing over here?" she asked, wandering over. "Can I get you anything?"

"You were right, Angel. This sandwich is excellent." Jack shoved the rest in his mouth.

"Best in town," she said proudly.

"That man you were just talking to, is he the town's official Santa?" Charley asked.

"R.C.? No. He just retired from the trucking business. Though, who knows? Maybe one day he'll want to be our Santa in our Christmas Day Parade."

"R.C. should change his name to S.C. for Santa Claus," Charley suggested.

"I don't know if he'd agree. His trucker handle is too perfect for him. Ever since I've known R.C., he's given great advice on every subject imaginable. The other truckers tell me it's sometimes a little harsh, but then they don't call him Reality Check for nothing."

"Did you say Reality Check?" Charley craned her head forward, certain she must have misheard.

"Yes. Isn't that a great name?"

Charley shot Jack a look with wide eyes.

"Does R.C. come in a lot?" he asked, and Charley already knew what he was thinking—that he was the guy who left the comment on her blog.

"Only when he's passing through town. And now that he's officially retired, I don't know if I'll ever see him again." Angel put her hand over her heart. "He's such a sweet man. I sure will miss him."

"Maybe he lives closer than you think," Charley said brightly.

"I don't think so." Angel took a big breath in and let it out on a sigh. "You know, I asked him where he lived once and he was very vague about it. All I got out of him was that he lived north of St. Nicholas. 'Very, very far north' were his exact words. But what am I doing jabbering on and on? Your soup's getting cold. Can I warm that up for you?"

"No need," Jack said.

"Don't trouble yourself." Charley put a hand over her bowl. "Mine's still pretty hot."

"Okay. Well, holler if you change your mind."

Once Angel left, she stared at Jack in disbelief. "Do you think he's the same Reality Check on my blog?"

"You bet I do." He wiped his mouth with his napkin and leaned back with a troubled look on his face. "I think it goes deeper than a blog comment. What if that guy isn't just a trucker? What if he's connected to the Scrooge Legend?"

"How?"

"Think about it. You're considered a Scrooge, so he makes a comment on your blog to lure you out in public where he can sit behind you and eavesdrop." He cupped his hand to the window in order to survey the outside.

Is he being cautious or paranoid? "I understand what you're saying, but if he really is what you suspect, why did he leave? What important information could he have possibly overheard? We were raving about our sandwiches."

"I'll tell you what he knows," he said sharply, as if he'd already condemned the guy. "He heard enough to know you suspected the comment was from me, he knows we were high school sweethearts, and now he knows I really care about you."

She let out a tiny gasp. The shock registering in his eyes told her he hadn't meant to express his feelings, but she was oh, so happy he did. A smile spread across her face, which triggered one on his—only his smile was that of embarrassment.

"Well said." She held his gaze.

"You think so?" He tossed his head back.

"I particularly liked the last part."

"Good," he said with finality, as if she wasn't allowed to change her mind. "Now you can understand why I'm all the more determined to figure out the identity of R.C."

"I understand that now." *If he wants to be my protector, who am I to stand in his way?*

"When we get back to the inn tonight, I'll trace Reality Check's IP address. I guarantee it comes right back here to St. Nicholas, and maybe right into the mayor's office."

"You lost me. How does the mayor fit into this?"

"I think this is an elaborate PR stunt. He knows you work at a popular magazine and can promote the town."

"You think they're having money trouble?"

"Money is often the biggest motivator. Here's how I see it. They targeted you by insisting you're a Scrooge. Now they have your attention, and because it's personal, you can't ignore them. They get paid actors to help promote the legend for you, and they also have spies, including R.C., who can report back on your opinions of the town in case they need to throw something else in your path. The goal is for you to have such a wonderful time up here that you write about how magical the place is, and then the town will be flooded with tourists."

There it was, her logical answer, laid out right in front of her. Like Jack, she had also assumed the legend was used for tourist intrigue, but she hadn't figured out why she received an invitation. Jack thought she was targeted because of her blog at the magazine. It made absolute sense. She should have been elated, but she wasn't. It would mean that all those interviews were lies, and everything in St. Nicholas was contrived.

And what about Jack? Would it mean his arrival at the Carrolls' B&B was truly a coincidence? *How depressing.* It was ironic to think that she felt more secure about their relationship when she believed a magic mailbox brought him to her, than knowing they happened to be in the same place at the same time. It was simply fate versus chance. But which one would win? Which one would decide her future with Jack?

Chapter Eighteen

With hot drinks in hand, Jack and Charley strolled down the street together in comfortable silence. He'd voiced his theory to her, which was solid, except for one thing. Why had Tony Braca been invited to St. Nicholas? He could see how the captain's brother would be targeted for his newly acquired money, but what was the angle on Braca? Jack needed to pay Felicity and Nolan a visit to get some answers, and he'd need to do it soon. But for now, he'd enjoy investigating the mailbox connection while spending time with Charley.

"My car's right over there if you're still up for a stakeout," he said, taking a sip of his coffee.

"Absolutely. You might call me a stakeout geek now, if there is such a thing. It's exciting to think about who we might catch."

And she just made me fall for her even more, he thought as they reached his car.

"I see you parked closer tonight."

"Just a little. We still don't want to be detected." He opened the car door for her. "Besides, I've brought extra ammunition."

Her eyes sparkled with anticipation. "What?"

He waggled his eyebrows as he closed her door. He

then circled around to the driver's side and climbed in. "I attached an audio bug to the bottom of the mailbox." He pulled out his cell phone. "Now we can hear any movement occurring near the mailbox, even if we can't see it." He dialed the number that connected to the transmitter.

A huge grin took over her face. "When did you set this up?"

"Before I found you at the diner." He tapped the speaker icon on his phone, and the rustling sound of pine trees moving in the wind filled the car.

"This is so cool." She laughed. "We're like spies."

"That's the idea. Hey, can you grab the binoculars out of the glove box?"

She popped the latch and handed them over.

"Tonight, we've got great eyes *and* ears." He surveyed the mailbox through the binoculars, adjusting the focus. "This guy's all but caught."

The two suddenly heard footsteps in the distance. Charley's eyes expanded in suspense. "Which direction is he coming from?"

Jack homed in on the mailbox. "I can't tell, but he's definitely moving toward us."

They stared at the mailbox, neither saying a word. The footsteps got louder, closer—

A sharp knock on Charley's window had her jumping with a yelp. She whipped around to find Angel holding up a takeout bag. Jack turned on the car to roll down the window.

"I didn't mean to startle you," Angel said. "I just got off my shift and thought you might like a couple slices of hot apple pie."

"That's so sweet of you." Charley took the takeout bag from her. "Thank you, Angel."

Jack leaned over the armrest. "How did you know we were here?"

"You think you're the first ones to come up with the Santa Stakeout?" She erupted with a short laugh. "Oh, please."

"Just how many stakeouts have there been?" Charley asked.

"Too many to count."

Charley slumped with a disappointed sigh.

Jack felt a little deflated too. If Angel had assumed they were on a stakeout, the guy collecting the Scrooge suggestions might also assume that. "Has anyone been successful?"

"Every single one of them." She raised a brow and flashed them an enigmatic smile before walking away.

"I don't think she was referring to past stakeouts," he said.

"No, I don't think she was."

Their eyes met, both sensing something was happening between them, but then a car door slammed behind them. Jack banged his head against the headrest, irritated by the interruption as Charley let out a big sigh.

Resigning himself to work, he raised the binoculars, surveying the mailbox and its surroundings.

Charley sat back and sipped her tea. "See anything unusual?"

"Not yet." He handed them over so she could take a look for herself. "It's colder tonight, which means fewer people will be out walking. Hopefully, that will cut down on the number of false alarms." He watched her concentrating on the mailbox, looking fascinated with what they were doing.

She lowered the binoculars and caught him staring. "What?"

"Nothing." He scratched his nose.

"The look on your face was more than nothing."

Man, she knows how to read me already. "I can't get over how genuinely interested you are in all of this."

"Is that a bad thing?"

"Just the opposite. It's one more thing we have in common."

Her eyes gleamed with an intensity he remembered in high school. "I guess it is."

He wanted more time with her than one week—to know if it was possible, if *they* were possible—but the days were going by too fast. If anyone was losing interest in stakeouts, it was him. "Time for pie?"

"What?" She laughed, lowering the binoculars. "You want pie now?" Her eyes ran over his body. "Where could you possibly put it?"

"There's always room for pie."

She let out a resigned huff before she rummaged around in the takeout bag for plastic utensils. "You seriously need to give me the details of your workout routine because if I keep eating like this, I'm going to need it."

"What are you talking about?" His eyes brazenly ran over her. "You're in perfect shape."

"And I have to make several food sacrifices to keep it. You, apparently, can eat whatever you want."

"It's not like I eat doughnuts for breakfast, lunch, *and* dinner."

"Ha-ha." She handed him one of the takeout containers with a set of plastic utensils. "I can't eat them at all."

When he opened the container, the aroma of cinnamon

and apples filled the air. He popped open the bag holding the plastic utensils, pulled out a fork and dug in. "Wow."

Charley could no longer resist and tasted it for herself. "So good."

He scooped up another forkful, froze, then scrambled for his binoculars.

"What?" Charley sat up on alert. "Did you hear something?"

"No." He scanned the area. "I just thought the pie might have been a planned distraction."

Charley gasped. "Is it?"

"All clear." He started eating again but kept his attention on Charley. "So, why have you been pinned as a Scrooge?"

"Not exactly sure. Probably my lack of enthusiasm for the holiday season."

He could relate and assumed it might be from losing her mom. Even though he'd only spent one Christmas with Charley, he remembered how much she was into it. She'd be listening to Christmas carols every time he came over after school. He helped her decorate her family's tree right after Thanksgiving. It had been difficult at first, but she had been so cheerful and excited about the placement of every ornament that she helped him remember what it was like before his uncle went missing.

"Did you shut out Christmas after your mom passed away?"

"I wanted to, but she left me and my dad Christmas letters and requests to carry on our traditions. We ended up finding comfort in Christmas because of her."

"That's beautiful."

"It was," she said with a pensive look on her face. "But

then my dad moved, I got busy with work, and, well, my last few Christmases haven't exactly been in the top ten."

"Top twenty?"

She washed down a bite of pie with a sip of tea. "Not even on the list."

"That bad?"

She shrugged. "I keep falling for guys who like to leave at Christmas."

He hadn't expected that answer and regretted pushing her. "You mean they went out of town because they were too cheap to buy you a Christmas present?" he joked, giving her an out.

"I never thought of that. Maybe that's why my ex-fiancé chose Christmas Eve to break up with me." She closed up her pie container and set it aside.

Jack immediately despised her ex for hurting her. "Nice guy," he said, putting a filter on his words. He watched her carefully, wondering how much she'd open up about it. "I can see why you might view the Christmas season differently." The distant look in her eyes told him she was reliving the breakup in her head.

"Do you want to talk about it?"

She let out a noisy breath. "I wouldn't know where to begin."

"I'm not going anywhere," he said softly, and a small smile touched the corners of her mouth.

She briefly made eye contact, then stared out the window. "Hunter and I had been engaged for five months. We were good together—except for when it came to our friends. He didn't care for a few of my girlfriends, and to be honest, I thought one of his buddies was a jerk."

"What did you do about it?"

"I suggested we try to meet couples in order to have more mutual friends."

"How did that go?"

"Good. I was surprised how fast we hit it off with two couples in particular. The six of us joked that someday a TV show would be made based on our friendship."

Jack smiled, picturing it. He and Charley had had a whole group of mutual friends. He assumed they would end up being lifelong friends. Of course, that was before his dad moved him to Denver.

"Hunter wanted us to host a small dinner party for our friends on Christmas Eve. Since I was getting off work at noon, we decided to have it at my apartment, and he said he'd be there around three. At four, I left a message on his cell. By five, I still hadn't heard from him. I left more messages, sent texts. I was getting really worried, thinking something horrible had happened to him."

"That wasn't like him—to not answer you?" Jack asked in his typical detective fashion.

"Not at all."

"I can see why you were concerned."

"I remember how I kept looking out the window, getting more worried by the minute. Finally, at six, right when everybody was about to arrive, he called. He was fine, but he sounded distant. He told me he needed to work late."

"What?" Jack couldn't hide his shocked reaction. "He didn't think to call earlier?"

"Apparently not."

"What does he do for a living?"

"He's a financial advisor, and I get it. My dad's in the business. I know there are sometimes last-minute client needs that require working late. But it was Christmas

Eve. The markets were closed, and the working-late-again excuse kept happening with Hunter more frequently."

"Did you ask him why he didn't answer your previous texts or voice messages?"

"Yes, but he wouldn't say. He actually got defensive. When he heard how disappointed I was, he went off on me, like I was the bad guy—as if I didn't have the right to be upset. He was the one who scared me half to death. He was the one who invited our friends over, but I was the one who had cooked and cleaned for hours and was expected to make excuses for him not showing."

"You know, that type of behavior is consistent with someone who's hiding something," he had to tell her, even though he assumed she already knew.

"I figured as much, but I didn't want to believe it." She stared at her hands. "Hunter finally showed up around eleven that night. Everyone had left, and I was cleaning up. He simply said the wedding was off. No reason, no warning." She got quiet for a moment as though she were trying to collect herself. "I can only assume there was someone else in the picture, but I don't know for sure. To this day, I have no idea what happened."

Like with his uncle's disappearance. It was the worst feeling to carry every day—the not knowing. "I'm sorry, Charley. When life comes at you so quickly and throws you for a loop, it's hard to catch your breath."

"That's exactly how I felt. I thought I had good instincts about people. Apparently, I don't."

"You have very good instincts. Don't question that. In my line of work, I can tell you that when the heart gets involved, the brain ignores a lot."

She blew out a quick breath. "Isn't that the truth." She stared out the window, probably trying to get Hunter and the pain of what happened out of her head. "Still, it bothers me that I didn't see it. It's not like I ignored one thing and then another. I felt like I was completely blindsided."

"I've been there, but I bet if I asked you specific questions about him, you'd see it. You'd start seeing a pattern of behavior you hadn't focused on before."

"Like what?"

"Take your girlfriends for example. Are they still your friends?"

"Of course. I've always had a close-knit group of friends."

"I remember." He nodded. "Even in high school you had a knack for choosing loyal, trustworthy friends who respected you, were there for you, and didn't play games."

"They were and still are," she said. "Hunter had actually suggested, more than once, that it was time I give them up. He said having six girlfriends was too many. How ridiculous is that?"

"Sounds like he was jealous."

"There was no reason to be. He always came first, and my friends treated Hunter with respect, even though he couldn't give them the same courtesy."

"Why couldn't he appreciate the honest, loyal bond you shared with them?"

She shook her head, mulling it over, and then she focused intently on him. "Because he wasn't loyal and couldn't be honest with me?"

"Fits the pattern."

"I can't believe I never made that connection," she said, sounding surprised.

"It's easier to see the situation when you're not directly involved."

"Not everyone has that ability."

He shrugged. "It's pretty easy to listen."

"And yet so many don't."

Her gaze wasn't wavering from his. He wanted to lean over and kiss her but knew it would be poor timing. The best thing about their past relationship had been their friendship, and he wasn't going to jeopardize that now.

He took her hand in his. "I want you to know that I'll always be there for you."

Her eyes moistened. "That means so much to me, Jack. Thank you."

After such an intense conversation, Charley offered to do a coffee run. She couldn't believe how comfortable she'd been telling Jack about her ex-fiancé, and how he so easily saw the problem. How had she gone from being attracted to such a great guy like Jack to picking out a selfish man like Hunter? Jack was being kind when he told her she was a good judge of character. When it came to her romantic relationships, insecurity had somehow taken over, clouding her ability to read a situation correctly, and without knowing what exactly caused her to become so insecure, she knew she could easily be blindsided again.

The barista called her name, and Charley picked up her drinks at the counter. As she turned to go, she caught sight of two teenagers sitting quietly in the corner. The girl was crying and the boy put his arm around her, trying to comfort her.

"It's not forever, and we'll FaceTime every day," he said. "I promise."

Charley knew exactly how the poor girl felt, and to have a separation happen at Christmas made it all the worse. The boy must have sensed her staring at them because he glared at her and pulled his girlfriend closer. Charley gave the boy an apologetic nod and hurried out the door, realizing she had been intruding on their private moment.

As she walked to the car, she thought of those teens, and it took more than a moment to shake it off before she got back inside the SUV.

"Any developments?" she asked, handing over the straight black coffee to Jack.

"Nothing yet." He offered her the binoculars. "You know, I don't think you told me your theory about this place."

She stared at the mailbox. "Before my plane landed in Denver, I had decided, like you, that the legend was nothing more than a tourists' trap. But now..." She lowered the binoculars and eyed Jack. "The people here are down-to-earth, decent folks who genuinely care about everyone, even strangers. And though I can't quite buy into the Scrooge Legend, where Santa's in charge and uses a magical mailbox for communication, I do feel many locals want to help visitors rediscover the true meaning of Christmas."

"They definitely nailed the atmosphere." He turned toward her, studying her.

"What?"

"Just trying to connect the dots between the legend, the Scrooge invitations, the swift attitude adjustments, and the reported life-changing events. According to the legend, you'll have a change of heart strictly by being in St. Nicholas for one short week. That's a high bar—the time crunch is bad enough, but what about the town itself? For someone like you who's only known big-city life, isn't St. Nicholas too quaint to have an impact on you?"

"I think that's the point. Because St. Nicholas moves at a snail's pace, I keep finding myself analyzing my life instead of being glued to my phone." She tucked her hair behind her ear and gazed out the window. "It's funny. When I'm so busy that I constantly have to multitask, I don't have time to think about how I feel. Do I enjoy my job? Do I like where I'm living? Do I want to be with the person I'm dating? Back home, I sometimes find myself just trying to get through the day."

"I understand that feeling very well," he said. "How do you feel here?"

"The Cold Hard Facts Queen in me wants to deny giving props to this town entirely. After all, it's really you who has made me think clearer, but we wouldn't be here if it weren't for the legend."

"I've made you think clearer?"

She nodded. "Spending time with you—being present, really listening—you've helped me see things differently," she said. "I mean, just tonight, as I was getting us coffee, I saw a teenage couple sitting by the window, and I—" She suddenly let out a small gasp as a revelation washed over her. She stared at Jack, then out the window, then back at him again.

"What is it?" He gave her a look of concern.

"I've just realized something." She locked her gaze on him. "My issue with Christmas goes back much farther than Hunter."

His brows raised. "To what?"

"Not what, but who," she slowly said, astonished that she hadn't made the connection before. "To the first guy who left me at Christmas."

"Another jerk?" He sounded incensed. "Who is this guy?"

"You." She met his gaze with total clarity. "It was you, Jack. I've actually had four guys leave me at Christmas, and you were the first one."

"Me?" Jack looked like he'd been slapped. "No. I didn't leave you. I mean, I guess I did, but that wasn't my choice. My dad got transferred out of state."

"I know you had to move when your family did. I'm talking about the way it all went down." She drew in a deep breath. "I remember standing on the edge of your family's driveway as we were trying to say goodbye to each other. The moving van had just pulled away, and your family's car was all packed up. Your mom and dad were sitting in the front seat, waiting for you, anxious to get on the road. I remember the quick, embarrassed kiss you gave me, knowing your parents were watching. I remember how I tried to tell you how much I loved you, but you were distracted—so I rushed my goodbye and I've regretted it ever since."

"You remember all that?"

"Every detail. I remember how we promised we'd talk every day, but we didn't. I called you, and it would take you three days to get back to me. It wasn't long before it took five days, and then ten."

"Charley, I had planned to keep our relationship going, I truly had, but we were kids. I was trying to adjust to a new school, a new neighborhood—"

"With new friends and a new girlfriend. I get it." Her sudden bitterness sliced through the air unintentionally.

"We were sixteen. A long-distance relationship is hard on anyone, let alone teenagers."

"I know. I'm sorry. I've been upset with you for years,

but tonight you helped me see things differently, and I now realize that my anger was misplaced. I should have been angry at the situation, not you. Like you said, we were young. Back then, all I felt was that you'd been taken from me, and you didn't seem to care."

"Oh, Charlotte." Jack put his arm around her, pulling her to him.

The tenderness in the way he spoke her name made her eyes well with tears. "I used to lie awake at night wondering why you had shut me out. I wondered what would have happened if you hadn't moved. Would we have stayed together?"

He intertwined his fingers with hers. "This might be hard to believe, but I did the same thing. I resented my dad for making me move. For months, I wouldn't talk to him. Then he started coming home from work early, and he'd throw the football around with me and talk about my future. It would make me feel guilty." Jack took a big breath in and let it out. "For the record, I do think we would have stayed together. I loved you very much, Charlotte. That's what made it so hard to let go."

She sat up, turning toward him. "I wish you had told me that before you left. Then we would have had a proper goodbye."

"Maybe I didn't because I never wanted it to be over." He stared into her eyes and she started to fall. Every fiber of her being was trying to resist falling for him again. The way he spoke to her, the way he held her, and those eyes of his were like unrelenting drills, creating hairline fractures, trying to split open the powerful dam holding back her feelings for so long. All he had to do was kiss her and the dam would burst wide open.

Jack cupped her face in his hands, staring into her eyes. He leaned closer to kiss her and—

Jingle bells filled the car. A split second later, a deafening screech had Charley covering her ears with her hands, and Jack scrambling to turn down the volume on his phone.

They bolted out of the car and raced to the mailbox.

"The flag's down!" She put her hands on top of her head and spun around, certain she'd see the culprit running away.

"No." Jack jerked his flashlight in all directions, trying to catch any movement within the trees. "Oh, come on!"

Charley ran in one direction, Jack in the other, searching for the mail collector. She was certain one of them would see him. No one could have run away that fast.

She made her way back to the mailbox at the same time Jack reappeared, still shining his flashlight over the immediate area.

"I swear I'm bringing in a bloodhound next," he said through gritted teeth.

Charley suppressed a laugh at that thought. She suddenly found herself secretly rooting for the bandit mailman. If he wasn't caught, they'd have to continue with their investigation.

Jack bent down and ran his hand under the mailbox. "The bug's gone." He shot up, fury building in his eyes. "You heard it, right, the jingle bells?"

"Yes. A few seconds before that ear-piercing screech."

"It was feedback on the microphone. Someone is definitely messing with us." He threw light over the base of the mailbox, examining boot imprints left on the hard-packed snow.

The guy was long gone but she kept glancing around for Jack's sake. "I can't believe this has happened again."

He paced, clenching his fists. "How do we get this guy?" He then froze, jerking his head up before meeting Charley's eye. "Are you up for another stakeout?"

"Sure, but shouldn't we figure out how to outsmart him first?"

"I just did, and tomorrow night he's mine."

Chapter Nineteen

He almost kissed me. She entered her room, sliding off her coat. *And I almost let him.* Their conversation had been so intense that she thought it might scare him away, but it didn't. He already asked her to dinner for the following night, and, of course, she said yes. A bit of insecurity caused her to wonder why he hadn't asked her to breakfast. Though she supposed Jack would be busy in the morning, rigging up something even more spectacular for tomorrow night's mail collector's capture.

She sat on the end of the bed, pulling off her boots, as her mind filled with Jack. He was such an amazing listener, which she found so rare in the guys she had dated, and his advice seemed right on target. He was confident, caring, gorgeous, and a true gentleman. Chivalry was very much a part of him, and she found that extremely attractive.

If their relationship were to keep moving in a serious direction, the big issue they faced was the same one that had broken them up in high school. They lived in different states, which meant one of them would have to move, one would need to compromise. Why were her love relationships always complicated? She pushed that thought away, choosing to immerse herself in the lighthearted feeling she had missed for so long. She sat at her computer, pulled up her blog, and started typing.

Hi All,
As I mentioned in my last post, I'm in St. Nicholas, Colorado, currently investigating the Scrooge Legend, which claims that any Scrooge—yours truly—who enters the town will end up loving Christmas as much as Santa. I've been here for a few days now, and I have to admit that there's something to the Scrooge Legend. There's a mysterious mailbox in the center of town where names of suggested Scrooges are deposited. No one has ever seen who collects the mail.

Although I can't yet declare myself a full-on Christmas enthusiast, this town has my attention. Aside from the mailbox, this place is downright gorgeous. Every bit of it is adorned with beautiful Christmas decorations, and the residents are incredibly welcoming, including my B&B hosts who make me feel right at home. I even went ice-skating. Stay tuned. This Scrooge might catch the Christmas spirit yet.

She smiled and hit Post. "I think I already have, dear readers, but you don't need to know that quite yet."

With a satisfied sigh, she sat back and glanced at the mantel. "Arthur?" She bolted out of her chair in search of the missing mouse. "Arthur, where'd you go?"

She moved the throw pillows, checked under the bed. She poked her head in the bathroom, rummaged through the armoire drawers, opened the closet, and inspected the floor. No Arthur. There was only one place left to look.

She snapped opened the curtains and found him sitting on the bench under the window.

"There you are! How did you get over here?" She curled up with him on the window seat, straightening out his jacket. "Did you talk to Santa for me?"

Arthur didn't react. She snagged her phone off the table and showed the stuffed mouse a picture of Jack.

"What do you think?" She studied his photo. "I was wrong to have been angry with him for so long. He's turned out to be a pretty great guy. We almost kissed tonight, but were interrupted." She let out a long sigh. "Oh, Arthur, what am I doing? We live in different states."

She eyed the mouse. "I know, I know. I kind of let him into my heart again and that terrifies me. What if I'm not reading him right? What if he doesn't feel the same way about me as I do him?" She played with the tiny bells on his vest. "You think he does? Yes, I know he's gorgeous with a killer smile. And those eyes can melt anyone. But no, I can't trust him completely until I know how he feels for sure, so don't try talking me into it."

She got up and set him back on the mantel. "Okay, fine. I'll think about it. Good night, Arthur." She hopped in bed, thinking fondly of Jack, and finally fell asleep.

When something happens once, it isn't a big deal; when something happens twice, it can become one. Jack thought back on his uncle's saying. It had been another sleepless night because he couldn't get Charley out of his head. Uncle Bill's saying was true. Charley had become a very big deal.

Last night, when they'd returned from their second stakeout, Jack immediately checked her blog. He couldn't confirm Reality Check's true identity, but who else could it be besides the trucker? Luckily, R.C. hadn't posted another comment. That was the good news. The bad news was Jack tracked the email account to the North Pole.

"Not possible!" He was incensed just thinking about it. He threw back the covers and marched into the bathroom where he flipped on the light and stared at his own reflection in the mirror. He'd always been good at his job because he left his emotions out of his investigations. Now all he could think about *were* his emotions. For Charley.

He spread shaving cream over his face and took a razor to his skin. What would his life look like in five years? In ten? Would he still be a detective in Denver? Would he be single? In a relationship? Would he be with Charley? He thought back on the night before and how vulnerable she'd been—how she had trusted him enough to open up to him. He hated to think how much pain he had caused her, and how that pain had negatively affected her love life.

After he moved away, he soon realized that missing her as much as he did wasn't going to get him back to Los Angeles, no more than missing his uncle was going to bring him back to his family. Their high school long-distance romance had been a no-win situation that only prolonged their inevitable heartache. At the time, he'd thought letting the relationship fall apart was probably the least painful way to end it. He'd assumed his actions would make her angry enough to forget about him so that she could find love again and be happy. For him, he had never stopped loving her, and he'd hoped that somehow they would find each other again.

By six-thirty Jack was headed downstairs. He wanted to spend the day with Charley, but he needed to set up an indiscernible trap for the elusive mail collector. Knowing breakfast wasn't served until seven, he poured himself a cup of coffee and thought about how he could pull it off. He wanted to impress Charley with his new idea. If she had thought the audio surveillance was cool, he couldn't wait to see her reaction to what he was cooking up for tonight.

With coffee in hand, he stepped out on the front porch and noticed he wasn't the only early riser. Joe and the handyman, Mike, were setting up an animated display of Christmas carolers in the front yard.

Joe plugged it in, then took a step back and scratched his head. "I don't know, Mike. Mary will love how the carolers move as they sing, that's a given, but no one's going to see them in the dark."

Mike glanced at the walkway, then at the carolers, as if he were noting the distance between the two. "What we need are motion sensor lights that will illuminate the display whenever anyone approaches."

"That's a great idea," Joe said.

"Yes, it is." Jack stared up at the trees.

"Morning, Jack." Joe greeted him with his usual friendly smile. "Can I help you with something?"

He couldn't believe his luck. He just might be able to get some help *and* question Mike without him knowing it. "As a matter of fact, you can."

After Jack pitched in to help with the lights on the carolers, the men grabbed some breakfast together. Jack explained what he wanted to accomplish with the mailbox, and it seemed as if Joe and Mike were more excited about it than he was. That was fine with him. Whatever got the job done.

By eight-thirty, the men were hard at work by the mailbox in the town square. The area was covered with ladders, drills, hammers, motion sensor floodlights and a vast array of extension cords. Several curious residents stopped to ask what they were up to, and Joe's answer remained vague—saying their undertaking was part of the upcoming Christmas festival. Still, their high visibility started to worry Jack. Would it tip off his stealth mail collector? Would someone from the town hall tell them to stop what they were doing?

"Are you sure we don't need a permit for this?" he asked Joe for a second time.

"Positive. I'm on the town council." Joe handed a light up to Mike. "This falls under assistance with the Scrooge Legend. As long as it doesn't impede walkways, roadways, or destroy public property, we're good."

Jack unwound another extension cord and began threading it through tree branches, attempting to conceal it along the way. "Everyone here in St. Nicholas really keeps the Scrooge Legend alive."

"Why wouldn't we?" Joe said. "Every Scrooge story has a happy ending."

Mike seemed a little quiet. "What about you, Mike? Do you believe in the Scrooge Legend?"

"No reason not to," he replied, climbing two more steps up the ladder to set a light on a sturdy tree branch. "I've always been curious about the mailbox, and I'd like to know who's collecting the mail as much as you."

"How long have you lived here?"

"It'll be two years this Christmas." Mike tied down the light to the branch and angled it toward the mailbox.

"It was perfect timing when Mike showed up," Joe said, handing Mike an extension cord. "Our town's three best handymen retired at the same time. I don't know what Mary and I would have done without him. There isn't anything Mike can't fix."

"I believe it." Jack smiled. "He fixed my shower yesterday."

Joe cast an eye on Mike, looking very disappointed. "I thought *I* fixed that leak."

Mike laughed. "What do I keep telling you, Joe?"

"Leave it to the expert, I know, I know."

"How did you come to St. Nicholas?" Jack glanced at Mike as he pulled out another floodlight from its box and got it ready to hand off. "Were you invited like my friend Charley?"

"No." He came down off the ladder. "I was passing through town and there was something so darn familiar and homey about this place that I ended up staying."

"I can see why you would," Jack said. "What did your family think of that?"

Mike suddenly looked very uncomfortable. "Oh… uh." He quickly broke eye contact with Jack and stared at his watch. "Hey, you know, I just realized I'm due at the Sweeneys' house. I promised Ian I'd help him install a new dishwasher today."

Joe tested out the light and it worked. "We got this, Mike. Thanks for your help."

"Yes, much appreciated." Jack pulled out his wallet. "What do I owe you?"

"You put that away." Mike waved him off as he grabbed his tool box. "Happy to help. Good luck tonight."

Jack watched Mike take off in a hurry. "Was it something I said?"

Joe took over for Mike, repositioning the ladder under the tree on the opposite side of the mailbox before Jack handed him another light. "Mike is one of the nicest guys you'll ever know, but he's had a tough time of it."

"How so?"

"He almost died twenty years ago."

Jack got instant chills. "Are you serious?"

Joe descended the ladder and grabbed a swig of bottled water.

"What happened?" Jack asked, joining him.

"He got hit by a car in New York City. When he was admitted into the hospital, the staff didn't find any identification on him. He was in a coma, listed as a John Doe, for over a month. When he came to, he couldn't remember who he was or where he lived. His doctor told him he had suffered a brain injury and that the amnesia could be permanent. The local news stations picked up his story and ran it every night for a week, but no one came forward. He didn't want to be known as John Doe, so he chose Mike Hodges for his name."

"Hodges?" Jack could barely get the name off his tongue.

"That name mean anything to you?"

"It's my mother's maiden name."

"That's a strange coincidence."

"Even more of a coincidence is that my dad's name is Mike." Jack felt a tightening in his throat.

"Is that so?"

Jack's mind was reeling. All those leads that never panned out. All those times he thought, *could this guy be him?* And now his twenty-year search could finally be over. He'd been talking himself out of it after Mike told Jack his name. He couldn't understand why his uncle would pretend to be someone else. Even his theory of a syndicate tie was a stretch.

His family had scoured all the Chicago hospitals for him and any admitted John Doe for months, originally thinking he'd been in an accident. They'd filed a missing person's report with the police to cover the amnesia, kidnapping, and foul play angles. Even though the FBI had searched for him out of state, it hadn't been the main focus because his family believed he wouldn't have gone out of town without telling them.

Jack remembered how his mom kept insisting that Uncle Bill had to be unresponsive in a hospital somewhere, but since there wasn't a central database of hospital admission records, there was no easy way to find him.

Mike could really be my uncle. He blinked back emotion threatening to spill over. Joe's story explained so many unanswered questions that he and his family had asked for so long. His uncle never called, never came back, because he didn't know who he was or where he lived.

He cleared his throat, forcing to fight back the flood of emotions banging around in his chest. He opened a bottled water and took a swig. "Did Mike ever tell you why he left New York?"

"He said the cost of living was too high. He also felt like he didn't belong there. He said his gut was telling him that he was in the wrong city, so he decided to hit the road, hoping something would jog his memory."

"Twenty years of searching," Jack muttered, shaking his head. "Poor guy."

"I sure as heck wouldn't have been able to do it for that long, always being on the road, always looking for answers," Joe said. "At least now he feels at home here, and everyone just loves him."

"I can see that. You're good people, Joe, to look out for him."

"That's what we do here." He crunched up his empty water bottle and threw it on their pile of trash. "Now, let's get you set up for tonight."

Chapter Twenty

Charley hurried down the steps of the bed-and-breakfast, irritated she had set her alarm wrong. She was hoping to run into Jack because she didn't want to wait all day before she saw him again. Now it was eight-thirty, and though she didn't know exactly when he preferred to eat, she assumed it was early.

She rushed into the dining room to find…no one. With a heavy sigh, she flopped down at the nearest table.

Mary wandered in to clean the rest of the tables. "There's the sleepyhead."

"Sorry. I overslept," she said, still a little out of breath.

"No need to apologize. Breakfast is available for another hour." Mary piled the dirty dishes on top of one another. "Can I get you started with some coffee? Tea? Hot chocolate?"

"I'd love some English Breakfast, if you have it."

"Be back in a flash." Mary grabbed dirty dishes with both hands, then headed to the kitchen.

Charley glanced out the window, wanting to relax and enjoy a leisurely breakfast, but she didn't know how to do that. At home, she'd be cramming down a bagel or gulping a fruit smoothie while answering work emails. Now she couldn't help but turn around in her chair every five seconds to see if Jack was descending the stairs. When Mary appeared with her tea, she couldn't stand it any longer. "Has Jack had breakfast yet?"

"I'm afraid so. He went into town with Joe and Mike."

"Who's Mike?"

"Our handyman," Mary said, setting down a small basket of mini muffins. "Those boys looked like they were up to something."

The corners of Charley's mouth turned up, thinking back on how Jack said he'd be catching the elusive mail collector tonight and wondered what more he could possibly be doing. The miniature microphone hadn't helped identify him at all. If anything, the sound of jingle bells captured by the microphone only supported the theory that it was one of Santa's helpers.

"Jack's determined to solve the mystery of Santa's mailbox."

Mary exploded with a laugh. "Good luck with that!"

Charley poured a splash of cream in her tea and gave it a stir. "How long have people been trying?"

"Gosh." Mary tilted her head, seeming to contemplate the question. "As long as I can remember. Probably as long as the town's been here."

"Oh. Guess I better not get my hopes up for tonight."

"It's always fun to try. I personally don't mind if we never find out. When a mystery is solved, the wonderment of that mystery goes with it."

She pondered that for a moment, but the Cold Hard Facts Queen in her needed to quash that wonderment for real facts—that was the only way she could know if the legend was a hoax. But how could it be real? Christmas magic didn't exist any more than elves did.

Of course, Komodo dragons were thought to be mythical creatures until they were documented in 1910. Admittedly, she couldn't explain how her invitation to St. Nicholas, the one she threw away, had landed on her boss's desk moments later. She also couldn't explain how she'd come across pictures of Jack, only to reconnect with him two days later. She'd buy into the idea of it being pure coincidence if she had run into him in a big city like Los Angeles, but to find him in a six-room B&B in a small mountain town she hadn't even known she'd be traveling to was mathematically implausible.

And what about the mailbox itself? She had firsthand accounts of how it brought loved ones to town. Would she have run into Jack had she not suggested him as a Scrooge? Would the person he suggested eventually come to town? She needed hard evidence of Christmas magic, and the easiest way of finding it was through the identification of the mail collector. The locals said it was one of Santa's helpers, so if the mail collector couldn't be captured on video, then she'd need to see him with her own eyes. If he, or she, proved to be out of the ordinary, then perhaps Christmas magic did exist, and maybe she'd get her happy ending after all.

But what if it wasn't an elf? What if Jack was right about the entire town having a hand at creating and sustaining the Scrooge Legend for profit? That would be a real disappointment. Charley would be forced to debunk the legend, and for what? To point out that there was a little less magic and goodness in the world?

Charley tumbled out of her thoughts when she heard Mary speaking to her. "And what about you, Charley? You arrived here, as you put it, not a fan of Christmas. Are we rubbing off on you, even a little?"

"More than a little," she admitted. "I can't believe I've

only been here a few days, and I'm questioning everything—my instincts, my job, my attitude, my insistence on staying single. How did this happen?"

Mary's eyes twinkled. "I think you know."

"The spirit of Christmas?"

"It works in mysterious ways."

Right after breakfast, Charley took off for town. She didn't want to intrude on *the boys* as Mary had called them, but at the same time, she wanted to say hi to Jack and let him know she was around should he finish early. By the time she arrived at the town square, they were already gone.

"Shoot." She inspected the mailbox and the surrounding area, but she couldn't figure out what exactly they had accomplished. She closed her coat a little tighter as she strolled through the square, keeping an eye out for Jack. It felt colder now that he wasn't near. She took out her phone to send him a text when she realized that she should grab a few more Scrooge interviews. So far, not one person had told her that the legend was fake. She couldn't even find anyone who was indifferent about it. The Scrooge Legend was as real as the earth beneath her feet. Period.

She crossed the street, thinking she'd go to the library first when a toy store caught her eye. Two beautiful dollhouses and three hand-carved wooden sailboats were on display in the window. She immediately thought of Jack's uncle and went inside.

"Afternoon," greeted a cordial saleswoman, wearing a red-and-green plaid dress. "Is there something I can help you find?"

"Can you tell me about the sailboats in the window?" Charley gestured to the display.

"We just got those in last night." The woman strode over to them. "My understanding is that both the sailboats and the dollhouses were made by a local artist."

"Is that so?" Charley admired the detail on all the pieces. "Do you happen to know the name of the artist?"

"I don't, though he would have left his card with the manager." The saleswoman looked around the cash register. "I'm sorry. I don't see it. Can I take your number and get back to you?"

"I can stop by later. Do you know when the manager will be in?"

"Hard to say. Her daughter went into labor this morning."

"How wonderful for them."

"Yes. This will be her first grandchild."

Charley smiled at the thought of being a new mom. At one time she had wanted two children of her own, but that was before her love life took a nosedive. When her second serious relationship fell apart, she realized her prospects of having children were diminishing. When Hunter said he wanted to wait three years before starting a family, she worried she'd never have children at all. She had finally forced herself to stop thinking about them, convincing herself she'd never have time for a family anyway.

"I'll check back with you later in the week." She was halfway out the door when she turned around. "On second thought, I'd like to buy one of the sailboats—the red, white, and blue one."

"What a thoughtful, lovely gift," the saleswoman said as she carefully took it off the display and carried it to the cash register. "Everyone wants the latest gadget these days. I never understood that because most are obsolete within months. You can't find many handmade gifts anymore."

"No, you can't." Charley checked out the beautiful Christmas ornaments by the register.

"Would you like this wrapped for Christmas?" The woman rang in the price.

"Please." Charley handed over her credit card. While she waited for the woman to add festive ribbons and bows to the bag, she pictured Jack's delighted reaction when he opened it. She'd need to get the information on the artist before she gave it to him. What were the chances of it being his uncle? Wishful thinking was more like it. Then again, the surprising town of St. Nicholas seemed to have better odds than any casino in Vegas.

Jack had planned to call Charley after he and Joe finished rigging the lights over the mailbox, but now that he had Mike's full name, he wanted to run a background check on him. First, Jack needed to get some answers for his captain.

At Felicity and Nolan's B&B, construction trucks lined the driveway. Jack parked and headed to the front right as Felicity pulled up behind him.

"Hey, Jack," she called, getting out of her car with two bags of groceries.

"Let me get those for you." He hurried over to help, then followed her inside. "I see you're getting the place back together." He stepped into the foyer and saw painters working at the top of the stairs.

"The son's father lived up to his word, and our repairs are moving right along." She walked into the kitchen with Jack trailing behind. "Everything okay at the Carrolls'?"

"Couldn't be better." He set the groceries on top of the counter. "In fact, I wanted to thank you for sending me over there. Out of sheer luck, I ran into my high school sweetheart who's also staying there."

"Sheer luck?" Her eyes twinkled as she began unpacking the groceries. "That's great to hear."

"You weren't kidding about unexpected things happening."

"Our town is very special." A secretive smile played on Felicity's lips. "Can I get you something to drink?"

"Don't trouble yourself, I can't stay. I just wanted to ask you about Tony Braca."

Felicity threw the perishables into the refrigerator, then gave him her undivided attention. "You're a friend of Tony's?"

"An acquaintance, but I know he had a change of heart after staying here."

"Of course, he did. He was a Scrooge," she said. "I couldn't let him walk out that door still being a Scrooge, now could I?"

"I suppose you couldn't." Jack stifled a smile.

"That's what we do here. We help people, like the Carrolls are helping Charley."

Jack's eyes widened in surprise. "You know about Charley?"

"Of course. We're all on the same team."

Jack rubbed his brow, trying to get his head around the fact that the locals appeared to be more interested in helping people than making a buck. "Do all the B&B proprietors make it a priority to help so-called Scrooges?"

"Only a handful."

"Who sends them?"

"Why Santa, of course."

"Santa, right. A guy who apparently lives at the North Pole invites whoever he wishes to your town and expects you to provide free room and board for them for a week? How do you stay in business?"

"Not everyone is a Scrooge, Jack. You're not."

"Charley thinks I am. She says I'm here because she put my name in the mailbox as a Scrooge suggestion."

Felicity leaned on the counter. "You're here because you're an intricate part of her happiness—and yours."

"Forgive me, but I'm here because my boss sent me. He's very concerned that people are getting brainwashed up here."

She laughed. "Is that what he told you?"

"Not in so many words, but Tony and his own brother had an attitude adjustment while they were here. When they returned home, they were completely different."

"Different or happier?"

"Happier," he had to admit. "But that doesn't mean their happiness didn't come at a price."

"Like what? Your high school sweetheart is a current Scrooge. Hasn't she told you that her invitation cost her nothing?"

"Yes, but—"

"But what?"

"You can't expect me to believe that Santa, or whoever is pretending to be Santa, sends you unhappy people, and in one week, you change their way of thinking and instantly fix them."

"No one can receive help unless they want it. You know that," she said. "I think the more important question you should be asking yourself is why are you really here? Do you honestly think you're in St. Nicholas to expose a scam that results in making people happier?"

He ran a hand over his face. "I don't know what to believe anymore. I've got a stealth mail collector, a guy named R.C. leaving cryptic messages on Charley's blog, and I don't have any logical answers for my boss."

"Again. Why are you really here?" she asked, sounding far wiser than her biological age. "You appear to be very good at connecting the dots, so I'm surprised you haven't noticed how, here in St. Nicholas, people are more connected to each other's happiness than they realize. Unrelated situations tend not to be so unrelated. It's all connected. It's right in front of you. You just need to give yourself time to see the whole picture."

A part of Jack wanted to buy into it; he really did—but his years of being a cop wouldn't allow it. Felicity wasn't going to be straight with him about who was truly behind the Scrooge invitations, and he had no concrete or logical explanation as to why people were returning home happier than when they left. If he was right, that the legend was merely a marketing tool to increase tourism, there was no crime in that. Though he refused to believe Felicity's whole Santa explanation, he was willing to take her advice and focus on what was in front of him—Charley and Mike.

He thanked Felicity for her time, then drove back to the Carroll Inn and got to work. While he waited for his laptop to boot up, he dragged out his cell and dialed his partner at the precinct. "Hey, Adam. Can you do a background check for me?"

"Sure. What's the name?"

"Mike Hodges."

"I'll run it and let you know."

"Thanks." He disconnected the call and began checking out Mike's digital footprint. Jack found his current address, which was a rental, two prior addresses in other towns, and an insufficient credit history. The handyman didn't have a website, wasn't on any social media site, he hadn't shopped online, and he hadn't left any reviews.

Abandoning his research, Jack pulled up his family photos and scrolled through them, stopping on a picture of his uncle working on a toy airplane. Studying the image, he noticed something he'd missed before. He magnified the image and zeroed in on his uncle's right hand, revealing a long scar that was a good inch in length between his index finger and thumb. Jack had forgotten all about that scar—one he vaguely remembered his uncle receiving on a construction site that sent him to the hospital for stitches.

Jack sat back. He'd finally found a way to physically identify his uncle. *Does Mike have a scar?* He thought back to earlier in the day. He couldn't recall seeing one, but then again, he hadn't exactly been looking for it.

Jack continued scrolling through the photos until his phone rang. "Yeah?"

"That's how you answer the phone these days?" Lisa teased.

He pinched the bridge of his nose, wanting to kick himself for answering without seeing who was calling. "Hey, I can't talk right now."

"I only called to make sure you made it up there safe and sound."

Why was she so concerned about his well-being? He should have made a clean break with no friend strings attached.

"Are you still there?"

He cleared his throat. "Look, I know I said that we could still be friends, but I don't think—"

"How's the bed-and-breakfast?" she asked. "I hope it's not run-down like you thought it would be."

"I'm sorry, but I've got to go."

"Okay, I'll let you get back to work. I just wanted to say thank you for staying late the other night, so we could have a real heart-to-heart."

"No problem. It was good we did." *Let that be the end of it.*

"Nothing like a good talk to build a strong relationship," she said. "I was reading an article the other day, and did you know the best marriages start with solid friendships?"

He sighed. "You know my feelings about marriage."

"Who's talking marriage?" She laughed. "*I* was talking about friendships."

She was like a good magician with a perfect sleight of hand, only she did it with words. He was about to hang up when he remembered what Felicity had said about people being more connected to each other's happiness than they realized. Could this include Lisa? *No.* Then again, she was making him uncomfortable because she was uncomfortable, and wasn't he the cause of that? *No.* He wasn't going to second-guess his actions due to what Felicity told him. Lisa was attempting to manipulate his emotions, and he needed to shut that down immediately.

"Lisa, I don't want to hurt you, but I don't think it's a good idea for us to remain friends. I think it's best that we go our separate ways."

He listened to the silence, waiting for her response, but instead he heard two beeps, telling him the call had been dropped. "No!"

Jack threw down the phone and dragged his hands through his hair. Things were going so well with Charley. He didn't need anything messing that up for him—especially Lisa. The fact that she wasn't accepting the end of their relationship had him worried. Loose ends that didn't get tied up tended to unravel very quickly.

Chapter Twenty-One

With her arms full of Christmas gifts, Charley's cell began ringing right as she opened the door to her room. She dropped the packages on the table and answered the call before it went to voice mail. "Hey, Liv," she said, out of breath.

"Have you checked your blog lately?"

She hadn't and was embarrassed to admit it. She was always on top of it, especially after she posted something, but she honestly hadn't found the time. "No, sorry. I've had spotty service since I've been here." She felt guilty for telling her best friend a little white lie. "Is there a problem?"

"Just the opposite. Several of your readers are sharing their stories about their stay in St. Nicholas, and your loyal fans are asking you for an update," Liv said. "Who's Jack?"

"What?" Charley ran to her computer and turned it on.

"Someone named Reality Check mentioned a Jack. Are you dating someone there?"

Charley's laptop finally booted up and her blog filled the screen. She had over a hundred comments and was having trouble locating the one from Reality Check. "I don't understand why I wasn't alerted to all of this activity," she said, exasperated.

"I guess it's because of the spotty service."

Slack-jawed, Charley skimmed the comments.

Don't waste your time debunking the Scrooge Legend. It's the real deal. Take it from a rehabilitated Scrooge.

She scrolled down to some more.

Are there other Santa mailboxes around the country or just the one in St. Nicholas? Can you put a Scrooge suggestion in for me? I'll email you his name.

"Liv, let me call you back."

Charley hung up and scrambled to find Reality Check's new comment.

Glad to see you're back on track with Jack. With true love, your heart will sing a song, and bring you to the place where you belong.

"What? What!" She catapulted out of her chair just as there was a knock at the door. She barely managed to open it before Jack barged in, red in the face with anger.

"Who *is* this guy?" He shook his phone. "Did you see this?"

"Just now," she said. "Were you able to trace R.C.'s IP address?"

"Yeah. It went to the North Pole."

"What?"

"As if we're supposed to believe that Santa is leaving comments on your blog. I have no idea if that trucker named R.C. is the same R.C. on your blog, but I guarantee the one from your blog is here in town, and I don't like it one bit. That guy is *watching* us."

Santa? North Pole? Charley hid her smile. "We need to talk to Angel."

Jack was still in a foul mood when he and Charley arrived at the diner. First Lisa, and now R.C. He could handle Lisa, but how was he supposed to deal with a guy he'd never met and didn't know where to find? *The North Pole. Unbelievable.* Anyone who redirected their IP address was hiding something. Now this guy was getting a little too personal with Charley, and Jack didn't know how he could protect her. He hated social media. Sure, she loved her blog, and her readers loved it as well. But if he had anything to say about it, he would insist on doing a background check on anyone and everyone who visited her site.

"We'd like to sit in Angel's section," Charley requested.

"Away from the window," Jack added.

"No problem." The young hostess, looking no more than eighteen, took them to a quiet table away from any windows.

"Do you by chance know Reality Check?" Charley asked as they sat down.

"You mean Santa Claus?"

Charley immediately caught Jack's eye.

He shook his head, refusing to buy into it. The hostess was obviously playing her part in advancing the Scrooge

Legend for their star guest, Charley Dawson, a popular magazine blogger—he was sure of it.

"That's what I call him because he looks so much like the Santa Claus you see in movies."

"He does," Charley said.

"He's such a sweet man. He always knows what to say, and he gives everyone little rhymes that seem to address personal issues."

Charley shot Jack a look. "Like what?"

"Well, like last year, when I was a senior in high school, R.C. was in here, having dinner, when my friends came in and asked if I wanted to hang out with them after I got off work. Of course I said yes, even though I needed to study. I had a big history exam the next morning that counted as a quarter of my grade. After they left, he asked me how I was doing in school. I said great even though my grades had been slipping. It's like he knew I wasn't being a hundred percent truthful. I don't know how he knew about the test, or that I wasn't going to study, but he left me a note when he paid the bill that said, 'Studying hard will pave the way. Don't mess up getting an A.'"

"Did you go home and study?" Charley asked.

"Yes, ma'am, and I got an A."

"Good for you," Jack said. "Now, stay off social media."

The young hostess gave him a bewildered look, as did Charley, before a large party came in the front door to end the awkward moment. "I better go take care of those customers," she said. "Have a good dinner."

A teasing smile played on Charley's face. "Gosh, Detective, aren't you being a little overprotective?"

"She's a teen. I'm doing my job."

"That's not it."

He groaned, sitting back. "I hate it when things don't add up."

"Maybe Reality Check is like you—just looking out for folks."

"That guy knows way more than he should." Jack clenched his teeth.

"But how?"

"I don't know. Maybe this whole darn town is under surveillance." He blew out an irritated breath, then rubbed his eyes. His conversation with Felicity had gotten under his skin. There was some truth to what she had said and that's what bothered him. He couldn't cherry-pick what he wanted to believe and what he didn't. "Why is it that no logical explanation sticks to anything here in St. Nicholas?"

"Welcome back," Angel said, walking up to the table. "How's your day been going?"

"Interesting..." Charley looked to Jack to fill in the rest, which he was not about to do. He already knew he'd get more questions than answers in return.

"Do tell," Angel said with glee in her eye. "Is it something juicy?"

"Hate to disappoint, but it's nothing like that," Charley said. "Someone named Reality Check left me a couple messages on my blog."

"How nice!" Angel snapped back into her professional friendly manner.

"Not nice," Jack said. "More like overstepping boundaries."

"What Jack is trying to say is that *I* don't know your trucker friend. The comments are very specific about me and Jack, and we're having a difficult time making the connection."

"If you're worried about him, don't be." Angel waved the thought away. "He's been a real help to many of the folks here in town. One customer described talking to him as a 'warm friendly hug.'"

"I'll bet," Jack said sarcastically. There was something off about the man. He was hiding something, and Jack didn't like that one bit.

"Thanks for letting us know," Charley said, stepping in.

"Anytime. Now, what will you be having for dinner this fine evening?" Angel bounced her gaze between the two. "In addition to our regular menu, tonight's special is homemade chicken potpie."

Charley's face lit up. "I'm sold."

"Make it two."

As soon as Angel left, Jack fixed his eyes on Charley. "I'm still not convinced Reality Check isn't a threat. And what if he's not a sweet old man?"

"According to Angel and the hostess, that's *exactly* what he is. Besides, we can't confirm that it's him. Anyone could be posting under Reality Check."

Jack looked away, drumming his fingers on the table. "Did you feel like someone was following you today?"

"No," she said with a laugh. "In fact, while I was Christmas shopping, I kept looking around for you, so I would have noticed. Seriously, Jack, I live in LA and I'm always aware of my surroundings. I think you're making too much of it."

He let out a resigned breath. "Okay, I'll drop it, for now." She was probably right, but once he discovered Reality Check's true identity, he'd be doing a very deep dive on the guy, just to be sure.

* * *

It took a while before Jack emerged from his surly mood. Charley asked him if something had happened aside from finding R.C.'s comment, and he dodged the question, which didn't sit well with her. She was most likely making too much of it, like Jack was doing with R.C.

"You went Christmas shopping?" Jack squeezed lemon into his tea. "I thought you didn't like it."

"I don't, but today was different. It didn't feel like a chore this time. I kept running across the perfect gift for everyone on my list. That never happens. Now I can hold my head high because everyone will get a real gift from me this year instead of a gift card."

"*Everyone*?"

Charley wanted to laugh at the adorable expression he had on his face. It was an excited, hopeful look, like he was wondering if he made her list, mixed with worry that he hadn't. "I might have a little something for you."

His face split into a huge grin. "What did you get me?"

"I'm not going to tell you. You'll have to wait." She almost said he'd have to wait *until Christmas* but stopped short. She didn't know if they'd be together at Christmas. They hadn't exactly talked about it. After her complimentary week was up, what then? Was she supposed to go back to her life in Los Angeles—a life without Jack? She didn't want to think about that. It was too depressing.

"I have to wait? For how long?" His eyes implored, almost as if he were daring her to open the topic they were dancing around.

"Depends," she said, playfully, as though that would somehow make her feel less vulnerable. "Maybe tomorrow, maybe Christmas…"

Jack's grin widened. "Christmas, huh? Sounds like I better get some shopping done."

Her heart felt like it was going to leap out of her chest. There wasn't the slightest hesitation in his reaction. He wanted to spend Christmas with her.

"Here you go. Two chicken potpies." Angel carefully set them down. "They're piping hot inside, so be careful."

Charley admired the gorgeous golden crust. "I'm starting to think St. Nicholas should also be known for its food."

"I'll back you up on that one," he said, already with a mouth full.

"Here's a crazy thought..." She pierced the top of her potpie with a fork to let the steam out. "What if a child is picking up the mail?"

He nodded, finishing a bite. "I thought of that, but he would have to be a very focused, smart kid whose parents would allow him to stay up late every night."

"Maybe he's a very short adult."

"It's possible. He could hide behind the mailbox a lot easier if he were, which would also explain why the lock is in the back."

"We'll know tonight when we finally catch him," she said, confidently.

"Speaking of which, you're going to love the new setup. There are now four motion sensor floodlights covering the mailbox. No matter which direction the mail collector comes from, he or she will be seen. Guaranteed."

"So, *that's* what you were doing." She assumed as much but was happy to hear it from him. "Mary said you and the boys were up to something."

"The boys?" Jack chuckled. "She said that?"

"Yeah. You, Joe, and their handyman?"

"Mike. I guess he's the number one handyman here in town."

She took another bite of her potpie. "That was nice of him and Joe to help you out this morning."

Jack leaned back and had a look on his face that she was beginning to recognize. He was analyzing something or someone.

"Did something happen?"

He stared into his glass of iced tea. "I actually met Mike yesterday. He was fixing my shower when we returned from ice-skating. He called me young man, and he has the same blue-gray eyes that I do."

"That's a strange coincidence, considering we were just discussing your uncle," she said. "I'm guessing Mike reminded you of him?"

He rubbed the back of his neck. "Every year I run an old photo of my uncle through an age progression program. I did it a few days ago, but I neglected to take weight gain into account. I reworked it, adding forty pounds, and now he looks a lot like Mike."

"Are you serious? Did you show him the photo?"

"No. Joe said Mike had been hit by a car twenty years ago and has no long-term memory."

Her heart stilled. A phrase and the color of one's eyes could be coincidence, but what about the gift she bought Jack? Had the toy sailboat been carved by his uncle's hand? She opened her mouth to tell him, then closed it. What if she was wrong? Wouldn't she be giving him false hope? She ran a hand over her lips. "Do you think he's your uncle?"

He sat back with a big sigh. "I want to believe he is, but I'm not a hundred percent sure." His eyes were uncertain, vulnerable. "And what if I'm wrong? I don't want to freak the guy out, or get his hopes up."

"I can certainly understand that." She needed to talk to the toy store manager as soon as possible. "Maybe we can somehow get confirmation that it's him, or maybe you can figure out a way to talk to him."

"I tried earlier. I asked too many questions this morning, and he shut down. I need to find a way to approach the subject without making him feel uncomfortable."

She fell silent, thinking of a solution. She was in awe at the constant synchronization that continued to happen in her life, and in Jack's. If ever there was a place to find his missing uncle, it would be St. Nicholas. "Is there anything you can say or do that might jog his memory?"

"Maybe—if I were still ten."

Charley took a deep breath, wanting to figure something out for Jack. "Let's say it's him. There has to be a way to trigger his memory, something from the past. What was the biggest project you two worked on together?"

His eyes lit up. "A few months before he went missing, Chicago was getting ready for their annual Christmas expo. He was hired to build a no-frills model train display, but Uncle Bill went all out and built a massive one. I helped out every day after school, and over two consecutive weekends. It turned out great. My uncle even won an award."

"That's awesome. I wonder if a model train display could trigger his memory. With so many Christmas decorations in this town, there's got to be one somewhere."

Angel stopped to check on them. "I'd ask how you like our potpie, but I can see that for myself." She eyed their almost empty plates.

"Another winner," Jack said.

"Hey, Angel, are there any model train displays around town?" Charley asked.

"No, but our Christmas festival starts tomorrow, and if you're looking for Christmas activities, there'll be door-to-door caroling, the Christmas cookie crawl, the best snowman competition. You've probably noticed an increase in decorations around the residential homes this week. Sunday night is the home decoration contest and the winner will be announced Monday. Whoever wins will get their electric bill paid by the city for an entire year."

"Now there's an incentive." Charley glanced at Jack, only he seemed far away.

"What dessert would you like me to set aside for you?" Angel asked. "It's Friday night, so our pies are going fast."

"Oh no. Not me." Charley put a hand up to stop Angel from suggesting anything tempting. "I'm already stuffed, and I still have a few bites to go on my potpie."

"As much as I love your apple pie, it's a hard pass for me," Jack said.

"But you're going to need something for later tonight." She fisted a hand on her hip. "You're having another Santa stakeout, aren't you?" She threw glances between the two.

Jack shook his head. "Are we that obvious?"

"Never." A playful smile touched her lips. "So, what will it be? I've got snickerdoodles coming out of the oven in five minutes."

"How can we turn down freshly baked snickerdoodles?" Charley asked Jack, knowing she couldn't.

"They might even help you catch one of Santa's helpers," Angel added.

"I can't argue with that." Jack put his hands up in surrender.

"Good. I'll bring them when you're ready for the check." Angel left to wait on other customers.

"So that's how you do it," Charley said, bursting with excitement.

He pushed his brows together. "I'm not following."

"The contest. Ask Mike to help you make a small train display for the B&B."

"Genius," he said as a smile took over his face. "I could just kiss you."

Charley bubbled with laughter. *And I could just kiss you right back.*

Chapter Twenty-Two

"Happy hunting!" Angel called to Jack and Charley as they left the diner and headed over to the town square.

Jack stared at the takeout container in his hand. "I can't believe we're armed for the stakeout with warm cookies and a cup of milk."

"Me, neither," Charley said on a laugh. "Of course, Angel's help has kind of killed your theory."

"How so?"

"If this town wanted to perpetuate the Scrooge Legend, they wouldn't be aiding us in trying to debunk it."

"Or maybe what we're doing right now *is* perpetuating it."

"You are a true cynic."

"How can you say that? I'm currently using milk and cookies to catch a person of interest." In truth, he would have baked the cookies himself if that kept her by his side. "Okay, here we go." He set the container of snickerdoodles on top of the mailbox.

She placed the cup of milk next to it. "We're going to expose him. I can feel it. No one can resist milk and cookies."

"Yeah, I'm sure they're really going to slow him down," he said in jest, but secretly he hoped they would.

Not that the elusive mail collector would take time to have a snack, but the few extra seconds he'd waste to see what was sitting on top of the mailbox would give Jack the advantage.

"If this works, you'll have to roll out the How-To-Catch-A-Criminal-With-Cookies Initiative in Denver."

He smoothed out the snow around the mailbox with his glove in hopes of getting a better imprint of the mail collector's footwear. "This is St. Nicholas we're dealing with. Normal rules don't apply."

"You can say that again." She remained riveted to what was happening behind him.

Jack stood to see what held her attention. Small groups of people were strolling up the shoveled walkway carrying chairs, blankets, snacks, and hot thermoses.

"What's all this?" He watched the now steady stream of townspeople assembling in the town square. "Is there a concert tonight that we don't know about?"

"In the dead of winter?" She seemed equally stumped by the growing crowd.

Residents continued to pour into the square, where they began setting up camp, facing the mailbox.

A feeling of dread washed over him. "You've got to be kidding me."

She shook her head, not understanding. "What?"

His gaze riveted to Joe and Mary, who had just entered the town square. "Joe," he called, marching over to them with Charley in tow.

"Oh, hey, Jack, Charley." Joe's pleasant smile faded when he saw Jack's scowl.

"What did you do?" he scolded.

Joe shrugged, brushing off Jack's annoyance. "Everybody is as curious as you are."

"But you can't invite an entire town to a stakeout!"

Joe appeared completely clueless. "Why not?"

"Because it defeats the whole purpose of one." He groaned, taking it down a few notches. "Whoever is collecting the mail is going to hightail it out of here as soon as he sees this huge crowd of people."

"Not so." Mary stepped in. "When the flag is raised, which it is, the mail's picked up without fail."

Jack was getting nowhere with his sweet but maddening B&B hosts. He had no choice but to address the group. He climbed up on a park bench for a better vantage point. "Can I have your attention, please?"

A few people stopped talking long enough to glance up at Jack, but ignored him and continued to get settled in for the show.

He shot a frustrated glance at Charley, then tried again. "Excuse me," he shouted. "If I could have everyone's attention, please." The crowd finally quieted down. "Thank you," he said on a sigh. "I'm Jack and I'm a detective from Denver."

"Hi, Jack from Denver," everyone said in unison, then laughed.

He looked at Charley. "Do they think I'm the emcee for their evening's entertainment?"

"Uh…yes." Her eyes danced at that thought.

"Great." He rubbed his face and put his focus back on the townspeople. "Hi. Look, I know some of you have already met Charley—"

"Hi, Charley!" shouted a group of five in front.

"We really appreciate your support," he said. "It's great that you all want to be here, but I'm afraid I'm going to have to ask you to leave."

The crowd's reaction was an offended one—a cacophony of insulted groans and affronted tsk-tsks to which Jack immediately tried to amend.

"Wait! I'm sorry." He threw up his hands, hoping to fix the slight. "If you would quiet down, I can explain." He waited a few moments, and the crowd finally did as he requested. "Thank you," he said, speaking at a lower volume. "Look, I've done a lot of stakeouts, and I'm telling you from experience that the mail will not be collected if you're all here."

"Why not?" A young hipster with shaggy brown hair was bopping toward him. He cut through the crowd to reach the front in order to talk to Jack without having to yell. Setting down his chair and backpack, he said, "Why won't the mail be picked up if we're here?"

Isn't it obvious? The thought must have registered on Jack's face because he heard Charley break with a laugh. He had to remind himself that he was not in Denver anymore but in St. Nicholas, a clearly mystifying town.

He fixed his gaze back on the hipster. "Well," Jack clasped his hands together, "let's think about this for a moment. We all know that whoever collects the mail is doing it at night. Right?"

"Yeah, man, that's what I hear," the hipster replied, and a wave of mumbled agreements rose from the crowd.

"Why at night?" Jack asked. "Because he or she doesn't want to be seen. By anyone. If *you* were approaching the mailbox and saw a large crowd of potential eyewitnesses, would you continue to pick up the mail?"

The hipster thought about it. He was taking too long to answer, so Jack did it for him.

"No. You'd turn around and leave," he said to the young man before he addressed the whole crowd. "I guarantee that if everybody remains here, he won't pick up the mail and *none* of us will see him."

The hipster appeared to be mulling over Jack's explanation as a redheaded woman stepped forward. "Do you have any idea how many stakeouts have been carried out at this very mailbox?" she asked with a caustic bite, which seemed out of character with the other friendly people of St. Nicholas. She had the ear of the crowd, so Jack knew to tread lightly.

"No, ma'am."

"Over a thousand. And they all failed. Then you come along." The redheaded woman's irritation instantly turned to glee. "No one ever thought of using motion sensor floodlights before."

"It's true. They hadn't," someone in the back of the crowd called out.

"We have faith in you." The redheaded woman pumped her fists, cheering him on. "We think you're really going to see Santa's helper tonight, and we want to see him too!"

Several shouts of agreement wound up the crowd with excitement. Jack tried to get everyone to calm down, but he was drowned out by their chatter about how amazing it would be to finally see the mystery mail collector. He lowered his head in defeat.

Charley climbed up on the bench and stood next to him. "I got this." She faced the crowd and yelled, "You're all going to blow this!"

Silence sharply fell like an ax over the crowd, and Charley regretted chiming in.

"You must be the Scrooge," the redheaded woman scowled, pointing her finger at Charley. The woman then leveled her eyes on Jack. "I'd think a Scrooge and a good detective would *want* lots of witnesses."

The crowd agreed with shouts of support while Charley apologized to Jack.

"We're staying," the woman crowed triumphantly, riling up the crowd into a frenzy.

"All right, all right." Jack motioned for everyone to settle down. "You can stay on one condition."

Silence instantly fell over the crowd again. He finally had their undivided attention. He opened his mouth to speak but was cut off by the sound of bells jingling. Floodlights instantly snapped on behind him and Charley, lighting up the mailbox like a football stadium on game night. Within seconds a collective shocked gasp rippled through the air.

Charley and Jack whipped around just as the cookie container fell to the ground—empty.

"No." Jack catapulted off the bench and flew over to the mailbox, but he was too late. "Oh, come on!" He fisted his hands in the air, certain someone above was finding great joy in messing with him.

Charley stared with jaw-dropping disbelief.

Joe laughed, then shoved a handful of caramel corn in his mouth before he passed the bag to Mary.

Charley futilely searched the area with Jack. "How could we have missed it again?"

Jack raced back to the bench and leaped on top of it to inspect the crowd, certain he could still catch the collector. He scanned the townspeople, scrutinizing every one of them like a secret service agent. He was determined to find the culprit attempting to escape without notice, but no one was moving—except for the hipster.

He picked up his chair and threw a last look to Jack.

"We told you it was one of Santa's helpers," the hipster said. "Mystery solved." He threw his backpack over his shoulder and started to leave.

Jack scrambled off the bench. "What do you mean mystery solved?" he asked, frustration coloring his words.

"The elf." He swept his hand toward the mailbox. "Plain as day."

"Elf?" Jack could not believe what he was hearing. "There was no elf!" He raised his voice more than he'd intended.

"Yeah, man, whatever. Suit yourself." The hipster motioned to his friends to pack up, and then the four of them left together.

Jack threw his hands on his hips and faced Charley. "Are we the only sane people here?"

"Excuse me, Detective Jack?" a soft, frail voice called. He turned to see a tiny elderly woman come forward. "The young man was right. It was an elf."

Jack could feel the heat of anger building inside him. He couldn't exactly dismiss a sweet old woman—not without looking more like a Scrooge than Charley.

He set his mouth with a compulsory smile. "Thank you for your statement," Jack politely whispered to her before he sought out Mary for a sensible answer. "Mary?" His eyes pleaded with her. He wanted a simple, logical, reasonable explanation. That's all he was asking for.

"You did have your back to the elf," she said, as if that had been his fault.

"That's right," the redheaded woman spat. "You were too busy chastising all of us."

Jack wanted it to stop. He wanted to make this headache go away. He glanced at Charley. She had attempted to rescue him before, but this time she shook her head and shrugged in a helpless gesture. He was on his own.

"Okay." He regrouped. This was no different than speaking to a bunch of eyewitnesses after a robbery. "Mary, what exactly did you see?" he asked, feeling confident that he was back in control.

"I saw an elf hat sticking up from behind the mailbox, and then I noticed a skinny little arm covered with a red-and-green-striped shirt and a tiny gloved hand reaching up for the cookies."

Bad idea. "Joe?"

"Same."

Keep it together. Jack wearily eyed the redheaded woman. "Is that an accurate description of what you saw?"

"No. The lights were too bright, so I lowered my gaze. That's when I saw elf shoes under the mailbox."

Poker face, Jack. Stay professional. "And…uh…what exactly do elf shoes look like?"

"They were green and were turned up, with a bell attached to each tip."

Charley laughed and he threw her an icy glare. "You can't argue with that, Jack."

"Anyone else see anything different? Anything logical?" he called out.

The elderly woman huffed. "Seems to me you're the Scrooge." She pursed her lips with a grimace and tottered off.

"Anyone else?" He searched the group of people near him. "Did anyone see his face?"

Jack heard mumbling from the crowd, but he couldn't make out what they were saying, so he began weaving his way through the crowd with Charley. "What about you, sir?" Jack asked a man in his thirties collecting his things. "Did you see his face?"

"No, sorry."

Jack eyed the older man standing next to him. "And you, sir?"

"Nope."

Jack moved farther into the crowd and observed a young woman corralling kids. "Did you see his face, ma'am?"

"He was mostly hidden behind the mailbox," she said, "but I did see him in profile for a split second."

"That's great!" Jack erupted with excitement. "Can you give me a description? Did he have a beard or a big nose?"

"He had very big elf ears."

"Elf ears?" Jack faintly echoed. "Any other distinguishing features that you can remember?"

"Other than his pointy ears? No. Like I said, I only saw him for a split second."

"Well, that's it." Jack brushed off his hands, knowing when to give up.

As the residents packed up and left, they talked excitedly about the elf, leaving Jack with even more unanswered questions.

He wanted to get angry, but why? There was no sense in crying over spilled milk. "The milk!" He ran over to the mailbox. "Where did it go?"

Charley helped him search the ground. "It was just here."

Jack tossed his head back with a frustrated groan. "He hadn't left. He was here the whole time."

She stiffened and lowered her voice. "Maybe he's still here."

"No chance." His laugh was almost a cry. "I heard bells jingle as the crowd was leaving, but I thought it was a kid."

Charley's eyes widened with that revelation. "He left with the crowd?"

"Wouldn't you?"

"Clever. He's very clever." She collapsed on the nearest bench and he joined her. "Here's a fun fact: over fifty percent of the Icelandic population believe in the existence of elves."

"Well, here's a cold hard fact. We're not in Iceland."

Her mouth twitched with amusement as she turned her coat collar up around her ears. "Are you sure about that?"

"I'm not sure about anything anymore. Cases take twists and turns, but this is ridiculous. Three stakeouts, and I've got nothing."

"What about the cookie container?" She pointed to the box lying on the ground.

He went over to the container, pulled out a plastic bag from his jacket and picked it up. He was hoping for a half-eaten cookie to collect DNA. "Barely a crumb left." He wrapped the plastic bag around the container and closed it. "I don't expect the lab will find much."

"What about fingerprints?" she asked, joining him.

"Ours are on the container, and so are Angel's. Mary said she saw a gloved hand reach for the cookies, so I doubt forensics will find any prints at all from our mystery mail collector. But that was a good idea, Detective Dawson."

"I learn from the best," she said as he inspected the snow. "Any elf footprints?"

He frowned. "Not a one."

They finally gave up and meandered along the path

around the town square, shaking off the frustration from the stakeout fiasco. He was enjoying Charley's company, and he hoped she was serious about spending Christmas with him. But what would happen after the holidays? He didn't want their relationship to end. He didn't want his existence to be just about work. He wanted to experience life again, and he wanted it to be with her.

"Jack!"

He turned to see Mary and Joe approaching. "I thought you should know that if you're thinking about doing another stakeout, you might want to hold off. Our annual Christmas festival starts tomorrow."

"Angel was telling us a little bit about it," Charley said.

"You're going to love it." Mary's eyes lit with anticipation. "All the stores and restaurants stay open late for Christmas shoppers. Smaller vendors set up here in the town square. We have ice sculptors and carolers and a lot of great Christmas games, like the Christmas stocking races and pin the tail on the reindeer."

"If you're like me, Jack, I'm sure you don't mind skipping the shopping," Joe said, "but you're definitely going to want to take advantage of all the Christmas-themed treats." He patted his belly. "Tomorrow is eggnog, which is one of Mary's favorites. But Sunday is English toffee, which is mine."

Jack was instantly propelled back to the first Christmas when Santa left him a small box of handmade English toffee in his stocking. He and his dad loved that toffee. They'd eat the nuts and chocolate first, by scraping it off with their teeth, and then they'd save the toffee for last. It had become a tradition. What had also become a tradition was for Uncle Bill to slip Jack his own tiny box of toffee when his mom wasn't looking. Jack would hold onto it until New Year's Day, so he could start off the year by having the sweet treat.

"…and every food establishment has at least one item on the menu that features the Christmas-themed treat," Mary explained. "The foodies go crazy this time of year."

"We can't miss out on that, can we, Jack?" Charley nudged him with her elbow.

"Definitely not," he agreed, clicking back into the conversation.

"You weren't planning on doing another stakeout, were you?" Joe asked.

"Not with the festival."

"Not ever," Mary said. "It's a big waste of time, Jack. You'll never catch an elf."

"Right you are. No more stakeouts." He wasn't going to allow a so-called elf to get the best of him. He was, however, going to take a break from it. "We heard your town has a house decoration contest. Maybe Charley and I can help you with that."

"That would be wonderful!" She clapped her hands. "We've never won. Joe keeps adding Christmas decorations to the front yard, but it never puts us over the finish line."

"Have you ever thought about a model train display?" Charley took the words right out of his mouth.

"That's a fantastic idea," Joe said, "though it might be too late to put one together for this year."

"Not if you have a few extra hands. We can help you all day tomorrow." He glanced at Charley since he'd just volunteered her time without asking.

"You've done so much for us, Mary. It would be our pleasure," Charley said. "Maybe Mike could advise us on how to set it up."

With that one gesture of support, Jack could see how much he needed her in his life. They were completely on the same page. She realized how important it was for him to know whether or not Mike was his uncle. Not only was she supporting him in his effort to discover the truth, but she also wanted to be involved in it, and that touched him beyond words.

"Great idea, Charley. I'll give him a call right now." Joe walked away, pulling out his cell.

"Guess I better get back to it." Mary shoved her hands in her pockets. "Thanks for the enjoyable entertainment tonight. You two should think about moving here. St. Nicholas could really use you."

Move here? If he and Charley wanted their relationship to continue past Christmas, one of them would have to move. He'd never thought about *both* of them moving…

"Oh, uh…" Charley seemed taken off guard, struggling to answer Mary, and he didn't know how to read it.

"It's definitely beautiful here," Jack said. "Though I'm not sure if your town would be able to use a guy like me. There doesn't appear to be enough crime to keep me busy."

"Work isn't the only thing that keeps people busy." Mary raised a brow to him before walking away.

Charley tucked her chin and stared at the ground, holding back a smile.

"Boy, the locals know how to speak their minds." He rocked on his heels.

"Yes, they do."

"They also know how to tell a tall tale," he added, trying to change the channel that was privately playing in his own head. "An elf picking up the mail?"

"Several eyewitnesses claim the same thing, Detective. Who's to say it wasn't an elf?" A challenging smile played on her lips.

"Listen to Miss Scrooge now," he said, teasing her, and she finally laughed.

"I have to admit, I'm even surprising myself." She moved closer as they walked along the path toward Main Street. "Here's something more shocking. I'm craving an old-fashioned, decadent cup of hot cocoa."

"I believe we're in the right town for that. But where to go..."

"Anywhere warm has my vote."

Would she ever like cold weather as much as he did? He didn't want to move back to Los Angeles. It was so crowded and expensive. He would, of course, if that was what Charley wanted, but maybe he could convince her to give Colorado a chance. "Close your eyes."

"What?" She laughed. "Why?"

He waggled his brows. "I'm going to spin you."

"To choose a restaurant?"

"Do I need to get a blindfold?"

"Okay, okay." She closed her eyes.

For a moment, Jack saw her as the sixteen-year-old he'd spun around on her birthday. When she opened her eyes that night, a bunch of her friends were standing in front of her, ready to take her to a concert.

"Do you remember doing this before?" He studied the beautiful woman that Charley had become—the way her delicate nose turned up, the way her lips curved into such a gorgeous smile.

"Yes. Did you fly in my high school friends?"

"I thought it should just be you and me tonight." He slowly turned her, watching her stiffen with anticipation, and then he stopped her facing the restaurants and stores across the street. “Now point.” She did, and he chuckled. “Your hot cocoa is going to be decadent all right. Take a look at what you picked.”

She opened her eyes and saw the Candy Cane Sweet Shoppe before her. “No way.”

“You chose well.”

Charley fixed her gaze on him and held it. “Yes, I did.”

Chapter Twenty-Three

Charley loved the look of the Candy Cane Sweet Shoppe. The walls were painted with tiny red-and-white-striped candy canes, and the tables were in the shape of candied hearts. Sweet treats and baked goods were displayed under laser-focused lights on glistening glass shelves. The store not only offered all the traditional Christmastime favorites from old-fashioned peppermint-flavored ribbon candy to maple walnut fudge, but it also sold other goodies like Australian Christmas Fairy Bread, German Christmas Pudding, and Irish Christmas Cake.

"I thought English toffee was extravagant," Jack said, equally wide-eyed with wonder.

"What a beautiful yule log cake." She admired the lifelike pine-tree needles made from green frosting. "Perhaps you'd care for some miniature snowflake fritters dusted with powdered sugar." She ran her hand along the display shelf, as if she were a model on a TV game show.

Jack laughed. "Check these out. Christmas fortune cookies dipped in chocolate with candied sprinkles." He held one up by the corner of its plastic wrapping.

In an instant, her mind whirled back to the night she wished for her soulmate, the night she received two fortunes telling her that she'd reunite with Jack.

"What's going on in that head of yours, Ms. Dawson?"

She snapped her attention back to Jack. "It's all connected somehow."

He eyed her with a surprised look on his face. "What did you just say?"

"It's all connected, though I'm not sure how, exactly. I had Chinese food the other night, and both fortunes in my cookies said I would reunite with the one that got away."

His mouth curved into a lopsided grin. "Am I the one that got away?"

She rolled her eyes at him. "Obviously."

"I like that," he said, standing taller. "But, yeah, unless Reality Check, or Santa, or one of Santa's helpers was communicating with you through cookies, I'd chalk that one up to coincidence."

"I suppose so." She sighed, not entirely convinced.

"Do you want to get that hot chocolate, or do you have an eye on something sweeter?"

"That's a loaded question."

"It was intended."

She laughed, grabbed his hand, and got in line. They gawked at the beverage board with their mouths hanging open like identical twins. There were over twenty hot chocolate choices.

"Maybe I'll just get coffee," he said, which made her laugh.

"Evening, folks," a young freckle-faced employee spoke up. "Can I help you?"

"I'll have your salted caramel hot chocolate," Charley replied, then looked to Jack.

"And I'll take your s'mores hot chocolate."

"Would you like the elf size, snowman size, or super Santa size?" the employee asked.

They shared a smile, then at the same time, said, "Elf size."

While Jack got their drinks, she found them a small table tucked in the corner by the store's Christmas tree.

"Here you go." He handed over her drink as he sat down.

She took a sip and hummed with pleasure. "This is crazy good."

"So is mine." He smacked his lips. "It actually tastes like a s'more." He passed it to her to try.

"Wow, it does. This reminds me of those weekends on the beach—swimming and playing volleyball with our friends, and then roasting marshmallows as the sun went down."

"Those were good times."

The tiny smile on his lips seemed bittersweet. Was he thinking about the end of their high school days, or was it about their present situation? Her departure date was looming near. One of them would need to move or else they'd be forced to carry on a long-distance relationship, and she already knew how well it turned out last time.

"Do you miss living in California?" she asked, wondering if he'd ever move back.

"Sometimes. I miss the ocean, the great places to eat, the incredible weather." He set his eyes on her, then lingered, searching her face. "And for a very long time, I've missed you."

Charley's breath hitched in her throat, and she swayed from the lightheadedness that followed. It was something she had wondered for years—had he ever truly missed her after he moved away?

They had talked about their breakup the night before, but she was the one who had done most of the talking.

Jack had blamed it on his family's move, and though he'd said some nice things to her, he hadn't really bared his soul—not the way she had. Now he was volunteering information. He had missed her for *a very long time.* Did that mean he'd suffered the kind of deep pain she had from their breakup as well?

"I've missed you, too, Jack. Very much."

He took her hand in his. "I should have had more faith in us."

"Thank you for saying that." She caressed his hand. "But as you said, we were kids."

"Maybe now we can continue this new chapter we've started as adults."

"I'd like that." She scooted her chair closer to him, and he put his arm around her while they enjoyed their hot cocoa. *A new chapter. Will it be a short one or one that goes on forever?*

"What about you?" His voice was smooth and gentle. "Would you ever leave LA?"

It appeared Jack had been pondering the two-state dilemma as well, but who would be the one to compromise? He could be a detective in LA, though the crime rate was higher, and she supposed it would depend on if he could get transferred. She liked working at the magazine, though much of her job was done from a computer, so she might be able to work from anywhere. She loved the weather and the beach and had great friends. She had a decent one-bedroom apartment, but her rent had gone up again. When she thought about it, she was starting to grow weary of the daily grind. She was getting tired of the constant traffic. It took forever to get anywhere in LA, and the cost of living was almost as bad as New York. Maybe she *should* think about moving.

"Yes," she finally said. "If the reason was important to me, I would."

He tilted his head so he could look directly into her eyes. "My California girl would move?"

She loved her new nickname. "To Antarctica, no, but for new adventures I'd consider it."

He held her tighter and gave her a tiny kiss on her cheek. "What do you think of Colorado?"

"I've only been here for a few days, but I like it so far."

"Not too much snow for the beach enthusiast in you?"

"I guess I'd have to see." She shrugged. "It's definitely not beach weather, but it's much warmer than Antarctica."

He laughed and pulled her closer.

Wrapped in the comfort of his arms, it was warmer than any Southern California day.

After the Sweet Shoppe, they headed back to the B&B and slowly ambled to their rooms.

"I had a great time tonight," she said.

"Even with my total failure on capturing you know who?"

"You mean the elf?"

"The mail collector yet to be identified."

"I'll never forget the look on your face," she teased.

"Yeah, well, I'll be getting the last laugh when I finally catch the guy."

He stopped at her door and reached for her hand. She met his gaze and she found herself getting lost in the deep pools of his blue-gray eyes. They were beckoning her, mesmerizing her. She drank in the perfect shape of his mouth, the soft look of his lips. She so desperately wanted him to kiss her, and he must have wanted the same because he slowly leaned into her, asking her for permission. She leaned into him, saying yes, and without hesitation, he gently kissed her. The sensation was warm, sensuous, and electrifying.

He finally pulled away, and in a sexy, low voice, he said, "Until tomorrow?"

She nodded, lightly biting her lower lip, as he slowly let go of her hand. Tomorrow couldn't come fast enough.

Jack tossed his key on the table, then went into the bathroom to splash cold water on his face. That one short satisfying kiss had practically rendered him useless. Talk about a spark.

He shook his thoughts of Charley from his head as he sat in front of his computer. He checked her blog and thankfully found that Reality Check hadn't posted any additional comments. He then spent the next hour trying to find anything he could on the trucker. He looked over several trucker blogs and discovered that the guy had been traveling all across the country for years. Every mention of him was positive.

"You're a regular Boy Scout," he said under his breath as he continued to read all the glowing comments about R.C. The man mostly gave great advice, but once in a while, he brought someone an inexpensive present that had priceless sentimental value to that person.

Jack sat back, trying to figure out how R.C. fit into the Scrooge Legend. Like everything else he had experienced in St. Nicholas, Reality Check was also an enigma. He went back to Charley's blog and began reading comments from people who had actually been to St. Nicholas. There were Scrooge accounts that seemed in line with the interviews she had collected. So many of them talked about how they found love or a purpose in life, or both. No one had a negative thing to say about the town, and if Jack was being honest with himself, he didn't have a negative thing to say, either. Sure, he got frustrated with his failed stakeouts, but no more than some of his previous cases in Denver. The rest of the time had been bliss. That's what Charley created—bliss. And he didn't want it to end.

Charley woke to her cell ringing. She rolled over, noticed Liv was on FaceTime, and took the call. "What's wrong?" She rubbed her eyes, trying to focus. "Did something happen to Clarence?"

"He's fine," Liv assured her. "I was worried about you. Is everything okay?"

"Yes," she said groggily. "Why wouldn't it be?"

"You were supposed to call me back yesterday," Liv said, a little miffed, as the camera on FaceTime jerked around.

"Oh, right." She winced. "I'm so sorry. Jack and I ran out the door to—"

"That's why I'm calling. Why haven't you told me about Jack? That Reality Check person mentioned him on your blog. Is Jack, *the* Jack Brody?"

"Uh-huh." She smiled and stretched. "And he's staying at the same B&B as I am."

"Get. Out." Liv's eyes bulged wide with shock. "Is Jack the one who sent you the invitation?"

Charley sat straight up. "I never thought of that. He showed up right after I suggested him as a Scrooge, so I assumed it was because of my suggestion, which sounds crazy, I know."

"I wouldn't have understood any of that if I didn't already know about the legend and the Scrooge suggestions," Liv said, her phone jostling around again. Her hand went in front of the camera for a second, but when she removed it, Charley could see Liv sitting on the end of her bed, zipping up her boots with Clarence and Liv's dog, Murphy, lounging on the bed behind her.

"How do you know about the Scrooge suggestions?" Charley finger combed her hair.

"Hello? Your blog?" She smirked into the camera. "You really must start paying attention to it again. There are some wild stories from people who commented on your post." Liv's face filled the screen, appearing to be on the move.

"Thanks for the reminder. I promise to do that."

"Sooo." Liv drew out the words, applying her lipstick. "Give me the highlights."

"Jack was the one that got away, and now we've reconnected," Charley said, still surprised that it actually happened.

Liv stared at her. "Is it serious?"

"It might be, which scares me. It took me years to cut off my feelings for him."

"That never works," Liv grumbled.

"I know that now. It made me miserable." She got out of bed, walked over to the window and opened the curtains, instantly bathing her room in the morning sun.

"Then take a chance. Love is one thing that's worth it."

"You're right. You always are."

"Not always." Liv made a kissy face to something off camera, and Charley could only assume she was feeding her fish. "I said yes to a date last night that was the worst ever."

"Uh-oh. What happened?"

"Everything. I won't bore you with the details, but

you'd think out of the thousands of single men in LA, I'd at least be able to find one decent guy."

"I'm sorry, Liv. Maybe it's time for a break. I can totally recommend St. Nicholas. There's more positive energy in this one small town than there is in all of Los Angeles."

"That's shocking to hear, coming from The Cold Hard Facts Queen."

"Tell me about it. I'm thinking of changing my blog to *The Warm, Heartfelt Facts*."

"And readers will demand to know what happened to you," Liv said, on the move again. "But you sound happy."

"I am."

"I'm glad to finally hear it." Liv picked up her keys. "Keep me posted on Mr. Jack."

"I will." Charley blew her a kiss, then hung up before discovering that Arthur was sitting on the table. "Morning, Arthur. I see you've been getting your exercise around my room." She straightened out his jacket. "Is that because you've been waiting for an update?" She picked him up. "Well, you'll be happy to know that things are going really well with Jack." She set him back on the mantel and patted him on the head. "Thanks for not giving up on me."

Chapter Twenty-Four

Jack slept only a few hours. Thinking about Charley and wondering how he could get Mike to open up to him occupied his thoughts until three in the morning. After he had breakfast with two of the inn's guests, Tom and Matt, the guys went outside and listened to Mike's instructions on how to build the model train display. Jack kept getting flashbacks of his uncle's incredible display in Chicago and knew Mike *had* to be him.

As they began erecting a circular raised platform in front of a decorated pine tree, Charley came down the porch steps toward him.

"Morning," she said. "Looks like I'm late."

"Not at all. Let me introduce you to Mike." He reached for her hand, and they walked over to where Mike was attaching three-foot legs to the platform. "Mike, I want you to meet Charley."

Standing up, Mike took off his glove to shake her hand, and Jack immediately noticed a faded one-inch scar between his index finger and thumb. His body went numb. *It's him.*

"Hi, Charley. Are you up for some decorating?" Mike asked.

"Anything you need."

"Great. Jack, you want to give her the rundown while I finish getting the foundation together?"

"Uh…sure, no problem." Jack inhaled sharply, trying process the fact that he had finally found his uncle.

Mike went back to work while Charley walked with Jack toward Mike's truck in the driveway.

Charley eyed him. "Are you okay?"

"Yeah." He wiped his watery eyes. "I think I just—"

"Morning," Rebecca said as she and Kim approached. "Mike said to come see you."

"Uh… Yes." He cleared his throat, pushing aside his emotions. "Mike's brought literally a truckload of miniature pieces for the town that will be positioned around the train tracks. We're unloading the boxes and sorting the pieces over there." He pointed to a couple of long worktables that had been set up to make the assembly process move faster. "Can you take these last two boxes over to the staging area and get started on them?"

"Sure thing," Kim said as she and Rebecca grabbed the boxes, leaving him with Charley to finish their conversation.

Charley leaned against the truck, staring at him with concern. "What's going on?"

Jack glanced at Mike, making sure he was still out of earshot. "My uncle had a long scar on the back of his right hand. I just saw an identical scar on Mike's right hand when he took off his glove."

"Oh, Jack." Charley covered her mouth, stunned. "You found him?"

He cast an eye on Mike. "I think I did."

"I'm so happy for you," she said, hugging him. "How are you going to tell him?"

He leaned against Mike's truck. "I was trying to figure

that out last night. It's been twenty years. I don't know how fragile his memories are. Does he recall bits and pieces, or nothing at all?"

"I can't imagine going through something like that." She shook her head. "What if you stay close to him all day and feel it out?"

"That's what I was thinking. If he works with me and feels comfortable around me, then I can try to weave some memories into the conversation."

"That seems like a good way to go."

"Hey, Jack," Mike called. "Can you help me a minute?"

"On my way." He took a nervous breath.

"Good luck."

He squeezed her hand, then hurried over to Mike.

The guys had been at it for over two hours. Tom and Matt finished tacking down the fake snow on the wooden platform while Mike and Jack screwed in the last of the tracks.

Jack moved on to setting up the miniature pieces for Mike's approval. He kept the conversation strictly about the train display, but the nerves in his stomach were starting to be too much for him. "Do you want the bridge in the center or on the side?"

Mike stood to get an overhead view of the layout. "Let's put it on the right side, like it's situated here in town."

"You got it." Jack placed the bridge on the right side. "This is really starting to look like St. Nicholas."

"That's the plan." Mike connected the caboose to the rest of the train. "I have Charley working on a miniature Santa's mailbox."

"You couldn't have chosen a better person for the job." He situated three pine trees next to the bridge. "You have a pretty extensive collection here."

"Yeah." Mike adjusted one of the pieces not yet glued down. "I've only been at it for ten years. Imagine if I had started earlier."

He didn't have to imagine. He'd seen his uncle's equally impressive collection when he was a kid. "Have you always been interested in miniature train displays?"

"Don't know." Mike rummaged around in one of his boxes and pulled out a couple of crossing signals. "But it kind of looks that way."

Jack chuckled. "The uncle I mentioned to you, Uncle Bill, he gave me a train set one year for Christmas and helped me set it up." He watched Mike for any recollection, but couldn't detect any.

"So you're not a novice, either?"

"No, I am. I was seven at the time, so my uncle did all the work."

Mike laughed. "Where are you from, Jack?"

"I live in Denver." He placed a miniature clock tower where he believed it should be. "I'm a police detective in the city."

"Is that right?" Mike set his eyes on him. "Do you work on a lot of homicides?"

"I saw a few when I was a police officer, but now I mostly deal with financial crimes—fraud, embezzlement." He took a deep breath. "Sometimes my cases involve missing persons."

Mike stilled for a moment, then stared at the miniature truck he held in his hands. "Missing persons?"

"Yeah." Jack stood, turning toward him. "I have a lot

of databases at my fingertips. We're able to connect the dots much faster these days than say…twenty years ago."

Mike looked off in the distance before he hesitantly glanced at Jack. "How much success do you have?"

"Depends on each case, but I've reunited half a dozen families over the years. There's nothing more gratifying about my job than that."

Mike moved closer, lowering his voice. "Did Joe tell you about my situation?"

"He did, and I can help." *Please, let me help.*

"Oh, boy." Mike blew out a breath. "I don't know." He ran a hand over his mouth. "No memories have resurfaced for me in quite a while."

Jack suddenly heard Charley laugh. He looked over to see she was heading in his direction with Rebecca and Kim.

"Okay, Mike. I think we got it," Rebecca said, carrying over a box of selected miniature pieces. "These might work for the town."

Mike appeared a little shaky, but he recovered quickly. "Those are great," he said, looking them over. "Jack and I haven't started on the town square, so feel free to place and glue wherever you see fit."

Charley caught Jack's eye, wondering how it was going.

He nodded. "Mike and I are going to take a short break, if that's all right with you."

"Sure thing," Charley said. "We've got it covered."

He and Mike strode over to the front porch where Mary had set up a small table with hot coffee and sugar cookies.

Jack poured coffee for the two of them while he dove back into their conversation. "I know you said your memories haven't surfaced for a while." He handed him a cup. "Sometimes it takes a song or a location, a photo or a voice to trigger someone's recall."

"I've tried remembering for twenty years," Mike said on a sigh before taking a sip of his coffee. "No one came for me in the hospital. Maybe I don't have a family."

It was painful for Jack to imagine lying in a hospital, feeling totally and completely alone. He blinked away the moisture beginning to flood his vision. "I think you do have a family, Mike. Maybe they didn't know where to look, and you didn't know where to find them. Please, let me help."

Mike got a little teary-eyed and cleared his throat. "What if you find them and I still don't remember them? That'd be horrible for everyone."

"As someone who's dealt with missing persons, I can tell you that knowing and working with whatever the current situation may be is far better than never knowing what happened at all."

Mike crossed his arms and stared off into the woods with a troubled look on his face.

Jack leaned against the railing. "We had a teen go missing a few years back who was connected to one of my cases. When we finally found her eighteen months later, she had changed dramatically because she'd been forced to let go of her old life. When she returned to her real family, it was tough at first—on her and on everyone she knew. But their love and support got her through it. Her family helped her to find the way back."

"That's a great story, but it's a big leap for someone like me who's been missing for twenty years."

"It's also been twenty years for your family," he reminded Mike. "They're still wondering where you are."

"You mean, if I actually have a family."

"You do. I'm sure you do." Jack desperately wanted to tell him, but not in the middle of building the model train display. Jack handed him his card. "Here's my cell. Let's set up a time when we can talk about this further."

Mike took the card and looked at it. "Brody." He tapped the card on the rim of his coffee cup. "I think I used to know someone named Brody. Do you—"

"Who wants some white chocolate gingerbread croissants?" Mary walked out with a basket of pastries. "Mike, Jack, would you care for one?"

"Why, thank you, Mary." Mike reached in and snagged one for himself.

"Jack, how about you?" She held out the basket.

"Much appreciated," he said, taking one, even though food was the last thing on his mind.

Mary descended the steps and took the pastries around to the other guests.

"I'd like to talk about this more," Mike finally said. "Maybe in a couple of days?"

"Anytime, day or night." Jack was relieved that Mike might soon know the truth.

Mike bit into the croissant and smiled. "That woman knows how to bake," he barely managed to say with his mouth full.

"She sure does," he replied, tasting one for himself as Charley came over.

"How's it going?" Charley split her gaze between him and Mike.

"It's always better with Mary's baked goods," Mike said. "I think I might need another one." He set out to find Mary's goodie basket.

"Don't leave me in suspense." She turned toward Jack. "What happened?"

"Mike knows I'm aware of his memory loss."

"That's good," Charley said. "Did you tell him what you suspect?"

"I was leading up to it, but I didn't get that far. I told him I wanted to help him."

"What did he say?"

"He was hesitant." Jack took a long breath. "After twenty years, it's a lot to take in. He finally agreed to talk with me about it later, and I hope he doesn't change his mind. He's worried he won't remember, and that he'll hurt his family more because of it."

Charley bit her lip as the crease between her brows deepened. "What if he met your parents?"

"It would help, but I don't know if they could handle it."

"*You* are," she said, "and if they could help jog his memory, I'd think they'd want to at least try."

Charley was right. If Mike was going to remember, he needed to see his brother again and at Christmas—their favorite time of year.

Mary returned with her goodies. "Charley, would you care for a white chocolate gingerbread croissant?"

"I'd love one." Charley picked one out of the basket and took a bite. "Mmm."

Jack retrieved his phone from his back pocket. "Mary, do you have another room available, or are you completely booked up?"

"I'm always booked solid this time of year, but it just so happens that I received a cancellation for tomorrow night not ten minutes ago."

"Isn't that fortunate?" Charley looked at Jack.

"How long was the reservation for?" he asked.

"One week."

Hope shot through him. "Can you hold the room for me for an hour? I want to see if I can get my parents up here."

"Yes, of course, dear. Take your time."

"Thank you." Jack strode away, his heart racing. His parents had been so hopeful when he'd become a detective. They'd assumed he'd be able to find his uncle quickly, but that hadn't been the case. Now Jack would be putting them through a lot, and what if his uncle couldn't remember his own brother?

Jack took a deep breath and dialed his parents' number. There was only one way to find out.

Chapter Twenty-Five

A little after four in the afternoon, Jack and Charley trudged into the bed-and-breakfast.

"I can't believe we built an entire model train display in one day," Jack said, physically exhausted.

"I can't either," she replied as they slowly climbed the stairs. "Mary told me the contest judges will be making their rounds tomorrow night. Hopefully, Mike's creation will give them the edge they need to win."

"How can it not? We built a miniature St. Nicholas."

"It really looks amazing. I took a ton of pictures, and I bet they go viral when I post them," she said. "When are your parents coming?"

"Tomorrow morning sometime."

"Good. I'm looking forward to seeing them again." She pulled out her room key. "Hey, do you have a mouse in your room that keeps moving?"

He gawked at her. "A mouse?"

"Not a real one. You know, one of Mary's Christmas decorations. Come take a look." Charley unlocked the door, and he followed her inside where she pointed out a tiny stuffed mouse sitting on the mantel. "He just showed up."

"You mean he walked into your room and made himself at home?"

"Ha-ha." She set down her things. "Though, come to think of it, Mary said she didn't bring him in here, so anything's possible."

"Another St. Nicholas oddity." He stood by the fireplace and examined it more closely. "He's cute, as far as decorations go."

"I named him Arthur."

"He looks like an Arthur." Jack noticed a light scent of gardenias as Charley stood next to him. He hadn't recalled smelling her perfume earlier that day. Maybe it was because they'd been outside. He was very aware of it now, and there was something stirring about it. He stared at her and the thought of the kiss they shared the night before pushed to the forefront of his mind.

Charley, however, still had her attention on the mouse. "What decorations do you have in your room?"

"Reindeer," he said. "All nine of them."

"Aren't you lucky?" She met his gaze.

Standing so close to her, face-to-face, brought back memories of dancing with her at prom. How they slowly swayed to the music, how she put her head on his shoulder, how he kissed her that night after the dance, how he couldn't think of anything else but her.

He stepped away from the fireplace, pretending he was comparing mantel sizes when, in reality, he was taking a step back from Charley in order to think clearer. "It's the same size. The reindeer are tiny and don't take up too much room."

"Can you name all nine?"

"Of course, I can," he said before he realized Charley would want him to prove it. She crossed her arms, waiting. "Uh...let's see." He scratched the back of his head. "There's Rudolph."

"Such a tough one to remember. Looks like I should have bet you serious money."

"Give me a minute." He started singing, badly out of tune, the beginning of "Rudolph the Red-Nosed Reindeer" while counting on his fingers. "There's Dasher and Dancer and Prancer, and Vixen. Uh... Comet and...and blah-blah and Donner? And...uh... Blitzen!" He held up his hands with eight counted off.

Charley held back a laugh. "There's a reindeer named blah-blah?"

"No, hold on." He began humming the tune to himself but got stuck in the same place.

She ever so softly said, "Cupid. How could you forget Cupid?"

Jack stared into her intoxicating eyes. "No idea." They moved closer to one another in such synchronicity that he didn't know who moved first. But now they were inches apart. He could hear her breath quicken, as did his. He could feel the intensity building between them, charging the air. His gaze fell on her sensuous, parted lips and he ached to kiss them. He set his hand on the mantel to steady himself and must have touched Arthur because one of the tiny bells on his vest jingled, instantly ruining the moment.

Startled, they broke apart, catching their breath.

Jack glared at Arthur. "Is it me, or is that mouse staring at us?"

"He's staring," Charley said beyond question. "His eyes are like the eyes on the Mona Lisa. They'll follow you around the room."

Jack jerked to the right of the mouse and then the left. "You're right. His eyes move with me. That's just—"

"Normal for this town," she finished for him. "He's actually a good listener, which is why I think he's gotten protective of me."

Jack heaved a dramatic sigh. "First, I had to get permission from your dad to date you, and now a stuffed mouse?"

She laughed, and Jack realized how much he loved the sound. She had a sweet, melodious laugh that made her light up from within. And her exuberance was infectious, for it made him want to make her laugh every hour of every day. "Arthur, do you mind if I take Charley to the town's Christmas festival?"

They looked at Arthur as if waiting for his approval.

"I think Arthur would love it," she said, speaking for him. "That way he can watch Christmas movies while I'm gone."

"Good plan." He ambled toward the door. "I'll swing by in an hour?"

"Works for me."

He hesitated, marched right back to her, and took her in his arms. He felt a rush of heat between them as she stared at him with beckoning eyes. He slowly lowered his mouth on to hers and gave her a long, passionate kiss. To have her in his arms after so many years apart was euphoric. Her body melted into his, and it took all of his willpower to at last break away.

"See you soon." He moved toward the door, then withdrew from her room, leaving her utterly speechless.

Smiling to himself, Jack rambled down the hallway, pleased he had as much of a dizzying effect on her as she had on him. *This is going to be a great night.* They'd enjoy the festival together, and then later they'd sit down and figure out their long-distance issue. Now that he'd finally found her, he wasn't going to let her go.

As he reached his room, his cell rang, and he saw that it was his boss. "Hey, Cap."

"How's it going out there?"

"Not as expected," he said. The understatement of the year. "No cult, no timeshare, no Ponzi scheme. No one taking advantage of anyone. I'm finding just the opposite. This town is filled with decent people who look out for one another."

"That's it?" Captain Wollin sounded clearly surprised.

"The town has a huge affinity for everything Christmas, but other than that, nothing nefarious."

The captain blew out a disappointed breath. "Did you at least find out who's sending the invitations?"

Yes, apparently Old Saint Nick is on the case and one of his little elves delivers Scrooge suggestions to him every night. "I haven't met the sender personally, but I'm in the process of tracking him down. However, I can confirm that I haven't come across anyone who's been hurt emotionally, physically, or financially by these letters. Only positive experiences to report at this time, although I'd like to stay a few more days to make sure I've covered every angle."

"You're trying to tell me that Braca and my brother were turned into good people by a town that celebrates Christmas twenty-four-seven?"

"The Christmas spirit is hard to ignore, sir."

"Huh. I suppose so. Maybe I should send my mother-in-law up there."

Charley poked her head out of the bathroom to check the time on the alarm clock by the bed. Jack would be arriving any minute. She applied her lipstick before hunting for her cell, which she found lying on the mantel next to Arthur.

She smiled at the cute stuffed mouse. "Didn't I tell you he was amazing? He's charming, funny, adorable, handsome." She let her own words sink in. "He's pretty much everything I asked for. He has to be my soulmate, don't you think?"

She heard Jack's three light raps on the door, wiggled her brows at Arthur, then went over to let him in. When she opened the door, she gasped. Jack was standing there in a giant Christmas stocking. Her jaw dropped as her mind whirled back to what she had said to Arthur her second night in St. Nicholas. *If Santa wants me to stop being a Scrooge, he will need to put my soulmate in my stocking this year instead of a lump of coal!*

Jack chuckled. "You should see the look on your face." He stepped out of the stocking. "Charley Dawson is at a loss for words?"

Yes, she was. Santa handled deliveries exceedingly well.

"Mary asked me to take a bunch of these stockings to the festival." He held up a big bag, overflowing with them. "I guess they're for the Christmas stocking races in the snow."

"You make an adorable stocking stuffer," Charley said, at last finding her voice.

"There it is." He grinned. "I knew you'd have a clever remark."

"Hard not to when a grown man shows up at my door in a Christmas stocking."

He laughed. "Ready?"

"Just a sec."

While Jack waited in the hallway, she snatched her coat off the back of the chair, threw Arthur a quick kiss and whispered, “Good job.”

Chapter Twenty-Six

The Christmas festival was in full swing with locals and tourists enjoying the first night of events. Charley and Jack entered the town square where dozens of vendors featured specialty items—beautiful glass Christmas ornaments, wooden sleds, handmade scarves. One vendor sold his-and-her matching pajamas. Jack held up a pair printed with tiny reindeer. He nodded enthusiastically to Charley with a big grin on his face.

She laughed, thinking what an adorable dork he was. How she missed being with someone who made her laugh. "If you're not careful, I'm going to buy those for you. Then maybe you'll remember poor Cupid next time."

His face was aghast. "I'll never forget Cupid again." He dropped the pj's and grabbed the big bag of Christmas stockings he still needed to deliver.

"Is that it?" She gestured to a booth off to one side.

"I think so." They strode over, and Jack glanced around for the vendor. "I wonder if I should just leave them."

A teenage boy wearing a Santa hat popped up from below the counter. "Are you here for the races?"

Jack jerked back, startled. "Maybe later, but Mary

Carroll wanted me to drop these off to you." He threw the bag onto the counter.

"Thanks, man. We totally ran out last year." The teenage boy dragged the bag closer and unloaded it. "You know, it's only ten minutes before the next race. Whoever wins gets awesome vendor coupons."

"That sounds great, but…" Jack turned to Charley.

"I've never done a Christmas stocking race. Have you?" She lifted a brow.

Ten minutes later, Charley, Jack, and several other competitors stood in oversize Christmas stockings at the starting line.

Charley narrowed her eyes at Jack. "You're going down," she said with glee.

"I wouldn't count on it," Jack threw back, confidently.

The blare of the horn sounded. Everyone began hopping across the well-lit, carved-out path in their Christmas stockings—Charley and Jack neck-and-neck. Charley was having a hard time hopping because she couldn't stop laughing at how funny Jack looked. His jaw was set with determination; his eyes danced wildly with excitement. She got too close to him, lost her balance, and tripped him by accident. They fell into the snow while a little girl from behind jumped across the finish line.

"I did say you were going down," Charley said. The second she stood, Jack pulled her back into the snow, making her laugh.

"I can't believe we lost when we were in the lead." He watched the little girl's family congratulate her. "Who knew little kids could be so ruthless?"

She couldn't help but think how fun it would be to do a race with their own kids one day.

"Are you getting hungry?" he asked, interrupting her daydream.

"I could eat," she said, tucking away her musings for later.

"Good, because I'm famished." He reached out and helped her to her feet.

Once they returned the oversize stockings to the teenager, they wandered around the festival, checking out food choices.

"How about we go French tonight?" Charley asked, standing in front of the Paris in St. Nicholas booth.

"Sure." He slid his arm around her shoulder as they glanced over the menu.

"*Bonsoir*," a peppy woman said. "Welcome to Paris in St. Nicholas. Tonight's Christmas theme is eggnog, which means you'll receive ten percent off any eggnog item."

"We certainly can't pass that up." Charley snuggled into Jack. "Are you still a splitter?"

"Now that brings back memories. I haven't split food with anyone since you."

"Time to reinstate a good thing," she said, then turned to the vendor. "We'll take the eggnog Monte Cristo, and the eggnog crepes with mixed berries for dessert." Charley glanced at Jack. "Good with you?"

"Great with me." Jack grabbed plastic utensils and napkins from the counter while they waited for their food. "Remember Homecoming, when we double dated with my buddy Chris and his girlfriend?"

She very much remembered dancing with Jack but had forgotten about their dinner. "Yeah. What was her name? Hannah?"

"Heather." Jack groaned.

"That's right. Heather," she said, rolling her eyes.

"You and I had been splitting meals for months, even that night."

"Didn't we split a Caesar salad and a filet mignon?"

"Good memory. Then you probably remember that Chris and Heather got into a huge fight. She wanted fish, which Chris hated, so he said they should just order separately, but Heather insisted they split their entrees."

"Didn't they break up that night?"

"Yeah," Jack said. "I guess not being splitters split them up."

Charley laughed.

"Jack?" A woman's voice rang out.

He glanced over and the color instantly drained from his face. An attractive woman with dark hair stood glaring at them. "Lisa!" Jack's voice filled with shock.

Lisa? Who's Lisa? Charley didn't recognize her but clearly Jack did. A feeling of dread began churning in the pit of her stomach.

"What are you doing here?" His tone was sharp.

Lisa shifted her focus between Charley and Jack. "I thought you were on a case."

"I am," he said coldly.

She gave Charley a onceover before setting her gaze back on Jack. "I expected more from you, Jack. Why did you lie to me?"

Fear of betrayal began building in Charley. *Is she Jack's girlfriend? Don't jump to conclusions.* Charley regarded Jack carefully. He'd obviously been taken off guard, but now he looked trapped, which didn't make any sense to her. If Lisa was an ex-girlfriend, or even a friend who had hoped for something more, he'd look uncomfortable, not trapped. Charley's breath snagged in her throat.

"I didn't lie to you," he said. "I told you I was on a case, and I also told you it was over between us."

Lisa drew her arms tight to her body. "I've got eyes, Jack. The body language between you two tells me you've known her a lot longer than a few days. Just how long were you dating the both of us?"

"You have it all wrong," Jack shook his head. "Charley and I dated in high school. We ran into each other at the B&B."

Lisa's eyes welled with tears. "You mean the B&B that I wanted to go to?"

"I'm not doing this," he said calmly, taking Charley's hand. "Let's go."

But Charley hesitated. When exactly did he break up with her? How serious had they been?

"Did he even tell you about me?" Lisa asked Charley in a trembling voice.

Charley met her gaze, seeing the pain in the woman's eyes, and slowly she shook her head, unable to speak.

Lisa let out a small laugh. "You'd think I'd at least get an honorable mention after treating him to a romantic dinner Monday night."

Six nights ago? Charley felt a ball of hurt lodge in her chest. She blinked repeatedly, keeping the inevitable tears from betraying the tough façade she was desperately trying to hide behind. She wanted to believe he wasn't an insensitive jerk, but she couldn't deny the wounded woman in front of her. Her mind reeled back to high school. How Jack stopped emailing and returning her calls and how their love fizzled out to nothing, as if it had never existed in the first place. The indifference had been more painful than if he had just ended it before he moved away.

Charley clenched her jaw before fixing her gaze on Jack. “You were still in a relationship less than a week ago, and you didn’t think that was worth mentioning?”

Bewilderment flooded his eyes. “The relationship was over.”

“Then why is she here?”

Charley and Jack turned toward Lisa, waiting for an answer.

She stepped forward, wiping the tears off her cheeks, and focused on Jack. “After we spoke yesterday, I was—”

“What?” Charley’s threw glances between the two. Something else he neglected to tell her? She’d known Jack in high school, and she thought she knew him now. Jack Brody was not a two-timing jerk, and he would confirm that. The Jack she knew would never stay in contact with someone he had already broken up with, especially since he had rekindled the relationship with her. “Did you talk to her yesterday?”

Jack’s shoulders slumped and his expression was that of deep regret. “Charley, I—”

She put her hand up to stop him, her eyes moistening. “It’s a simple yes or no,” she said, her voice shaking.

He hesitated, his eyes imploring her to see his innocence. “*She* called *me*.”

Charley choked with emotion as tears stung her eyes. She couldn’t believe what she was hearing. Instead of owning up to the fact that he’d been lying to her through omission, he chose to lay blame elsewhere. This couldn’t be the man she had fallen in love with.

She blinked, clearing her vision as her eyes met his, and in a voice as faint as a ghost’s she said, “If you no longer have feelings for her, why did you take her call?”

But Jack had no words for her. He just stood there, staring at her, shaking his head.

She backed away and hurried off before she broke down in front of him. She wouldn't allow him the satisfaction of seeing the devastation and pain he'd inflicted on her as he cut out her heart once again.

"Charley, wait!"

Lisa quickly grabbed his arm. "Jack, please."

He yanked it free. "Why are you here? We're not together anymore."

"I'm sorry," she said quietly. "It's just… I didn't hear everything you said before we were disconnected. I thought maybe you had changed your mind, that you realized our breakup was a mistake. Jack, all I did was ask you one little question."

"It wasn't a little question. It was *the* question."

Lisa cast her eyes to the ground, appearing as if she finally understood. Jack then turned and ran after Charley.

He rushed through the town square, scanning the crowds, desperate to find her. He raced to the mailbox, praying he'd find her there, but to his great disappointment she wasn't. "Charley?" he called, searching the town square, panicked. "Charley!"

He flew down to the frozen pond, and then to the diner. He stopped to catch his breath and texted her: Where are you? She's an ex-girlfriend. Please let me explain. He waited for a reply, but none came.

He scrambled into his SUV, worried she was walking back to the B&B. Halfway down the road he spotted her. He let out the breath he'd been holding and slowed down. He lowered the passenger-side window and pulled up alongside her. She had her coat wrapped tightly around her body and she was crying. A lump clogged his throat. Seeing her tears twisted his gut, and all he wanted to do was to take her in his arms.

"Charley?" he gently called her name.

She refused to look at him or acknowledge his presence. She simply marched on, staring straight ahead.

"She's not my girlfriend anymore." He kept pace with her, not backing down. "Didn't you get my text?" he asked, attempting to keep desperation from coloring his voice.

She wouldn't answer. She flipped her coat collar over her ears, shutting him out even more.

He stayed with her, creeping along the road by her side. Ignoring him wasn't going to get rid of him. "Would you please get in the car and let me explain?"

She continued walking toward the inn.

"I'm not leaving you out here on this road. It's not safe. You could get hit."

"At least that would put me out of my misery." Her voice cracked, sadness seeping out of it, and the sound tore at his heart.

"Don't say that. Don't even think it."

She picked up the pace, staring straight ahead.

"I'm in law enforcement, Charley. Don't make me use it."

She flicked him a look of uncertainty. "You wouldn't."

"For your safety, you better believe I would."

She faltered, came to a halt, and turned toward his car. Her fists were clenched and her beautiful face was marred with black streaks of mascara. *I did this* was all he could think.

Charley opened the door and climbed in. She put on her seat belt, but refused to look at him.

Jack realized he was only two minutes away from the inn. *I have two minutes to make it right.* He opened his mouth, ready to explain how everything went wrong with his breakup with Lisa, but he worried he'd sound too defensive, therefore guilty, and she'd bolt from the car. He needed to clarify his statements, and that was going to take time.

He slowed the car to buy him a little more time, and then he dove right in. "Lisa and I dated for a little under three months," he began, keeping his eyes on the road. "I knew about a month ago that our relationship was going nowhere. I had planned on breaking it off with her, but I got involved with a complicated case, and it never seemed to be the right time." He cast a glance in her direction. "We had dinner the night before I came up here because it was my birthday, but it was no celebration. We were fighting the minute we sat down. By the end of the night, I had ended it." He pulled up to the B&B and parked. He didn't make a move to get out, hoping Charley would do the same.

She glanced at the front door, then tucked her chin, staring at empty her hands. "So you didn't invite her up here?"

"No. In fact, I told her she couldn't come because I was working. That's what ignited our fight. I had no idea she was going to show up."

"Why did you take her call if you had already broken up with her?"

"I was in the middle of something, and I picked up without checking to see who was calling."

"What did she want?"

"To make sure I made it up here safely."

Her brows knitted together. "Why would she care—if you had broken up with her?"

The more he tried to explain, the bigger the hole he kept digging for himself. "I don't know. I was very clear."

"Yet, she drives *all the way* up here knowing you clearly ended it?" Charley puffed out a small ironic laugh. "You weren't clear with me all those years ago, and I got the hint."

He knew how bad it looked, and he didn't know how to get past it. "Charley, let's not do this."

"Do what? Revisit the one thing that messed with my head for the past fourteen years? Something isn't adding up, and I'm not going to spend the next fourteen years trying to figure it out."

"Charlotte—"

"No. You don't get to call me that." Her voice became suddenly sharp. "I can forgive you for not being forthcoming about your breakup with her, but the phone calls and her following you up here? This whole time I thought you were only with me, but you weren't. Whether you really ended it or you only think you did, she didn't get the message."

"How is that my fault?"

"You're the one who doesn't know how to end relationships."

"That's not true."

"Isn't it?" She eyed him. "Stellar job on breaking up with me."

"You're not being fair. I was a kid."

"But you're an adult now, and it appears like nothing has changed." She took a deep breath, lowering the temperature. "I can't do this again, Jack, I just can't." A tear rolled down her cheek but her voice remained steady and in control. “I think what’s best for us—for me, is to end this now and forever.”

His heart plummeted. “You can’t mean that.” His voice cracked as he looked at her, but his emotion didn’t seem to move her. It was as if she’d suddenly nailed a barrier up against him.

“I’m sorry, but I do,” she said barely above a whisper. “We’re through, Jack. It’s over.” She got out of the car, then looked back at him one last time. “And *that’s* how you break up with someone.”

Chapter Twenty-Seven

Right when Charley came barreling in the front door, Mary ambled out of the living room. "Evening, Char—" Mary's smile disappeared the second she saw Charley's tear-streaked face.

Charley forced a polite nod and hurried up the stairs, taking two steps at a time. She flew into her room and barricaded herself safely behind the door. Only then did she allow herself to break down in uncontrollable sobs.

After everything she'd been through as a teen with Jack, and then last year with Hunter, why had she allowed Jack into her heart so swiftly? She knew better. People didn't change. They only learned how to hide their deception better.

Ten minutes later, she heard a soft rap on her door. *The guy just doesn't get it.* "Go away, Jack." She ripped a tissue out of its box and wiped her nose.

"Charley, honey, it's me, Mary."

Great. Just what I need. She desperately wanted to tell her to go away too. She wanted to be left alone and remain alone for the rest of her life. Why wasn't anyone getting that?

"I'm not my best right now," she called, her voice hoarse.

"That's why I'm here. Will you please open the door?"

She couldn't resist how sweet and caring Mary sounded, reminding Charley of her own mother's tenderness when she'd fallen into a depression after Jack had moved away.

"It will only take a minute," Mary said.

Against her better judgment, Charley cracked open the door and saw her standing there with a tray of comfort food. "Thank you, Mary, but I'm not hungry."

"I brought you the most delicious mac and cheese. It's a secret recipe from a very well-known chef." Mary stepped closer to the door and lowered the tray so Charley could see the dish for herself. "Did you know pasta is one of the best endorphin-inducing foods you can eat? One bite will make you feel so much better."

Charley smelled the Gruyere and sharp cheddar cheeses, tempting her to let Mary in. She honestly didn't want company, but maybe if she took one or two bites, Mary would leave her in peace. She let out a sigh. "Come in."

Mary sashayed in and set the tray on the table by the window. "I also brought you a pitcher of iced tea since I hear you love it so much. Oh, and a few sugar cookies for dessert." She unloaded the items on the table and set the tray aside.

"Did Jack put you up to this?" She narrowed her eyes on Mary.

"Of course not. I haven't seen him. Is he in as bad shape as you?"

Charley slumped into a chair at the table. "I don't know and I don't care."

"And I think you don't mean that." She pulled out the chair opposite her and made herself at home.

"I trusted him and he lied to me."

"Jack lied?" Mary said as if it were impossible.

"He didn't tell the whole truth. Same thing."

"Is it? Sometimes people don't tell the whole truth because they don't *want* to lie."

"I know the difference between little white lies and big, fat, hurtful ones. He has a girlfriend."

"Jack?" Mary looked completely bewildered. "Our Jack?"

"*Your* Jack, if you want to claim him. He's not mine anymore." She crossed her arms. "He probably never really was."

"I'm sorry, Charley." Mary pushed the mac and cheese closer to her. "It's just…so hard to believe. I see the way he looks at you and that's head-over-heels in love."

"Yeah, well. I'm guessing it was all an act." She stared at the mac and cheese, then reluctantly took a bite. The flavor of cream and deliciously baked cheese exploded in her mouth—all she could think about was how much Jack would love it.

"Some act. So he has a girlfriend and he's dating you?"

"Not exactly." Charley shoveled in another mouthful of the best mac and cheese she ever tasted. "He said he ended it before he left Denver, but she drove all the way up here tonight, so she obviously doesn't see it that way."

Mary cocked her head with a perplexed expression on her face. "If he ended the relationship and she came up here anyway, then isn't that *her* problem?"

"It should be." She set down her fork and eyed Mary. "But she believes they're still together."

"Ah." Mary nodded. "So now you're trying to figure out whom to believe."

"No, I'm worried they're both telling the truth. Jack never officially ended our relationship when we were in high school. He stopped calling one day, and I was left to figure it out on my own. I don't know anything about Jack's ex-girlfriend, but what if he's done the same thing to her? What if he thought it was over, even said it was over, but he never conveyed it properly to her?"

"It's possible, but to me he seems pretty direct. Maybe this woman doesn't want it to be over. Jack's a solid, sturdy, level-headed guy who thinks before he acts, who cares about others, and who can be very charming. What woman wouldn't want that?"

She wanted that. But she also wanted to be right. "He should have told me about her. I felt blindsided, like the way I've felt too many times before."

"Do you think that's why Jack chose to keep it from you?"

Charley stopped mid chew. Could it be that simple? Had Jack decided not to say anything in order to protect her feelings? He'd seen how hurt she'd been by Hunter, and he had sincerely sympathized with her. Had she misjudged the whole situation?

"If he thought the relationship was over, what reason would he have to bring it up?" Mary asked.

"Either the endorphins from your mac and cheese have kicked in, or you're making too much sense for me to ignore what you're saying."

"I'm pointing out my observations, is all."

She wanted to believe Mary. She wanted to believe that things could be right with Jack again—if not for her own insecurities. "I'm trying to move forward, but I have trust issues."

"Then work with what you know. What does your gut tell you about Jack?"

"Putting aside what happened tonight, deep down I know he's the kind of man I want to be with."

"Can you see yourself with him long term?"

A tiny smile tugged at the corners of her mouth. "That's all I've ever seen."

"Then trust in that intuition of yours. It's rarely ever wrong."

Charley let the wisdom of Mary's words wash over her. She was angry with Jack because he blamed Lisa for his own shortcomings, but wasn't she doing the same thing? She had blamed him for making her insecure when in reality her insecurities were of her own making. If she wanted to move forward, she needed to have faith in herself and in her instincts again.

But that was easier said than done.

Mary came back into the kitchen to find Joe cleaning up. She grabbed dirty mixing bowls and cookie sheets off the counter and stacked them next to the sink to be washed. "This one's more complicated than I imagined," she said, feeling a little anxious.

"More players?" He drizzled soap on one of the cookie sheets and took to scrubbing.

She let out a long sigh. "An ex-girlfriend who wants to remove the 'ex.'"

Her husband processed the new information before he spoke. "I'm not worried. Jack and Charley are meant to be together."

"No doubt, but it seems like everyone can see that except Charley."

"That's why she's the Scrooge."

She nodded. "Our boss might have known she needed our help, but it's still up to her to do something about it. Charley, Jack, Jack's parents, his ex-girlfriend. There are a lot of moving parts." She eyed Joe. "What if I miss something?"

He dried off his hands and turned toward her. "You won't because you're always up for a challenge. Plus, you have me. Why don't I keep an eye out for Jack's parents in the morning, get them settled, and be on alert for any unwelcome ex-girlfriends?"

"Thank you, honey." She gave him a kiss. "You are my rock."

"More like a sturdy oak. I like to get watered and fed."

She laughed, then opened the cookie container and fed him one. "All right then. Let the challenge begin."

Chapter Twenty-Eight

Jack started out of his room a half dozen times. He was going to march down to her door, demand that she see him, take her in his arms, and tell her to stop being so foolish. They belonged together. Period. But he knew he couldn't do that. He couldn't force Charley to believe him. If only he could rewind the last few days…

Jack's cell rang and he jumped for it, only it was Lisa. *Unbelievable.* He immediately blocked her number. Why was she still calling him? He couldn't understand it. He knew she expected to always get her way, but this was borderline stalking. What had gotten into her? A month ago, she would have never followed him on an investigation. She would have accepted their breakup and probably told him it was his loss. Now he didn't even recognize her.

Santa's mailbox suddenly popped into his head. *No.* He had jotted down her name and thrown it into the mailbox, but he'd only done it to get the door to open. Besides, he didn't believe in Christmas magic. *Don't even consider it.*

Then again, he was back with Charley. By Christmas magic? And Mike could very well be his uncle. Jack huffed out an irritated breath and paced off a few brisk steps.

What if Felicity is right? She said it was all connected,

which meant if he had suggested Lisa as a Scrooge, it was his fault that she showed up. What had he been thinking?

Well, for one, he'd thought he was doing her a favor. She was obsessed with social media and being the center of attention. She put value in expensive gifts over forming a real bond with someone, and he suspected it was all because she had yet to find her true passion. He'd figured, like Braca and Captain Wollin's brother, Lisa could benefit from seeing things with a different perspective. He'd also assumed the town hosted one Scrooge at a time. Had he known that wasn't the case, he would have never suggested her.

He pinched the bridge of his nose. What did it all mean? How was everyone connected? Had he and Charley been drawn into something he wasn't seeing? He'd come to St. Nicholas for answers—now he had more questions and no answers.

Jack went into the bathroom and splashed water on his face. What did it matter, the how and the why? The only thing he cared about was getting Charley back. Maybe he should stand outside her door and pour his heart out to her. With his luck, she wouldn't be in her room. She refused to respond to his texts and his calls. He needed to get her attention.

He opened his laptop and turned it on. He didn't want to speak to her through her blog because it was such a public forum, but what other choice did he have? He pulled up *The Cold Hard Facts* and reviewed the latest comments. Many were inquiring about who he was, which felt very surreal to him. He scanned each comment, hoping Charley had replied to one or two, but she hadn't. She'd said she was done with him forever, and he was starting to believe that she meant it.

"I can do this." He laced his fingers together, turning his palms out for a good stretch. He was not a wordsmith. Clearly, if he were, he wouldn't be in his present predicament. *What should I say? Give me another chance? Please come back?* Staring at her blog for inspiration, he saw Reality Check had posted a new comment.

Jack sat up straight, clicked on the comment, and couldn't believe what he was reading.

> You say it's done, and you think you've won, but have you lost to hate? I heard your plea, Jack is the key, this isn't up for debate. Never say forever, unless love is your lever, he is your soulmate.

"What!" Jack flew back in his chair, cradling his head in his hands. *She's going to think I wrote this. She's going to think I've been Reality Check all along and that I kept that from her too.*

He shot out of the chair and paced, worried about how she'd react when she saw it. He reread it again, attempting to calm down, only then realizing that the comment also painted her in a bad light. It portrayed him as the good guy, and she appeared to be messing it up. "That's just fantastic."

He stared out the window, wondering how Reality Check knew about their private conversation. Only he and Charley had been in the car when she declared their relationship done forever. Jack scrubbed his weary face. Was he ever going to find a logical explanation for anything going on in this town?

He reread the comment one last time. "Yup, she's definitely going to think I wrote it."

* * *

"He didn't write it," Charley protested through the phone, staring at the comment on her blog.

"Who else could it be?" Liv sounded exasperated.

She knew Liv was only trying to protect her—that's what best friends did. "The author already identified himself. It's Reality Check."

"Jack *is* Reality Check."

"No, he's not. Jack and I have been through this already. Turns out there's a retired trucker named R.C. who frequents the diner we've been eating at and his handle is Reality Check."

"A trucker?" Liv's voice was laced with serious doubt. "Why would a trucker care anything about you and Jack? It's got to be Jack. He's a police detective. Reality Check is the perfect username for him."

"I thought that, too, but I swear, Jack had no idea about the first comment Reality Check left, and he was furious about being identified by name in the second."

"Then that's weird." Silence on the end of the phone meant Liv was truly stumped. "I'm assuming this guy lives in St. Nicholas?" she finally asked.

"He apparently lives up north."

"Then Jack needs to trace the IP address, find out exactly where he lives and tell him to butt out of your business." Liv seemed upset enough for the both of them.

"He already traced it. The location came back as the North Pole."

"The North Pole?" Liv laughed. "No one lives at the North Pole. I suppose you're going to tell me the trucker looks like Santa."

Charley sighed loudly.

"I hate to say this, but maybe *you* need a reality check,

or maybe you need to get out of that town. Santa eating at a diner, an elf picking up mail. St. Nicholas sounds obsessed—so obsessed that maybe they put a bug in Jack's car."

"I think Jack would know."

"Would he?"

"I don't know," she said wearily.

"Charley, you're tired, you're emotionally exhausted. If no one was in the car but you and Jack then that means either you or Jack wrote the comment, and I'm pretty sure it wasn't you."

She stared at her computer screen. "It does sound a little arrogant stating that he's my soulmate, and I'm the one in the wrong."

"I'll give him props for reaching out after you said you were through."

"Yeah, and so publicly, which is not like Jack at all." She bit her lower lip.

"So, what are you going to do?"

"I don't know. My instincts seem nonexistent these days. When it comes to men, I make the wrong choice every time."

"Do you love him?" Liv's voice softened.

"I never stopped," she confessed.

"You never told me that."

"Yeah, well, I knew professing my love for him wasn't going to bring him back. Jack was gone, he'd taken my heart, and that was the cold hard fact. Maybe that's why every guy I've dated after him has felt like I was settling."

"Settling sucks. I did it for a year and regretted it," Liv said. "The big question is, does Jack love you?"

"He acts like it, but I don't know for sure."

"You need to find out." Her suggestion was more of a command.

"Not going to happen. I told him I never wanted to see him again."

"And I said I was going to win the lottery last Saturday night."

Charley had missed Liv's no-nonsense advice. She wanted to take it, but how could she when her wounded pride was still stinging? "He should have told me."

"You're right. He should have. But what's done is done." Liv's doorbell rang, causing her dog to bark.

"I hear Murphy's on intruder alert."

"Always. I wonder if he could learn how to sniff out the jerks *before* I go on a date with them." Liv opened the door and greeted her date. "Hi. I'll be right with you."

Murphy growled loudly. "Sounds like he already has."

"Ha, yeah. I'm thinking the same thing," she said, sounding deflated. "Can I call you later?"

"Sure. Have a good evening." Charley hung up, went into the bathroom, and washed the black streaks of mascara off her cheeks. Was she making a mistake? She stared at herself in the mirror and took a deep breath.

"Hi, Jack. Remember when I said it was over? Well..." She shook her head. "Hey, are you Reality Check, or is your car bugged?" She rolled her eyes. "Jack, I love you, so do you love me, too, or what?" She groaned, flipping off the bathroom light. *I can do this.*

Grabbing her room key, she headed out the door, shaking the nerves from her hands. She took a deep breath and marched down the hallway to Jack's door. She stood there for a moment, gathering her courage. As she raised her hand to knock, she heard laughter coming from inside his room. It was Jack. Laughing hard.

Who's he laughing with? She put her ear closer to the door, but couldn't hear anyone except Jack. Was he talking to her on the phone? Again? She backed away, did an about-face, and hurried back to her room where she slammed the door and sank onto the end of her bed. She glanced at Arthur sitting on the fireplace mantel. "You're a stupid stuffed mouse. I don't believe in the Christmas spirit. Jack is not my soulmate. It's all an illusion, just like love is an illusion. That's the cold hard fact."

The comment on her blog was still up on her laptop. She went over and slammed it shut. She sat back in the chair and tucked her feet up under her, crossing her arms over her body. She wished Jack's so-called ex had never shown up. She and Jack had been so happy the past few days. Why did this continue to happen to her?

She opened her laptop, refreshed her blog page, and stared at the comment, chewing on her fingernail. Was she going to let him get the last word like he had in high school? She unfolded herself and started typing.

Hello, Jack. Don't try to pretend. I meant what I said, this is the end.

She posted her reply, and this time, she shut her computer down for good.

Jack sat on the end of his bed, laughing. "That's what I thought, too, Charley. I'm glad you found it funny," he said to himself, and then he groaned, clenching his fists. He began pacing in his room again, trying out anything that might work.

"I know you never want to see me again, but...but what?" He rubbed the back of his neck and tried something else. "I didn't write that pithy comment, but it sure makes a good point or two, don't you think?" He forced another laugh. "I know you hate me, but I love you, so whaddaya say?" Jack threw up his hands, grabbed his key, and yanked open his door.

He stormed down the hallway and stopped in front of Charley's room. He raised his hand to knock, hesitated, then chickened out. He needed to talk to his hosts.

Jack jogged downstairs, poked his head in the living room, then proceeded toward the kitchen where he found them at the sink. "Joe, Mary?"

The couple turned to see him standing there. "Good evening, Jack." Joe picked up a dish towel and dried his hands. "Can we help you with something?"

"Yeah, I, uh..." He rubbed his forehead.

"You look a little tired. Did you get yourself some dinner?" Mary asked, putting away the clean mixing bowls.

"No, uh... I kind of missed that." He clenched his jaw, not understanding why he was feeling so emotional.

"Let me make you something." She removed a dinner plate from the cabinet.

"I couldn't. You folks have been working hard all day, and your kitchen's all clean."

Mary walked over to the refrigerator. "I can make you a turkey sandwich, or I've got leftover mac and cheese. Your choice."

"Seriously, I—"

"She won't stop," Joe said. "You better choose or she'll choose for you."

"Mac and cheese would hit the spot," he said gratefully.

"All right then." She took a casserole dish out of the

fridge, transferred a good-size portion into a microwave dish, and heated it up. "Come on in and have a seat."

"Thank you." He wiped his hands on his jeans, suddenly feeling like he was sixteen again.

"Looks like you have something on your mind." Joe leaned against the kitchen counter.

"It's Charley," Jack said on a sigh. "We had a bad fight, and I'm worried about her leaving before I can fix things. Has she said anything about leaving early?"

"Not to me." Joe glanced at his wife.

"I talked to her earlier tonight, and she didn't make mention of it."

"You talked to her?" He perked up. "Is she all right? What did she say?"

Mary set the hot mac and cheese in front of Jack with a fork and a glass of water. "She was pretty upset, which tells me she loves you."

"You really think so?"

"I do." She gestured for him to eat.

Jack took a quick bite and swallowed. "Then maybe she'll give me another chance." He shifted his gaze between Mary and Joe. "I messed up. I didn't handle a breakup well with an ex-girlfriend, and she showed up here tonight."

"Where is the ex now?" Joe asked.

"I assume she's on her way back to Denver, but now Charley won't speak to me. I wanted her to be with me tomorrow when my parents arrive. I know I haven't shared this with you, but my uncle went missing when I was ten, and I think it's Mike."

"Oh, my goodness." Mary's hands flew up to her cheeks, her eyes instantly misty.

"It all makes sense." Joe eyed Mary.

"What does?" Jack asked, confused.

"More Christmas wishes coming true." A big smile took over Mary's face. "Now that you told us, I can definitely see a family resemblance between you two."

"There's a resemblance all right." Joe stared at Jack. "I knew something was up the other day with you and your twenty questions."

"I wish he would have recognized me." Jack shook his head. "If Mike doesn't remember my parents, it could be more painful for them than if I hadn't told them what I suspect."

"It'll work out as it's meant to," Joe said. "What can we do to help?"

"I know!" Mary clapped her hands together. "I'll host a little get-together tomorrow afternoon with Mike as the guest of honor. It will be a thank-you to him for creating that beautiful train display in our front yard."

"What a great idea." The heaviness in his chest started to lift. "My parents will have a chance to observe him before I make the introductions." He sat back, picturing it in his head. If his dad could get Mike to remember who he really was, it would be one of the happiest moments of his life. But without Charley? "I've got to get through to Charley. The last thing I want is to lose her while I'm focused on my uncle."

"When you're with your folks in the morning, we'll make sure Charley doesn't go anywhere," Joe said.

"Thank you." Jack released a big breath. "Mary, Joe, you have no idea what this means to me. With your help, I just might get them both back."

Chapter Twenty-Nine

After thinking things through, Charley regretted her decision to end her relationship with Jack. She'd planned on taking it all back, especially the part about it being over forever, but when she heard him laughing, she couldn't get it out of her head. Even if he hadn't been laughing with his ex-girlfriend, how could he have sounded so cheerful when she'd just broken up with him?

It was all Charley could think about, which was why she hadn't fallen asleep until four in the morning, and exactly why she'd slept through her six o'clock alarm. When she finally awoke, it was almost nine. Convincing herself that Jack's feelings for her weren't as deep as he led her to believe, she had planned on packing and slipping out the door before anyone, especially Jack, knew she was gone. But now she would have to do it the hard way.

She turned on her phone and immediately noticed she'd received a reply on her blog from Reality Check.

Open your eyes and you will see that you and Jack are meant to be.

"What?" Liv was right. R.C. *had* to be Jack, and by referencing the high school poem, he was toying with her emotions. She reread the comment. What was he doing? If he honestly felt they were meant to be, why hadn't he come to her room last night instead of laughing it up with someone on the phone? She sat back, staring at her computer screen. She had to be missing something. It didn't add up. Why couldn't she see it? Irritated, she stormed out of bed, marched to the bathroom, and slammed the door.

With a loud bang, the front door to the bed-and-breakfast flew open. Tom, leaning on Jack for support, hobbled into the house on one leg while his wife, Rebecca, followed close behind.

"Easy now." Jack maneuvered Tom around the large table in the foyer.

Mary raced out of the kitchen, hearing the commotion. "What happened?"

"Tom fell on the ice and badly twisted his ankle," Rebecca replied.

"I'm fine," he grumbled.

"Take him to the living room," Mary said. "I'll get some ice."

"Don't put any weight on it." Jack led the way. "I got you." As he helped Tom to an oversize chair and ottoman, he spotted Charley coming down the stairs with her bags. They made eye contact, but Charley immediately broke it off.

Mary appeared with an ice pack in one hand and a couple of pillows in the other. She spied Charley with her bags and instantly dropped one of the pillows. "Oh, shoot. Charley, can you get that for me?"

"Of course." Charley set down her bags, retrieved the fallen pillow from the floor, and followed Mary into the living room.

"I don't want everyone worrying about me," Tom said as Mary put the pillows under his knee and injured ankle.

Jack fixed his eyes on Charley, but she ignored him.

"It looks really swollen." She stared at Tom's ankle. "What happened?"

"I was showing Rebecca some of my great hockey moves and, I don't know, someone must have gotten in my way."

"*You* got in your way by showing off, but you'll live." Rebecca sat on the edge of the ottoman and set the ice pack on his ankle.

"That's cold!" Tom jerked his leg back.

"It's meant to be." She waited for him to settle, then placed the ice back on. "At least it's not broken."

"What else can I get you?" Mary asked.

"You've done more than enough," Tom said. "Thank you."

"I'm glad you'll be okay." Charley smiled at Tom. "And I just wanted to say goodbye to everyone."

"What do you mean goodbye?" Rebecca threw glances between Charley and Jack. "I thought you weren't leaving until Tuesday."

"I…uh, can't stay. Besides, I've already called a car service, which will be here any minute."

"But you'll miss seeing my parents." Jack sounded a little desperate, even to his own ears.

Surprise, hope, and sadness crossed Charley's face in quick succession. Was she questioning her decision to end their relationship, or was she wondering why he was acting like they were still together? He wanted to give her every opportunity to hit the reset button, but it was up to her to actually do it. She didn't look at him, like he had hoped. Worse, she pretended not to hear him.

"Anyway, it was great getting to know you," she said to everyone but him.

Tom eyed Jack, who shook his head in disappointment.

"And thank you, Mary, for everything." She handed over her room key before giving Mary a heartfelt hug. She then picked up her bags and started toward the door.

Jack could feel his heart racing. His eyes darted around the room as he silently pleaded for help.

Tom bellowed with a sudden cry of pain, holding his ankle. "Oh, it really hurts!"

Charley whipped around, regarding Tom carefully.

He groaned again. "Charley, do you have any ibuprofen on you?"

"Sure." She dropped her bags and opened her handbag.

Jack caught Mary's eye, panic gripping him.

She gave him a quick nod. "I'll get you some water," Mary said to Tom, then hurried out.

"I'm actually a walking pharmacy." Charley pulled out a tiny travel-size pillbox. "Did you know traveling is a big migraine trigger?" She opened her pillbox so Tom could help himself.

"Do you get migraines?" he asked.

"Luckily no, but I like to be prepared."

"Here you go." Mary hurried back in, handing Tom a large glass of water before she disappeared again.

He downed the pills. "If I had to get hurt, I'm glad it was here."

"This place is very special," Rebecca said. "That's why we come year after year."

Charley checked the time on her phone and peered out the window.

"Was your first visit to St. Nicholas related to the

Scrooge Legend?" Jack hoped to pique Charley's interest enough for her to stay awhile longer.

"No. However, it did involve Santa's mailbox." Rebecca caught her husband's eye, and they shared an amused look.

"Oh?" Charley sat on the couch, and Jack released the breath he'd been holding. "How?"

"Well," Tom began, "my friend, Dave, and I had been skiing in Breckenridge all day, and we decided to stop in St. Nicholas for dinner before driving back home. While we were enjoying some ribs at that barbecue place in town, we were complaining about all of our failed first dates. We were saying things like 'I wish I could meet a woman who was into football' and 'I wish she was an amazing cook.'"

Jack chuckled, pretending to be focused on the story but was actually keeping his eye on Charley, afraid she would abruptly dash to the door.

"Anyway, some kid in the booth behind my buddy and me overheard us using the phrase 'I wish' a lot. The kid turned around and told us that if we wanted a wish granted, we needed to put it in Santa's mailbox."

"A kid?" Charley asked.

"Yeah. He must have been eight or nine. He said that's how he got his parents back together." Tom took a swallow of water. "After a few beers, we found the famous mailbox. Dave was actually too afraid to do it, if you can believe that. He thought there would be a catch or a consequence to it later. I told him the whole thing was a kid's imagination, and to prove it, I'd throw a wish in there."

"What was your wish?" she asked.

Tom looked at his wife. "I wished for a beautiful woman who'd be willing to put up with me. One who was a great companion, who loved to cook since I didn't know how, a great listener, a great everything—and I got her."

"Aww." Rebecca leaned over and gave him a kiss. "He also got a woman who loves football." She lifted up her cashmere sweater to reveal a Denver Broncos jersey underneath. "Don't mess with my Broncos," she said, making everyone laugh.

Jack hated that Charley still wouldn't look in his direction. He wanted to see her smile again, even if it wasn't for him.

"How long after that did you two meet?" Charley asked.

"The very next day," Tom said.

"That soon?" She finally glanced at Jack, and he assumed she was thinking about the timing of their reunion.

"Not even twenty-four hours. After I threw my wish in the mailbox, it started to snow, so Dave suggested we stay overnight. We managed to get two rooms right here at this B&B. The next morning, I met Rebecca at breakfast. We hit it off instantly and the rest is history."

"That's a great story," Charley said.

"We were meant to be." Rebecca patted her husband's leg. "That's why this place is so special."

"What happened to Dave?" Charley asked. "Did he go back to the mailbox and make a wish?"

"No." Tom frowned. "Unfortunately, he doesn't believe in Christmas magic. I remember saying to him, 'Open your eyes, man, before it's too late.'"

"You said that?" Charley stared at him.

Tom nodded. "But sometimes people are too stubborn to take a chance."

"Dave's still single," Rebecca said. "Hon, maybe we should make a wish for him."

"Couldn't hurt," he agreed, and they kissed again.

Jack watched Charley carefully. It seemed like an inner battle was going on inside her head.

The room suddenly got quiet, and everyone heard a car honking from outside.

"Sounds like my ride's here." Charley stood, and Jack felt like he was going to be sick. "Well, Merry Christmas."

Mary and Joe hurried through the foyer toward the front door as Charley walked over to her suitcases by the stairs.

"Let me get those." Jack was instantly by her side. "Please don't go."

She, at last, met his gaze, and her eyes were glassy from tears. "Jack, we've been pretending. We live in separate states, we—"

The front door swung open with a burst of laughter. "Look who's here!" Mary announced.

Jack turned to see his parents. "Mom. Dad."

"Hi, son." His mom hurried over and gave him a big hug.

Charley, her head down and her bags in hand, was trying to slip out unnoticed.

"Is that the beautiful Charley Dawson?" his mom called to her.

She flipped around, plastering a smile on her face. "Hello, Mrs. Brody, Mr. Brody. It's good to see you again." She set her bags down once again and went over to greet them.

"It's been too long," his mom said, all smiles, and gave Charley a warm embrace.

"What a pleasant surprise to find the two of you together again," Jack's dad said, his eyes dancing between Charley and Jack. "Well, son, is there more to this reunion than you let on?" He clasped him on the shoulder.

"It's not like that," Charley quickly answered for him. "In fact, I was just leaving. My car service seems to be late. I should give them a call." She reached into her handbag and retrieved her phone.

"You can't leave now." Joe sounded alarmed. "We're supposed to get at least five inches of snow."

Mary cleared her throat.

"Ten. I mean ten inches of snow."

"I'm sure I'll be fine, I—" Charley's phone started ringing. "It's the car service. Hello?" She walked a few steps away from the group.

Everyone kept their voices down while she was on the phone. Jack anxiously looked at Mary. "No need to worry," she whispered.

Charley disconnected the call and turned toward the group. "His car broke down." She looked dismayed. "He said it'll be at least another hour." She glanced at Mary and Joe. "Can I get a ride so I don't miss my flight? I'll pay you for your trouble."

"Oh, dear." Mary fussed with the back of her hair. "We'd love to help you out, Charley, but we have a little get-together happening for Mike in a couple of hours."

Charley glanced at Jack, who immediately cast his eyes to the ground. He was *not* going to take her to the airport so she could fly away from him forever.

She released a discouraged sigh. "I guess I'll need to call another car service."

"Why don't you just stay?" Mary pleaded. "We so love having you here."

"Yes, stay." His mom voiced her support.

"I'll have to insist," Joe said. "I can't have any guests out there on icy roads."

"But I changed my flight." Charley looked dumbfounded, and Jack almost laughed. He had to remind himself that she was from LA where weather rarely interfered with travel plans.

"I'm afraid you'll just have to change it again," Mary said. "But you better wait until we know what's happening with this imminent snowstorm."

Charley checked the sky, which was partly sunny. "It doesn't look at all like it's about to snow."

Said the snow expert.

"Storms roll in awfully fast," Joe said.

"They really do." Jack could see impatience begin to boil under Charley's skin. She glared at him, as if he had commanded the weather to mess up her departure. "Check your weather app."

"I will," Charley huffed, pulling it up on her phone. She glanced up at the sky, then at the weather report, then at the sky. "It's supposed to start snowing in an hour? Really?"

"Oh, sure," Joe said. "I remember this one September day when it was eighty degrees at lunch and snowing by the time we went to bed."

Charley narrowed her eyes. "Then maybe Mike shouldn't come over."

"That man owns a snowplow, and he'll use it if he has to." Mary laughed, as did everyone but Charley. "Now, I've got to get back in the kitchen. Joe will show you to your room," she said to Jack's parents, "and, Charley, you know where yours is." Mary pulled out the key from her apron pocket and gave it back to her.

Charley stared at the key in her hand.

"I can't wait to catch up," his mom said, giving Charley a squeeze on her arm, and Jack finally saw a crack in that Teflon armor of hers.

Chapter Thirty

Charley staggered back into her room and dropped her bags. Her gaze immediately fell on the wrapped toy sail-boat she'd bought for Jack. She had left it behind with a note for Mary to give it to him after she was gone. She had known leaving would be difficult, but she'd had no idea it was going to be impossible. In truth, once she'd gotten downstairs and seen Jack, she hadn't wanted to leave. When he'd asked her not to go, she'd nearly bro-ken down. And then, when his parents arrived and were so happy to see her, she wished she'd never changed her ticket.

Tossing her workbag on the bed, she took out her lap-top to change her ticket again, but when she pulled up her itinerary, the changes she'd made in the early morn-ing hours were gone. She immediately got on the phone with an airline representative and discovered there was no record of her rebooking the return flight. Truly mys-tified, she hung up. She didn't know how it happened, but she was sure that St. Nicholas and the Scrooge Leg-end were behind it.

Okay, fine. She wasn't meant to leave, but what now? Was Jack posing as Reality Check or could it be some-one else? The phrases "open your eyes" and "meant to be" were in Reality Check's latest comment, the exact phrases that Tom and Rebecca used. Was it coincidence or was something far greater going on?

She couldn't deny all the magical things that had been happening ever since she stepped foot in St. Nicholas. Every interview she'd conducted with former Scrooges had told her the same thing—when they began to see things differently, their world changed for the better.

She had hated the holidays because too many Christmases had been without love, and the first love that left her had been Jack. Fourteen years had passed, and she had never made the connection until St. Nicholas changed that for her. Somehow, it had brought her Jack, and she'd discovered what had actually happened with their breakup. That one misinterpreted incident had created years of insecurity. For so long, she'd felt she was undeserving of love.

Less than a week later, she had regained some of her childlike wonder. She enjoyed laughing with someone again, daydreaming about the future, experiencing the sensation of an incredible kiss. She'd allowed herself to fall in love. There was no way she would debunk the Scrooge Legend now, even if she had solid proof that it wasn't real, because to her it was real—it had brought her Jack.

Charley stared out the window, watching the clouds roll in as everyone had said they would. What she didn't understand was how her and Jack's happiness could be so swiftly derailed by an ex-girlfriend. If the legend was all about love and light and healing emotional wounds, how could Lisa have been allowed to blow it all up? How did she fit into all of it? Why had she driven such a long distance for a guy who'd already told her it was over?

She remembered the pain she had seen in Lisa's eyes and she knew that pain. She understood that pain. Fourteen years ago, she had assumed Jack didn't love her. She'd misread the breakup and walled herself up in a prison of insecurity. Could it be that Lisa had done the same thing? Had some incident played with her emotions to the point she couldn't see clearly? It was the only thing that made sense.

And what about Jack? Were his feelings toward her real? Was he the one she'd been waiting for? Reality Check seemed to think so. He insisted Jack was her soulmate, and deep down, she believed that to be true.

"Okay, Reality Check." She took in a long deep breath. "My eyes are wide open. Show me that we're meant to be."

"Mike has no idea he'll be meeting you today." Jack sat at the table in his parents' room while they unpacked. "I can't promise he'll remember you because he still hasn't remembered me. This might be tougher than you think."

"We know," his mom said. "But you believe it's him, right?"

"I do. The way he walks, the way he talks, his scar, his eyes. He took Dad's first name and your last name. It's him."

His dad blew out a breath. "After all these years wondering." He shook his head as though the thought of seeing his brother again was simply implausible. "I… What should I say to him?"

"We're going to have to play it by ear," Jack said. "But what I do know from speaking to a psychiatrist friend of mine is that we can't bombard him all at once. He'll shut down. If it seems like he's starting to remember us or something about his past, then we'll need to gently feed him information."

"Okay." His dad sounded uncertain as he took his clothes out of his hanging bag and placed them in the closet.

"I still can't believe he was in New York." His mom set her makeup kit in the bathroom. "What was he doing there? He never said he was going out of town."

"I don't know," Jack said. "But according to Mike, he was hit by a car on the twenty-third of December."

"I can't imagine," she whispered in a voice layered with sadness.

"He's a survivor," Jack said. "Worst case, he doesn't remember us. If that happens, then we move forward and create new memories."

"We can do that." She came over to Jack and put her arm around him. "You always said he was out there. You never gave up, and your father and I are so grateful for that."

"As much as I'd like to take credit, I'd say it was divine intervention. How else can I explain that I found my uncle while I was on an investigation in a small mountain town, where I stayed at a bed-and-breakfast in a room with a shower leak, so that he would be the guy to fix it? Talk about right place, right time."

"Someone is definitely looking out for our family," she said, sitting down at the table with Jack. "And how does Charley fit into all of this?"

"That's a good question and a long story." He sighed. "These past few days have challenged my beliefs about what seems reasonable or logical and what doesn't."

"What do you mean?" his dad asked, closing up his empty suitcase and setting it aside.

"You know how someone says a place is cursed? I actually think this town is blessed. It's the only explanation for all of the unbelievable things I've seen and experienced. To find my uncle *and* my high school sweetheart in the same B&B—I'd say that's more than coincidence or sheer luck."

"You two didn't come up here together?" His mom looked surprised.

"No. She still lives in LA. We ended up working on the same investigation, but my ex-girlfriend showed up, and now Charley's not speaking to me."

"Oh, is that all." She waved it away as she got up to finish unpacking. "She'll come around."

"I don't know, Mom. She was on her way out the door when you arrived."

"But she stayed, and it's starting to snow," she said, glancing out the window.

Jack watched the beautiful white flakes gently glide to the ground. He loved snowfalls—the fresh, clean look of the landscape, the stillness they brought to his surroundings. The quiet forced him to reflect on the current challenges that faced him and helped him find the better path forward. Charley was his path forward, and he needed her to know that.

"I think you might be right about this town being blessed," his mother said. "Look who just walked outside."

Jack dipped his chin and spotted Charley stepping into the snow. She was staring up at the sky with her hand out, trying to catch the flakes. He abruptly turned from the window and ran to the door.

"Where are you going?" his dad asked.

"To get her back."

* * *

Jack went out the front door and walked over to Charley. The sound of the snow crunching under his boots had her twisting around to see who was approaching. When she saw it was him, she turned away and stiffened. *At least she didn't walk away.*

He shoved his hands in his front pockets and stood without saying a word. He waited for her to speak, but she didn't, and the strained silence between them remained. Their surroundings were so hushed that he could hear tiny snowflakes falling on his parka.

"Fun fact," Jack said, breaking the silence. "No two snowflakes are alike."

Charley stared at him like she'd been taken off guard. He waited for her to tell him to never speak to her again, but the startled look on her face turned to curiosity. "How do you know? Have you examined every single snowflake in existence?"

He chuckled. "Good point."

"And we're in St. Nicholas, mind you, where logic doesn't apply. Maybe here the snowflakes are all alike."

"Another good point. Why don't we begin our own investigation?" He took two steps toward her and held out his arm, where snowflakes continued to fall on his jacket. "See? The snow isn't sticking together yet, and because my jacket is black, you can see that this snowflake looks like a fern, and this one looks like a star."

Charley moved closer so she could inspect the tiny flakes. "Oh, wow. Here's a daisy-shaped flake."

"Here's one with tree-like branches."

"Look how beautiful this one is," she said in awe, studying a snowflake by his shoulder.

"I am," he told her in an almost aching voice.

She raised her eyes and met his unwavering gaze.

"I'm sorry," he said softly. "I should have told you that I recently ended a relationship. I handled it poorly."

"I'm sorry too." She gently laid her hands on his chest. "I jumped to conclusions. I should have trusted you."

He tucked her hands inside his. "Can we start over?" He searched her face for her answer.

"I don't want to start over." She stared into his eyes, not letting go. "But I wouldn't mind picking up where we left off."

He tipped up her chin and gently kissed her. He could feel her melt into him, and he knew he never wanted to be without that sensation again. When they at last broke apart, he took her hand in his. "Do you have your gloves and hat with you?"

"I do." She pulled them out of her pockets.

"Then let's go for a walk."

It was so charming how Jack helped her put on her hat and gloves. She'd noticed over the past few days how he innately protected her in every way. He walked on the side closest to the street. He made sure her seat belt was fastened before he started driving. He even directed her around foot traffic when they were holding hands. With his six-foot-two-inch frame and his muscular build, it was incredibly romantic.

And now they were out walking together enjoying the quiet, peaceful beauty of their first snowfall. Soft, cottony snowflakes danced and twirled in the air, and she hummed a small laugh when they hit her eyelashes.

She and Jack strolled down the Carrolls' long driveway, which looped around their front yard. With a town of only twelve thousand, sections of forest, not fences, separated residential homes. Charley could seriously see herself living in St. Nicholas, enjoying the privacy, while being surrounded by such stunning nature.

"I love this." She swept her arm across the landscape. "I really do."

"It's difficult not to," he said. "I love how snow muffles everyday noise, leaving the world calm and serene."

They traipsed a short distance into the woods, taking in the tranquil solitude.

"Are those birch or aspen trees?" She pointed to the line of trees along the Carrolls' property.

"Aspens. And they're gorgeous in the fall."

"I've only seen pictures, but I know what you're talking about—the bright yellows, the shimmery golds." She could almost picture them in front of her. "I don't recall exactly what I was researching, but I remember learning that a huge grove of aspens in Utah is one of the world's largest living organisms."

"No kidding?" He sounded surprised.

"Yeah, it's thousands of years old."

"We should go there for the changing of the leaves sometime."

"I'd like that."

"What are you doing next fall?" he asked, as if he were setting up a golf game with one of his buddies.

"Oh, gosh. My calendar's so full, but I might be able to squeeze you in."

"Good, then it's a date." He grinned. "And what are you doing for Christmas?"

She stopped and met his eyes. "I…don't know," she faltered, too terrified to dream that she could actually have a Christmas filled with love again. "I don't have any plans."

"Would you like to spend it with me in Denver?"

She blinked back the tears, smiling. "I would."

"I was hoping you'd say that." He leaned over and gave her another kiss. "We have a lot to talk about."

"I know." She took a deep breath. "I don't want to live in two different states."

"I don't either, so we're going to figure it out. Okay?"

She nodded because she couldn't speak, too overwhelmed with joy. She could finally see a future that wasn't the loveless, lonely existence she had come to accept. For the first time in so long, she could see a future filled with love and happiness.

He took her hand and they walked awhile longer—until the flurries turned to snow. "We should probably head back. The party will be starting soon."

She studied his face. "Are you anxious about what will happen with Mike today?"

"A little." Traces of nervousness colored his voice. "But I'm more worried about my parents."

"I imagine it will be a shock for them to see him. Is there anything I can do?"

He turned and stared into her eyes, his intense gaze holding her. "Just be there for me?"

The strong, protective man by her side was asking for her support, trusting her to help get him through whatever was about to happen that afternoon. That meant more to her than he knew. She touched the side of his face. "Always."

Chapter Thirty-One

Mary was preparing food in the kitchen, a little frazzled, since many of her guests decided to show up early. Joe had quickly gotten the word out that their beloved handyman could potentially be receiving good news today, so twenty more people asked to come to Mary's not-so-little get-together. Now she was cranking out as many appetizers as she could.

"Okay, Mrs. Carroll, I'm reporting back that our guests are being watered and fed as I speak," Joe said. "What's next?"

"Thank you, Mr. Carroll." She threw breaded mozzarella sticks on a baking sheet right as the oven timer went off. "Can you take the pigs in a blanket out of the oven?"

"Sure thing." He slid his hand into an oven mitt and retrieved the pan. "Oh, boy. You haven't made these in a long time."

"Jack said they were one of his uncle's favorite foods. I thought they might help with his recall."

"They'd certainly help me."

"You can have as many as you want, as long as you keep an eye on Mike today. Jack and his parents are going to be sharing a lot of their memories with him. If he can't remember and gets upset, I don't want him jumping in his car and driving on icy roads."

"Don't you worry," he said, taking the mini hot dogs off the pan and placing them on a large platter that Mary provided him. "I've got a bunch of little things on my to-do list that I can always ask Mike to help me with should something go sideways."

"That's a relief." She set the honey-mustard dipping sauce in the center of the platter, then took a saucepan of hot cider off the stove and poured it into several mugs.

"You'll be happy to know that Jack and Charley are back together again." He lifted the platter in one hand and a Christmas tree made of fruit in the other.

"Hallelujah." She looked up to heaven before grabbing the tray of mugs with two hands. "One Scrooge rehabilitated. One Christmas wish to go."

Jack gave a light rap on Charley's door as he heard people arriving downstairs. He already had knots in his stomach, worried that his uncle wouldn't remember his parents or anything about his previous life. But when Charley opened the door and he saw her beautiful smile, his nerves managed to subside.

"Do you have a moment before we go downstairs?" she asked.

"Sure." He stepped inside as she walked over to the table by the window.

"I was going to give this to you at Christmas," she said, handing him a wrapped present. "But considering what is about to happen, well, I thought you should have it now."

He looked at her curiously as he untied the bow and tore off the paper, exposing a red, white, and blue hand-carved wooden sailboat. He put a fist to his mouth as his eyes welled up. "Oh, Charley," he said with a cracking voice. "This is just like the ones my uncle used to make." He swallowed hard, then cleared this throat. "Where did you find this?"

"The local toy store." She brushed away a stray tear. "I've tried to get the artist's information, but I still don't have it."

"I do." Jack wiped his face with the back of his hand, then took Charley in his arms and held her tight. "Thank you."

It took more than a moment for Jack to collect himself, and by the time he and Charley made it downstairs, the living room was packed.

"There they are." Charley pointed to his parents standing by the living room picture window.

As he and Charley made their way over, his mom instantly beamed at the sight of the two of them together.

"I'm so glad you were able to stay longer." His mom reached for Charley's hand.

"So am I, Mrs. Brody."

"Please, call me Allison."

Charley smiled and squeezed her hand.

Mary nudged in. "I've got hot apple cider here, if anyone would like some."

"Yes, please." His mom eagerly took two mugs off Mary's tray—one for her and one for his dad.

Jack reached in. "Cider, Charley?" She nodded, and he grabbed two. His mom appeared casual, but he knew she was a wreck inside.

"There's plenty of appetizers on the table and over on the bar, so help yourselves."

"Thank you, Mary," Jack said gratefully, realizing just how much work she and Joe had put into the party for his family.

His mom blew on her cider, then took a small sip. "Absolutely delicious. This B&B is a real gem. How did you ever find it, Jack?"

"I was booked at another place, but they had a flood, so the Carrolls took me in."

His mom cast a sideways glance at his dad, who looked anxious. "We might have to make a habit of this place, don't you think, Michael?"

"Huh?" His dad met her gaze. "What were you saying?"

"That everything is going to be just fine." She rubbed her distracted husband's back.

"He's still coming, isn't he?" Jack's dad asked, concern creeping in his voice as he kept glancing toward the front entrance.

"Yes," Jack reassured his father. "I already checked with Joe. He said Mike was finishing up a job and that he would be over soon."

Charley stepped back to get a better sightline of the front door right as it opened. "Someone just arrived," she reported, which had Jack and his parents craning their necks.

"I think it might be Mike," Jack said, his height allowing him a better vantage point. "Yes, he's here."

"Oh!" His mom took a deep breath, putting her hand over her heart.

"It's all right, Mom." He steadied her. "We have plenty of time."

At the front door, Mary and Joe appeared by Mike's

side. Joe took his coat while Mary handed him a mug of hot cider. She then turned to address her guests.

"May I have your attention, please?" she called to the small crowd, and the chatter slowly dissipated. "As many of you know, Joe and I have been trying to win the house decoration contest for years, and this year we really have a chance. We want to thank all of you who helped build our new, amazing, outdoor model train display, and we want to especially thank the man who designed it, Mike Hodges."

The room erupted with applause as Mike beamed with pride.

"Thank you, but I was more than happy to do it, and like Santa, I had a lot of great helpers." Mike gestured to the crowd and raised his mug to his volunteer crew. "Here's to everyone coming together to help the Carrolls. The judges will cast their votes tonight, so may they win hands down!"

The room erupted with cheers, whistles, and applause before everyone settled back into their conversations. The Carrolls' guests appeared to be having a good time, except for Jack's parents, who remained by the big picture window, tense and nervous.

Jack's dad wasn't taking his eyes off Mike.

"Honey, do you think that's your brother?" his mom asked.

"It's hard to tell from here," he said with a shaky breath. "I need to look into his eyes to know for sure."

The sooner they could get Mike's undivided attention, the better. "Mike loves Mary's food," Jack said. "Charley, maybe we can get him back here for some appetizers."

"Let's do it." They walked over to Mike, who was chatting with Rebecca and Tom.

"Charley. You stayed," Rebecca cried.

"I couldn't leave."

"We're all glad you didn't," Rebecca said, winking at Jack.

"It's good to see you're standing again, Tom." Jack tried to keep it light and casual even though his stomach was one big ball of anxiety.

"The swelling's almost gone," he said, staring down at his ankle. "Thanks to all of you."

Jack glanced at Mike. "Did Tom tell you what happened?"

"He was just filling me in. Setting big guys like us on any slippery surface is a disaster waiting to happen."

They all laughed.

"Have you seen the spread of food Mary put out for all of us?" Charley asked Mike.

"I haven't had a chance." His eyes darted around the room, lit with anticipation.

"We've been sampling everything," Rebecca said. "It's all so good."

Tom nudged Mike. "You better go over there and get some before it's gone."

"I think I will." Mike made a beeline for the two tables of food, leaving Charley and Jack to follow quickly behind. Jack motioned to his parents to grab a seat on the couch.

Mike studied the platters of food. "Charley, do you happen to know what these are?" He pointed to the closest platter.

"Bacon-wrapped water chestnuts."

Mike set a couple on a paper plate and continued to move along the table.

"This dish is roasted garlic shrimp," Charley said.

"Mary also made pigs in a blanket and a Christmas tree made of fruit."

"Pigs in a blanket?" Mike's eyes popped wide with excitement. "I love pigs in a blanket. Funny how I just remembered that. Gosh, I haven't had any since..." He looked as if he was struggling to remember, and then turned red with embarrassment. "Well, it's been a while."

Jack took a deep breath, feeling anxiety tighten his chest as Mike loaded up his plate. "I've got some seats for us by the couch," Jack told him, gathering a sampler platter for his parents, even though he knew they were too nervous to eat.

Mike snagged a handful of napkins, then followed him and Charley over to the sitting area. Jack's parents stood as he began the introductions. "Mike, I'd like you to meet my parents, Allison and Michael Brody," he said, regarding Mike carefully.

"Nice to meet you folks." Mike made direct eye contact with them before he sat with his plate of food and mug of cider.

Jack hadn't seen any recognition from Mike, which was truly disappointing.

"You've raised a good son here," Mike said. "He was a great help to me with the outdoor train display." He bit into a pig in a blanket.

His parents were suddenly very quiet. Both of them had watery eyes.

"And Jack really helped me with my investigation," Charley jumped in, since it looked as if he and his parents were going to lose it.

"He's a good son." His mom dabbed her eyes with the corner of a paper napkin.

"How's it going over here?" Mary asked, stopping by. "Can I get anyone anything?"

Mike took a drink of his cider, washing down his food. "Mary, you need to open a restaurant. This is killer food."

"I'm so glad you're enjoying it," she said before eyeing Jack.

"I agree with Mike. Only the rest of us are just getting started on it." Jack hoped she would understand his cryptic message.

"Very good." Mary nodded. "Holler if you need me." She walked away, and Jack watched her quietly ask the other guests to give them some space.

Mike didn't catch any of it, too focused on his food. "These are so good."

"They are," his mom said in a fragile voice. "I used to make pigs in a blanket every Sunday after church. Michael's brother Bill went crazy for them."

"I can see why." With no sign of recognition, Mike stuffed another one in his mouth.

His mom's chin quivered. Charley stepped in so she could get it together.

"When did you say you last had them?" Charley asked.

Mike shook his head. "I wish I could remember."

Jack cleared his throat, pushing down his emotions. "He suffers from memory loss," he said, pretending his parents didn't know.

"I'm so sorry." His mom stared at Mike. "My sister suffers from the same thing. She has to work on her recall all the time. Would you like to try a recall exercise? There's one in particular that works really well when eating food."

Mike gave her a questioning look, seeming to wonder if she was serious. "Uh…sure."

"Great." She forced a smile. "Take a bite, then close your eyes. It will help you to better concentrate on the full taste of what you're eating."

Mike did as she requested.

"Now, picture where you were the last time you tasted the same thing. Take yourself back, way back—even if it was twenty years ago."

Mike kept his eyes closed, slowly chewing. He stopped for a moment. His brows furrowed, and then he swallowed. Mike opened his eyes and glanced at Jack's mom.

"Do you remember anything?" she asked.

"I don't know." He blinked, then stared off in space. "I think I saw an oak table by a window. I want to say it was snowing, like it is today, but maybe I'm just imagining it."

"That's great," his mom said. "This is how it works. Do you remember anyone around the table?"

Mike stilled, trying to recall.

Jack's mom wiped away tears, beginning to lose control, so his dad took over. "Maybe there's a ten-year-old boy there, or his mom or another adult male?"

Mike shifted his gaze to Jack's dad and stared into his eyes. For a moment, Jack thought he saw a glimmer of recognition cross Mike's face. Mike couldn't seem to look away, as if he was desperately trying to place him. "It's funny, but you…have we met before?"

Jack inhaled sharply, unable to move.

"I think so," his dad replied in an unsteady voice as he reached for his mom's hand. "We lived in Chicago for years. Do you remember living in Chicago?"

Mike studied Jack's dad for several seconds before he shifted his focus to his mom. He then closed his eyes, appearing as if he were concentrating on images playing in his head. He opened his eyes, only to gaze off in the distance. "I… I think I…"

His mom and dad were barely holding it together. Mike kept taking long pauses and looking up. Jack had seen this behavior with victims of a crime who were trying to recall repressed memories. He held his breath, praying his uncle would remember. He could see that Mike was right on the edge of remembering something.

With confusion filtering through Mike's eyes, he cocked his head to one side. "I… I remember taking the subway."

Both Charley and his mom gasped as Jack's father continued.

"Just like my brother, Bill. He took the 'L' to work all the time."

Mike slowly nodded, as if his mind was seeking out fragmented memories to stitch together.

"Back then, Bill was in construction," his dad said. "He did a little bit of everything—plumbing, framing, electrical—you name it. He could do it all."

Mike began trembling as he listened intently.

"He'd feel right at home here because he lived for Christmas," his dad said. "He spent the holidays with us every year. Came over days in advance, and together we'd turn the house into a Christmas wonderland."

Mike stared at his dad again. "I feel like I know this guy. Bill, you say?"

"Yes, Bill Brody." His dad reached into his jacket and pulled out old pictures. "Here's Bill with Jack and me." He handed it to Mike, who stared at the picture.

Jack grabbed hold of Charley's hand, ready to come out of his skin.

"Here's another picture of Bill in his workshop." His

dad gave Mike the photo. "He used to make all kinds of things—coffee tables, bookshelves, airplanes, sailboats. He built beautiful dollhouses for sick kids at the hospital."

Mike's hands were shaking severely as he studied the picture. "This…uh…this sailboat here in the background looks like the one I carved out of wood just last week."

Charley let out a tiny gasp as she caught Jack's eye.

"Bill loved making miniature train displays. Allison and I both worked, so Jack would go over to his place after school and help him with his projects." His dad handed him one last picture. "This is Bill's train display that won an award in Chicago twenty years ago. That's Bill in front of the display."

Mike's eyes misted over. "Bill looks so much like a younger me."

"Yes, he does."

Mike wiped away his watery eyes. "Where…where is Bill now?"

His dad's voice cracked. "I think he's sitting right in front of me."

Tears splashed Mike's cheeks. "I'm Bill? I'm Bill Brody?"

Jack's dad nodded, his eyes welling with tears.

Mike mopped off his face with his sleeve, only the tears kept coming. "I'm *Bill*." And this time when he looked into Jack's dad's eyes, he finally recognized his long-lost older brother. "Mikey?"

Jack's dad nodded. "Little brother."

Both men got up and gave each other a tightly held embrace. When they finally pulled back, they were smiling.

"I'm remembering things," Mike said, who at last was Bill Brody. "This is unbelievable." He ran his hand through his hair. “Mikey, I just remembered how you and I would always watch football with Dad.”

“We did,” Jack’s dad said with a laugh.

Uncle Bill turned to Jack’s mom and gave her a big hug. She was already blubbering, overjoyed with their reunion. “Allison, you make the best pigs in a blanket, and a killer apple pie.”

“You loved them both.” She patted his hand.

He then turned to Jack, who wasn’t doing a good job of keeping it together, either. “What you’ve done for me today—” His uncle Bill grabbed him and held him tight. “Jack, I remember you now as a little boy.” He stepped back and looked him in the eye. “You were always so eager to learn what I did.”

Even though tears were streaming down Jack’s face, he couldn’t stop smiling. “I was, but I never had the patience. I never had your talent.”

“That’s not true. Being good at something takes time—”

“—and there’s always tomorrow.” Both he and his uncle finished the phrase together.

“You were the best teacher,” Jack said, remembering, his heart full.

Uncle Bill glanced at Charley. “You’ve got a really good guy here.”

“Yes, I do,” she said proudly.

Uncle Bill studied his family in front of him. “I’m sorry it’s taken me so long to remember you. After six months of trying, my doctors informed me that the amnesia was most likely permanent.”

“Jack told us what happened to you,” his mom said. “We had no idea you went to New York. We called your work, scoured all the Chicago hospitals, and filed a missing-persons report with the local police. Had we known you were in New York…" She started crying again.

Uncle Bill put his arm around her. "Thank you for trying to find me."

"There are so many John and Jane Does who walk among us," Jack said. "Do you remember why you were there?"

His uncle thought about it, then slowly nodded. "A job interview. A very rich, eccentric guy saw my work at the Chicago Expo and wanted me to build a similar display for his son's birthday in March. I didn't tell anyone because I had planned on buying everyone's gifts in New York, and I didn't want to ruin the surprise. Jack, I had just purchased your gifts from FAO Schwarz when I crossed the street and got hit by a car."

"Oh, Uncle Bill." Jack clasped him on the shoulder as tears ran down his face, and he couldn't seem to make them stop.

His dad stepped in. "Jack became a detective because he was certain you were still out there."

"And you said you didn't have patience," Uncle Bill said, which finally spurred on much-needed laughter. He then glanced at his brother. "Do you still live in Chicago?"

"No. We live right outside Denver now, about ninety minutes away."

"Jack called us yesterday," his mom said. "We arrived this morning, so we're here for another week."

"That's terrific." Mike clapped his hands. "I want to hear about everything."

"You will." His mom gave him a hug as Mary and Joe joined them.

"I'm judging by all the smiles and tears that Mike is Bill again." Mary's gaze bounced around the group.

"How did you know?" his uncle asked.

"We didn't," Mary said, "but Jack filled us in."

"And then we might have filled in everyone here," Joe confessed.

"What?" His uncle looked a little pale as he noted how everyone was staring at him.

"We've all known about your spotty memory," Joe told him. "A few of our young techie teens tried to find you online but didn't get very far."

"Everyone came here today to support you, no matter the outcome," Mary said. "So, Mike-now-Bill, can I break the good news to them?"

Uncle Bill looked a little confused. "Uh…okay."

Mary turned to the rest of her guests. "He remembers!" Everyone cheered. "Mike's real name is Bill Brody and this is his brother, Michael, his sister-in-law, Allison, and just about everyone knows his nephew, Jack. Come say hello."

His uncle was suddenly surrounded by all the guests.

"We've been rooting for you, Bill," Rebecca said. "We've been hoping you'd be able to remember who you were."

"This calls for a celebration." Charley raised her mug of hot cider. "To Bill!"

Everyone echoed Charley as Jack put his arm around his long-lost uncle. "Welcome home."

Chapter Thirty-Two

Charley woke the next morning feeling a little hungover from having experienced such an emotional day. Reuniting with Jack and then being part of his family reuniting with Bill after twenty years was truly miraculous. She now understood why so many people could attest to life-changing experiences in St. Nicholas.

She got out of bed, said hello to Arthur, then opened the curtains. “Oh!” She was in awe of the stunning view out her window. With several inches of freshly fallen snow, she couldn’t believe the pristine winter wonderland before her was real. Every pine tree had been dusted with glistening white powder; every bit of land was blanketed in a rich, velvety, winter white. She grabbed her phone and snapped some pictures. She had to take a moment to share such breathtaking beauty with the world.

After she logged on to her blog, she scanned the comments her readers left about the elf. The existence of elves had become a full-blown, passionate debate.

Her fingers paused over her keyboard as she stared out her window for inspiration, then began typing:

Morning Everyone!

I thought you might like to see the winter wonderland that's right outside my window. Isn't it gorgeous? St. Nicholas, Colorado, is inspirational, magical, and a definite must-see.

Speaking of magical, I love the debate going on about the elf. Does he exist? Is the Scrooge Legend real? I used to believe that something couldn't exist unless there was concrete evidence that it did. But I'm here to debunk my archaic way of thinking. I was sent to St. Nicholas as a Scrooge, and I'll be leaving loving Christmas as much as Santa. So, yes, for me the Scrooge Legend is very real.

I want all of you to know that I was wrong to advise skipping Christmas. We are blessed to have such a wonderful holiday because it forces us to step out of the daily, sometimes chaotic, grind and focus on what truly matters: family, friends, community. Can the days leading up to Christmas be a little hectic? Absolutely. But it's worth it. So, please, take my new and unwavering advice: Embrace Christmas with your whole heart. I promise you'll cherish the memories for years to come.

And one more thing, have yourself a very Merry Christmas!

Charley posted it to her blog and sat back smiling. She glanced out the window, taking in the scenery. Sadly, she only had one more full day in St. Nicholas—in its peace and serenity, which made her feel so alive. She never thought she'd enjoy spending time in a snowy small mountain town. Now she didn't want to leave. Did this mean she could move out of LA, the place she had lived her entire life? She took a deep breath, wondering what Denver was like. It wasn't as big as LA but certainly not as small as St. Nicholas. Could it be just right?

She picked up her phone to text Jack, then realized he might still be sleeping. They had talked with Bill well after the party ended. When she had finally called it quits, it was one in the morning, and the Brodys looked nowhere near wrapping it up.

The thought of taking a morning walk in the snow suddenly seemed very appealing. She got dressed and hurried downstairs. As she headed for the front door, Mary called out to her. "Good morning!"

Charley entered the dining room where the Carrolls were finishing breakfast with Jack and his parents. "Morning."

"We saved a seat for you." Jack patted the empty chair next to him as Mary rose from the table to pour her a cup of tea.

"Thank you." She slid in next to him, and he immediately found her hand under the table. "I can't believe you all beat me down here. What time did Bill leave?"

"Not until two," Allison said with a yawn.

"That was one amazing day," Charley said.

"One I thought I'd never see." Michael gave Jack a grateful look. "Thank you, son."

"I can't take all the credit. This town had a lot to do with it." He glanced at Charley. "And speaking of which, Mary and Joe were about to tell us about the very first account of Santa's mailbox."

"What?" She gasped with excitement.

"Before we do that—" Mary held up her hand "—let me get Charley something to eat. Are scrambled eggs, bacon, and cinnamon raisin bread all right with you?"

"Sounds perfect. Thank you." After Mary headed into the kitchen, Charley turned toward the family she already felt so comfortable around. "Did you see the gorgeous snow outside?"

"It's quite spectacular." Allison added lemon to her tea. "I never get tired of seeing the massive blanket of white after a heavy snowfall."

"That's because you don't have to shovel it," Joe said, which brought on a burst of laughter. "I bet we got eight inches of the white stuff, which is nothing for our little town. All the stores will be open, guaranteed."

"You just said the magic words for my wife," Michael said. "Stores and open."

"Very funny." Allison rolled her eyes. "You should be happy I like to shop, otherwise, you'd be getting nothing in your Christmas stocking."

"I'll go with you, Mom," Jack said. "I need to get a little shopping done myself." He squeezed Charley's hand.

"I haven't exactly done mine, either," Michael confessed.

"It looks like a family outing is in the works." Joe drained the rest of his coffee as Mary came back in with Charley's breakfast and set it before her.

"Now, what else do you need?" Mary asked, looking over the table.

"Nothing. This looks delicious. Please, sit down so we can hear about the mailbox."

"All right, dear." Mary topped off Jack's coffee, poured more for Joe, then made herself a fresh cup before sitting down. "The story I'll be telling you is about Santa's mailbox *before* the Scrooge Legend."

Charley and Jack shared an equally surprised look.

Mary poured milk and sugar in her coffee, gave it a

stir, and sat back. “Santa’s mailbox was here well before this town ever existed. The year was 1925, to be exact.”

“Wait? You’re saying there was a mailbox sitting in the middle of nowhere?” Jack asked, already skeptical of the story.

“Yes. On December 24, 1925, a small group of weary travelers were trying to make it home for Christmas, but one of their trucks broke down, and they got stuck out in the elements with no town in sight. With cold temperatures dropping quickly, they needed to set up temporary shelter for the night. That’s when they came across the mailbox. Nothing else was around for miles. They didn’t know what to think of it, so they built a fire and camped out right next to it. Realizing they’d never get home in time for Christmas, they decided to write letters to their loved ones. They wrote down their Christmas wishes for them, then dropped the letters inside the mailbox.”

“But why would they do that if they knew their letters wouldn’t get delivered?” Jack asked.

“Why do people toss coins in fountains or rub lucky statues? They did it because it was there. When the travelers finally made it home, they learned, to their great surprise, that all the letters had arrived on Christmas Day—a true Christmas miracle.”

Mary paused for a moment to take a sip of coffee. “Soon their story was told to the papers, and word got out about the mysterious mailbox. Curiosity had people going out of their way to see it for themselves. Many would deposit letters intended for a loved one with no postage and sometimes not even an address—and all the pieces of mail got delivered.”

“Every one of them, including business correspondence?” Charley asked.

"No, only heartfelt messages were received. The messages could be in the form of a letter, or a postcard, or even a short message scribbled on a piece of paper—it didn't matter. Love just needed to be the intention behind the message."

"Is there any proof that this happened?" Jack asked with skepticism still in his voice.

"Absolutely. Our library has a few of the original letters and newspaper articles on display."

"We've got to check them out," Charley whispered to Jack, realizing she'd never made it over there.

"Who delivered the messages?" Michael asked.

"Unknown. Which fueled curiosity even more. Families started coming from all over to find the mailbox. With so many people making the journey, a town with food and lodging sprang up around the mailbox. Heartfelt messages were deposited in it all year round, but the biggest delivery day was always on Christmas."

"Is that why they call it Santa's mailbox?" Allison asked.

"Yes, and that's why the town is called St. Nicholas."

"All those lives touched by one mailbox," Allison marveled. "That's a beautiful story."

"When did Santa's mailbox begin accepting Scrooge suggestions?" Jack asked.

"I don't know, exactly," Mary said, "but the mailbox became a way to send a Christmas blessing to someone who had lost their Christmas spirit."

"And the Scrooge Legend was born," Joe added.

"Incredible." Charley took out her phone and made some quick notes.

"Thank you for sharing that with us," Allison said. "This town is becoming more special by the minute."

"My pleasure." Mary rose and picked up the plates. "Now, all of you had better get going if you want to experience this glorious day."

"And don't forget about tonight." Joe got up with his dirty dishes in hand. "The mayor will be announcing the winner of the home decoration contest at four o'clock in the town square."

"There's no way we'll be missing that." Jack pushed back his chair.

"See you then," Michael said to his hosts as they disappeared into the kitchen. "I want to get some pictures of us outside and also by the Christmas tree."

Jack waited for Charley, but she wasn't getting up from the table. "Ready?"

"Why don't you go ahead? I'll meet up with you in a bit. I want to help Mary with the dishes."

"Where are my manners?" Allison came back to the table. "I'll help."

"No need." Charley waved her away. "I got this. You guys go get some great pictures."

"All right, we'll see you soon."

Jack gave her a curious look. "You know you're more than welcome to be in our family pictures."

"I know. I just want to help Mary. That's all."

"Okay. We'll be out front if you change your mind." He gave her a kiss on the top of her head and followed his family out.

Charley ate the last bite of her raisin bread before taking her dishes into the kitchen. Joe was on his way out the door, but Mary was at the sink rinsing plates and loading them into the dishwasher.

"Here's the last of them." Charley set the dirty dishes by the sink.

"You don't need to be doing that," Mary scolded. "Shouldn't you be out taking pictures with the Brodys?"

"It should be a family thing, which I'm not."

"Yet. It's only a matter of time."

Mary could actually be right. In less than a week, her entire life had changed. "I want to thank you for everything—especially the insightful talk you gave me the other night."

"I'm glad I was able to help," Mary said. "How does it feel to have the Christmas spirit again?"

"Amazing." She bubbled with a soft laugh. "I didn't think I could be this happy."

Mary turned off the water and dried her hands. "Charley, there is one thing I haven't told you about the Scrooge Legend."

"Oh?" Charley couldn't miss the serious look on Mary's face as she motioned her to have a seat on one of the barstools.

"There's one requirement Joe and I couldn't tell you about earlier, but now that you're no longer a Scrooge, I can."

Charley's heart skipped a beat. "What is it?"

"Now that you have the Christmas spirit back, you must share it."

"Okay," Charley said, not entirely sure she understood. "I can certainly do that. I can tell my readers to visit St. Nicholas, I can—"

"No." Mary put up a hand. "What I mean is, you'll meet a Scrooge soon, and you will need to do something for him or her that means a lot to you. Something that will affect you greatly."

Charley frowned in confusion. "Like what?"

"I don't know."

Charley let out a frustrated sigh. Mary was talking in circles like she had the night she arrived.

"I'm not just saying that. I honestly don't know."

"Can you at least give me an example?"

"I really can't."

Charley drew in a long breath, trying to understand. "If I'm supposed to do something for this Scrooge, something that means a lot to me, then shouldn't it be easy?"

"No. It might be difficult," Mary said, and that unnerved Charley.

"What happens if I don't help this Scrooge?"

"Things might turn out differently than expected, though I'm only guessing. I really don't know because reformed Scrooges always step up to the challenge."

Charley sat there wondering why Mary had told her about the requirement. It was just going to make her anxious.

"You'll be fine." Mary laid a hand on top of hers. "Trust your instincts. It will all make sense soon. I just wanted you to be aware."

Charley settled into a reluctant smile. "Thanks for the warning." *I think.*

Chapter Thirty-Three

Charley didn't want to worry about what Mary had said, but how could she not? Was she trying to tell her that her own happiness was at stake if she didn't give this Scrooge what he or she needed? That didn't make sense at all. According to other ex-Scrooges, they were all so happy and none of them had warned her about a last-minute requirement. Of course Mary knew about Charley's trust issues. Did she inform her so she wouldn't panic?

Charley heard a knock at the door and opened it to find Jack. "Hey." She let him in. "Did you get your pictures taken?"

"We did. Turns out my parents will be using one of them as their Christmas card."

"For this year?" Charley grabbed her coat and hat. "Not much time to get them out."

"That's exactly what I said." Jack laughed as they headed downstairs. "My parents already left. They're picking up my uncle at his place, so they're going to meet us in town."

Charley grunted a response, her mind occupied with the bombshell that Mary had dropped on her. Maybe she should try to find one of the locals she'd interviewed and ask them about the Scrooge requirement.

"Are you okay?" he asked, opening the front door. "You seem distracted."

"Mary just told me that as a Scrooge, I have one requirement to fulfill."

"I thought they told you there were no strings attached."

"They did." She scowled as they got into his SUV.

Jack gave her a sidelong glance. "What is it?"

"She said now that I have the Christmas spirit, I need to pay it forward. I'll be meeting a Scrooge soon, and I'll need to do something for this Scrooge. She said whatever it is will affect me greatly."

"That sounds a little ominous." He started the car and drove down the driveway, heading for town.

"It does." She glanced out the window, hoping this requirement wasn't going to cast a cloud over her happiness.

"You know, my captain thought something fishy was going on with the invitations. Maybe this requirement is the dark side of St. Nicholas."

She stared at Jack. "You think so?"

"There's good and bad to everything—maybe even St. Nicholas."

"I hope not." She shuddered. "This place truly feels magical."

Jack cracked a smile. "You've definitely got your Christmas spirit back."

"Don't you? With everything that's happened?"

"I guess I do," he admitted, turning onto Main Street. "You, and then my uncle. How can I *not* be all in?"

"You better be." She playfully slapped him on the leg. "Hey, do you mind if we stop at that gourmet coffeehouse before we meet your family? I want to talk to a former Scrooge about this requirement."

"No problem."

A few minutes later, Charley was scanning the place for Piper. "Shoot. I don't think she's working."

"Can I help you?" a young man behind the counter called to Charley.

"I was hoping to speak with the barista named Piper. Is she working today?"

"I think you mean Piper, the owner. She's right over there." He pointed to a woman who had her back to them, restocking a display case with coffee-related merchandise.

Charley looked over just as she turned around. "That's her. Thank you." Piper was the owner? It made the results of her Scrooge story even sweeter. "Excuse me, Piper? Do you remember me?"

Piper took a moment to place Charley, then smiled. "Aren't you the Scrooge I spoke to about the mailbox?"

"Yes, although I was told this morning that I've graduated, so to speak."

"Congratulations." Piper eyed Jack. "I can see that you have."

Charley blushed. "This is Jack…my boyfriend." She loved how that sounded again.

"Good to meet you," Piper said. "What can I help you with?"

"The Scrooge requirement." She got right to the point. "Can you give me some clarification on it?"

"Ah, the requirement." Piper nodded. "Why don't you sit down." She gestured to the nearest table, then grabbed her half-finished coffee off a display shelf. "Would you care for something to drink?"

"Oh, no, we're fine." She and Jack followed Piper over to the table and sat down.

"The requirement." Piper released a long breath. "It's difficult to describe."

"So I've heard." Charley frowned. "Can you tell me what yours was? Maybe it will help me to understand."

"Sure. When I lost my job, I had to move back home because I had a mountain of debt. A month later, my mom unexpectedly passed away."

"I'm so sorry." Charley put a hand to her chest.

"Thank you." She took a sip of her coffee before continuing. "With my finances being as they were, I couldn't pay my mom's mortgage. The house had fallen into disrepair, which was so sad to me. I wanted to restore it to its full glory, but I had no financial means to do so. A callous real estate broker, who happened to be *my* Scrooge, wanted to buy her house before it went into foreclosure. He wanted it badly, and I didn't want to give it to him because he refused to tell me what his plans were for the property. But letting the bank take it was no guarantee that they'd leave her home standing, either. It seemed like an impossible decision for me."

"That sounds horrible," Charley said. "How did you decide?"

"I thought about the people of St. Nicholas. They'd been like family to me. I couldn't allow my mom's property to fall into the hands of a corporate bank in Denver. What if they turned it into a huge apartment complex or a tacky commercial enterprise? I sold it to the Scrooge."

Charley looked mortified and grabbed Jack's hand. "That must have been so difficult for you."

"It was."

"What happened to your Scrooge?" Jack asked.

"He immediately began making all kinds of changes to the house, which I had feared—until I saw them. He restored the house to its original 1930s condition, and then sold it back to me for a dollar."

"What?" Charley stared at her in disbelief. "How could he afford to do that?"

"He said he was investing in his future because he had fallen in love with me during the renovations. And, of course, I fell in love with him too." She paused for a moment, thinking back on it with a smile. "You know, before I made my decision, I remember telling myself that I needed to have blind faith that it would all work out."

"Blind faith?" Charley echoed.

"It was so scary at the time, but the outcome was far better than I imagined. Now my husband and I have two beautiful children who are growing up in their grand-mother's gorgeous home, and being debt-free allowed us to purchase this place—my home away from home."

Charley took a deep breath. Hearing Piper's story made her wonder who could possibly be her Scrooge. She didn't live in St. Nicholas, or have a home that could be threatened by a Scrooge. At least she now understood why Mary found it difficult to explain. "That's a won-derful story. Thank you for sharing it."

"My pleasure," Piper said as they got up. "Good luck."

As they exited the coffeehouse, Charley was trying to wrap her head around Piper's story. It amazed her how every Scrooge story she heard had so many twists and turns. It comforted her to know that they all ended on a happy note. "I'm not sure who my Scrooge will be, but I feel better after hearing Piper's outcome."

"I don't," Jack said, looking concerned. "What if your

boss is the Scrooge and he offers you a job halfway across the globe?"

"Then I won't take it."

"But what if you have to?"

"Then you'll come with me."

"And what if I can't?" He turned to face her. "I don't want to lose you again, Charley. We still need to work out our issue of living in different states, and I don't want this requirement to complicate matters even more."

How could I have ever doubted his feelings for me? She couldn't explain it, but she suddenly felt so grounded and sure of herself, and quite confident of their success as a couple.

"Then we won't let it. Like Piper, we'll have blind faith that our relationship will not only survive, but thrive. And as far as our location issue is concerned, I've been thinking that a permanent change of scenery might be good for me."

Jack couldn't hide his stunned reaction. He searched her face. "Are you saying what I think you're saying, that you're okay with moving out of LA?"

"I think it's time. I still need to talk to my boss to see if I can work remotely, and I also have to like Denver as much as I like it here, but yes, I want to give it a try."

Jack's grin took over his entire face. "Oh, Charley, you've made me a happy man." He planted a big kiss right on her mouth. She laughed, never thinking she'd see analytical Jack get so excited. "This is turning out to be the best day ever." He let out a short little howl.

"Come on, you goofball. Let's go find your family."

They crossed the street to the town square, and as they approached the sixty-foot Christmas tree, the sun came out from behind the clouds causing the freshly fallen snow to glisten like silvery beads of glass. "This place is so gorgeous."

"Would you like me to take your picture?" a man called out.

Charley and Jack turned to see Uncle Bill approaching with a spring in his step.

"Hey, Uncle Bill."

"I sure do love the sound of that," Bill said, patting his nephew on the back.

Jack looked past him. "Where's Mom and Dad?"

"Oh." He sighed with a wave of a hand. "I lost them in one of the stores, but they're on the way. They were going crazy with all the Christmas sales."

Jack chuckled. "My dad has become more of a discount fanatic than my mom."

"Hey, now, I heard that," Michael griped, approaching. "A good deal is a good deal."

"And he'll be getting plenty of them before we leave town," Allison added, right behind him. "I'll wager the car will be so stuffed with packages there won't be any room left for me."

Charley and Jack laughed as his parents took note of the massive tree.

"It's a beauty, isn't it?" Bill stared up at the town's centerpiece. "It's brought in the day after Thanksgiving, and starting tomorrow, the Christmas lights will be synched to Christmas music, which will play day and night until New Year's Eve."

"How lovely." Allison took in all the beautiful ornaments.

As Bill kept Allison and Michael captivated, explaining the detail that went into the tree's trimming, Jack and Charley took a selfie in front of it. *Our first selfie.*

Charley couldn't stop smiling, even after the picture was taken.

"And now I want to show you the famous Santa's mailbox that has touched all of our lives." Bill led the way like the town's official tour guide.

Jack's parents eagerly followed Bill while Charley and Jack lingered behind. He put his arm around her, and she could easily picture all of them on vacation together in Italy or France. She'd barely be able to concentrate on the museum tours that they'd no doubt be taking because her mind would be filled with Jack—just like it was at that moment.

As soon as the group came around the winding path, Allison spotted the mailbox. "Of course it's red." She went over to inspect it. "I love the intricate design on the legs and the candy cane flag."

"When the flag's up, there's mail inside," Jack told his parents. "Charley and I were conducting stakeouts at night, attempting to catch the elusive mail carrier."

"Did you?"

"Uh..." Jack scratched his head, casting an eye on Charley. "We tried," he said, no doubt hoping to skate through the subject.

"Oh, but you haven't heard the best part," Bill said. "We rigged the area with floodlights and motion sensors, making it impossible for the mail carrier to go unnoticed."

"So, who was it?" His dad bounced his gaze between Jack, Bill, and Charley.

"I wasn't there, but I heard it was an elf," Bill said, causing Charley and Jack to groan simultaneously.

Allison laughed. "An elf?"

"The jury's still out on that one." Jack sounded annoyed. "Charley and I didn't see the so-called *elf*, but apparently everyone else did."

"Probably some kid dressed as an elf," Michael said. "But you know, I can think of a few Scrooges whose names I wouldn't mind dropping in there." He tapped the top of the mailbox.

"Michael," Allison scolded him.

Charley stepped forward. "I'm starting to think it really is a magical mailbox. I put in Jack's name, and he showed up within hours."

"Coincidence," Jack brushed off.

Charley squelched a smile. She could clearly see how Jack got his skepticism from his father.

"Now, Jack. Don't be a Scrooge," his mother said.

"Charley's right," Bill spoke up, glancing at the mailbox. "We're together today because of this mailbox."

"How so?" asked Jack, putting his arm around Charley.

"Do you know about the mailbox's original purpose?" Bill asked.

"Mary told us about it this morning." Charley snuggled into Jack. "Is that what you did? You sent a letter?"

"Not at first, but only because I didn't believe it," Bill said. "I thought it was nonsense. But when I was ready to leave town, Joe asked if I could stay and help him decorate the inn for Christmas. The thought of decorating someone else's house suddenly sounded very appealing to me."

Jack chuckled. "I wonder why that was."

"Yeah." Bill smiled. "When I began stringing the lights with Joe, I had my first memory recall in years. I saw flashes of your dad and me stringing Christmas lights all over the roof. I never saw enough to identify

Michael as my brother, but the fact that I had seen something, well, that made me stay in St. Nicholas indefinitely. On Christmas Day, I heard more stories about the mailbox, and I started to wonder if they could be true. After Christmas, I couldn't get the mailbox out of my head. Every time I walked by it, I'd wonder if I dropped in a letter without a name or an address, would it somehow get delivered?"

"Did you finally do it?" Charley asked.

"Nope. Too much disappointment over the years had hardened me against believing in any kind of miracle." Bill stared at the mailbox with a pensive look on his face. "Then a couple of weeks ago, on Thanksgiving Day, I set aside my stubbornness and sent a message to the family I couldn't remember. That's how I even addressed my letter. 'To the Family I Can't Remember: I have amnesia and I don't remember who you are or where you live. Please come find me. I'm in St. Nicholas, Colorado.'"

"Oh, Bill." Allison put a hand to her heart.

"Did anything happen when you dropped in the letter?" asked Jack.

"Nothing that I could tell, except that I finally felt relieved. I let go of having to wonder about it. In fact, I decided right here, at this mailbox, to let go of my twenty-year search and call St. Nicholas home. And then you showed up, Jack, and started asking questions."

"I remember how you kept looking at me," Jack said. "But you also appeared spooked. Why?"

"I was afraid to believe in a miracle, I guess. When you said you were able to find people who'd gone missing, I was overwhelmed. I thought it was too good to be true. I actually thought you were going to help me find my family. It never occurred to me that *you* were my family." Bill got teary-eyed again as he placed his hand on the mailbox. "So you see, this mailbox truly *is* magical. It gave me a miracle. It brought you to me."

No one could speak because they were overcome with emotion. Everyone surrounded Bill and gave him a big hug.

Several minutes later, Allison dabbed her eyes. "That is one magical mailbox. Where can I get one online?"

Everyone burst with a much-needed laugh.

Michael wiped his face with his handkerchief. "Okay, family, let's go have some fun at the Christmas festival before we start blubbering again."

That afternoon, Charley and Jack's mom watched the men try to outdo each other in the Christmas stocking races before Jack took her tobogganing—something she had never experienced. She and Jack flew down the hill on a tiny sled and she loved it. As the day progressed, Charley felt like she was already part of Jack's family. Would her work situation go as smoothly? Maybe she needed to tip the scales in her favor by adding a new travel list to her blog. The more she worked remotely, the better her chances were to make a move out of LA.

Chapter Thirty-Four

Jack watched Charley laughing with his mom as they worked on building a snowman together. He was finally ready to admit that his reunion with Charley and his uncle was nothing short of a miracle. To think that his car navigation system had actually sent him directly to his uncle's residence, but he had been too blind to see him. Jack shook his head, knowing he'd never call his navigation system stupid again.

Jack truly felt blessed. Even his last hurdle, the long-distance issue, appeared to have found a possible solution. If all went right with Charley's job, and if he could help her fall in love with Denver, then he knew he could make her happy.

"It's almost four," Jack called out. "We better go."

"Okay, son." His dad got up from a bench with his uncle.

"What do you think of our snowman?" his mom asked.

The little guy was out of proportion and leaning to one side, but his pink macaron eyes and his broken candy cane smile made him memorable. "Best snowman I've ever seen."

"We nailed it." Charley high-fived his mom.

Jack smiled, putting his arm around her, and then they

traipsed over to the town square for the announcement of the home decoration contest.

"It's a full house," Charley said, looking around at the ever-growing crowd.

There was a makeshift podium erected next to the Christmas tree, with a few city officials buzzing around the back of it. Jack heard a hearty laugh and glanced over to see a burly man in red who looked exactly like the trucker from the diner.

Charley gasped, also catching sight of him. "Is that R.C. talking to Mary?"

"I think so. Come on." He grabbed Charley's hand and tried to hurry over, but several locals suddenly got in the way. When they finally reached her and Joe, R.C. was gone.

"Where's Bill and your parents?" Mary asked.

"They're on the other side." He looked over his shoulder and waved at his family to join them. "Where did R.C. go?"

"Who?" Mary plastered on a smile.

"Reality Check," Charley said. "The retired trucker you were talking to a minute ago."

"Oh, *that* R.C." Mary nodded, casting a quick glance at Joe. "He had to run." She looked past Jack and Charley as Bill and Jack's parents made their way over. "Bill, we're so glad you're here. I've got a really good feeling about this." She crossed her fingers and held them up.

As Bill and the Carrolls began talking about the model train display, Charley pulled Jack aside. "*That* R.C.?" she repeated. "There's more than one? And did you catch the brush-off?"

"Hard to miss. R.C. is definitely connected to the legend."

"Good evening, St. Nicholas!" a short, jolly man in his early sixties called out to the crowd who answered him with cheers and applause. "Is everyone enjoying the festivities?" The crowd roared loudly. "Very good. As you know, I'm here to announce this year's winner of the home decoration contest. It was a difficult decision, and I must commend all the residents for going above and beyond with so many additional decorations. However, one home stood out among the rest. This home, or should I say inn, has a miniature town of our beloved St. Nicholas and a working model train to boot. Joe and Mary Carroll!"

Mary squealed while Joe let out a big belly laugh as everyone erupted in whoops and hollers.

"Come on, Bill." Mary grabbed him by the arm and swept him up to the podium with Joe. The mayor handed Mary a plaque, and she took to the mic. "Thank you, Mr. Mayor, and a thank-you to our guests and friends who volunteered a full day of their time. But mostly, I want to thank Bill Brody for his incredible design. Bill, this is as much your win as it is ours."

The crowd clapped for Bill while the mayor jumped back in front of the microphone. "Fantastic job, Bill. The judges and I were so impressed that I'm hoping you'll say yes to being our official Christmas decoration designer for the entire town."

Bill looked totally shocked. Jack, Charley, and the Brodys clapped furiously as he was gently pushed by Mary to stand in front of the mic. "I'm…so honored. I would love to be your designer."

"Wonderful." The mayor shook Bill's hand.

"Can I have you look over here, please?" The town's

official photographer took a picture of the mayor with Uncle Bill and the Carrolls proudly holding the plaque.

"Now, it's time to put this tree in sync." The mayor pushed a big red button, and the lights on the tree began dancing to "Jingle Bell Rock."

"Congratulations," Charley said as they came down from the stage.

Jack clapped for them. "Well deserved."

"We couldn't have done it without you all." Mary was all smiles.

"Time to celebrate," Jack's dad said to the Carrolls. "We're going to get a bite to eat if you'd like to join us."

"We'd love to," Mary said, "but unfortunately our work is never done. Have a good time."

Charley and the Brodys headed over to the diner, where the hostess sat them at a large table in the middle of the restaurant.

"Man, oh, man, I have worked up an appetite today." Bill rubbed his hands together, looking over the menu. "The food here is almost as good as Mary's."

"I can second that," Charley said. "Jack and I have eaten here almost every night."

"Evening, folks." A good-looking guy in his late twenties stepped up to the table. "My name is Gabriel, and I'll be taking care of you this evening."

Charley and Jack shared a look—Angel, now Gabriel—the continuous Christmas theme was not lost on them.

"What can I get started for you?" Gabriel asked.

A half hour later, Charley and the Brodys were sharing plates and enjoying good conversation. Michael was telling funny stories about Bill, keeping everyone entertained.

"I'll take some more of that delicious turkey potpie." Allison held up her plate for Jack to scoop two spoonfuls onto it. "Splitting meals is a great idea."

Jack smiled. "Charley got me hooked on it, way back in high school."

"I think you might have started a new tradition." Michael winked at Charley as he helped himself to some Italian meatballs.

Allison looked around the table. "Speaking of traditions, we need to decide where we're all celebrating Christmas. Will it be here, Denver, or Los Angeles?" She set her eyes on Charley, and Charley's heart soared. First Jack, and now his mom was including her in Christmas plans.

Jack spoke up. "I've already invited Charley to Denver."

"How wonderful!" Allison said. "Grandma Nellie is going to be very happy."

"Does she know?" Charley asked. "About Bill?"

"We spoke to her on the phone this morning, and it was one big cryfest," Allison said. "She always believed Bill was alive like Jack."

"She did." Jack nodded. "I gave her progress reports just about every time I spoke with her."

"I can't wait to meet her," Charley said.

"Bill, would you like to come to Denver for Christmas and stay a week or two after the New Year?"

"Like to?" He dropped his fork as a big grin took over his face. "I'd love to!"

"Excuse me, Jack?" a familiar female voice interrupted.

Charley glanced up to see Jack's ex standing at their table. *Lisa? What is she still doing here?*

"I'm sorry to intrude," Lisa said, looking at Jack anxiously, "but can I speak to you for a moment?"

"What do you want?" He put his arm around Charley.

"Can I talk to you *alone*?"

"No. *Please*. Go home."

Lisa frowned, wringing her hands. "I can't. I've tried."

"What do you mean?" Irritation rippled through his voice.

"I got a flat tire on the way out of town, so I tried again yesterday morning and my car stalled. It was completely dead. A mechanic helped me push it to the side of the road. Now he says it's going to take a week to fix."

"I'm sorry to hear that," he said on a sigh, "but I'm not sure there's anything I can do about it."

She glanced at the others, nervously biting her lower lip, before she put her gaze back on Jack. "The mechanic told me about the Scrooge Legend. He said my car probably conked out because I was meant to stay in town. He said it happens all the time to people who have no idea they've been swept up in the Scrooge Legend. Did you involve me, Jack? Did you suggest me as a Scrooge?"

The irritation on Jack's face instantly vanished, leaving him ghost white from shock, which told Charley everything she needed to know. "She was the one you suggested?"

He met her gaze, confusion filling his eyes. "I... I didn't think it was real. I just wanted to get the mailbox door to open."

She wanted to believe him, yet how could he have been thinking about Lisa while he was standing at the mailbox with her? When she'd suggested Jack, she had been testing the theory, but she'd also wanted him to show up in St. Nicholas. She'd wanted to see him again. She shook her head, not understanding. "Wasn't there another name you could have used?"

"We were talking about drug dealers and bank robbers. I didn't—"

"Couples reunite all the time under the Scrooge Legend," Lisa said. "At least that's what the mechanic told me. I'm sure Jack—"

"Stop!" Jack ran a hand over his face in what looked to be pure exasperation. He then took a deep breath and spoke slowly to his ex. "Let me say this as plainly as I can. You are not my girlfriend. Charley is my girlfriend, and you will never ever be my girlfriend again. Now, *please*, leave me alone." He turned to Charley. "I didn't suggest her for the reasons you might think. I—"

Lisa stepped closer to the table. "Jack, if I could just—"

Charley shot out of her chair. "I don't know why you refuse to listen to Jack, and I don't know why you can't leave St. Nicholas," Charley heard herself saying in a surprisingly calm voice. "Maybe you need to regain your Christmas spirit, maybe you're here to meet your soulmate, or maybe your car really *is* broken. But whatever you think is going on between you and Jack, isn't."

"How would you know?" Lisa stiffened, seeming offended. "You didn't even know we'd been dating."

"That's enough," Jack said, standing next to Charley, as if the two of them together became one united front.

And that was when Charley finally felt it, Jack's strong, unwavering loyalty to her. Why he'd suggested Lisa as a Scrooge no longer mattered. She had complete faith in him. She could see a real future with him, and she was going to fight for it.

Charley gently laid a hand on Jack. "You're right, Lisa. I didn't know you two had dated, but I do know Jack and how he feels about me. It's unfortunate you haven't come to terms with his decision on ending it with you, so this is what I'm going to do. I'm going to leave, in order for you to truly grasp the situation between you two. But let me save you some time. No matter what you tell yourself, no matter how hard you try, you can't make somebody love you." Charley gathered her things, then looked at his parents and Bill. "Thank you for a lovely day." She turned and walked away.

Jack ran after her. "Charley, wait." He caught her right at the door. "Please don't go."

"I don't want to." She searched his eyes. "But I need to, so that you're able to get things resolved with her."

"It is resolved. I broke up with her. Why she won't accept it is something she'll need to figure out on her own."

"I would agree if you hadn't suggested her as a Scrooge. Jack, anyone can see she's having a hard time facing facts. But you thought enough about her to put her name in the mailbox, and now she can't leave. Whether you like it or not, you're wrapped up in it."

Jack sighed. "I hear you, Charley, but what more can I do?"

She looked away, trying to understand, thinking about all the Scrooge stories she'd heard, and about everything that had happened between them, and then she saw it. "Do what you do best. Listen to her. That's how you helped me."

"Hey, guys," Tom called as he and Rebecca approached. "We're heading back to the B&B, if you need a ride."

"That would be great." Charley zipped up her coat, then looked at Jack. "You got this."

Jack opened his mouth to protest, but was cut off by Rebecca nudging him.

"We'll take good care of her, Jack, don't you worry," she said as Tom opened the door for his wife and Charley.

Before Jack could say another word, the door quickly closed behind them.

Chapter Thirty-Five

Jack could not understand what was going on. Charley thought he could fix things by listening to Lisa, only it hadn't helped when he listened to her for three solid hours while he'd broken up with her. Everything was going so well. Why had he made such a stupid mistake and put Lisa's name in that mailbox? All he wanted was for her to be happy without him. Why couldn't she want that too?

Jack trudged back to the table and discovered that things were worse than when he left. Lisa was sitting in Charley's chair and she was crying. Jack wanted nothing but to grab his keys off the table and go—only he couldn't. He had to stay and figure it out for the sake of his relationship with Charley.

"My job was the one thing I could depend on," Lisa managed through tears, "and now I've lost that too."

"You'll get another one." Jack's mom reached over and patted her hand.

"Is everything all right?" his dad asked.

"Better than here," Jack replied. "What happened?"

"Lisa's boss called to tell her she'd been let go."

"I'm sorry to hear that." He sat next to her.

"It's not your fault." She wiped her tears off with her napkin. "I didn't mean to barge in on you, I really didn't, but I don't understand what's happening. I got evicted from my apartment for absolutely no reason, which made me think I should come up here even though you told me not to." She looked at him with puffy red eyes. "I wasn't going to come here, Jack, you've got to believe me, but I kept hearing this phrase in my head, that if I drove to St. Nicholas, I'd find true love. How crazy is that?"

"After everything I've experienced here, it's not," he said. "To me, it sounds like you were listening to a gut feeling."

"I was. I thought that maybe you had changed your mind about our relationship. But when I discovered you had moved on from me so quickly, I realized what a fool I've been. I don't understand how my instincts could have been so wrong. I can't believe I came up here for nothing, and now I've lost my job."

"Maybe all of this is happening for a reason," Jack said. "Maybe you need to think about moving to a new town where you'll find a new job and make new friends."

"You think so?"

"Haven't you been wanting to move because of your noisy neighbors?"

She nodded, then gave him a sheepish look. "It was part of the reason I pushed moving on to the next level. I knew we weren't ready, but I figured we'd work it out."

"Oh." Jack couldn't hide his surprised reaction. "I wish you would have been straight with me. I could have helped you find another apartment."

"I know, I'm sorry. I've wanted to move for months. Come to think of it, I've also wanted to quit my job, so maybe the little voice in my head wasn't off after all."

"Now that you don't have anything to tie you down, you could make some major changes," he suggested.

"I'd like to." She shrugged. "I just don't know how to go about it."

"What are your career aspirations?" his mom asked.

"I don't know. I don't like to work. I like parties, and friends, and I just realized I sound like a snob." She shook her head with an embarrassed laugh. "What I meant was, work feels like work. I was an assistant to a cold, heartless boss, and I despised every minute of it."

"It's a good thing you got out of that toxic environment," his mom said.

"Yeah, the only days I enjoyed were when I was in charge of planning the office functions. My boss was so pleased with a reception I'd planned for important clients that he was nice to me for two whole weeks."

"How come you never told me about your caustic relationship with your boss?" Jack asked.

"You're out there catching criminals. My differences with him seemed petty."

He felt awful for missing how miserable she'd been at work. "Nothing is petty when it interferes with a person's well-being. I'm sorry I didn't know."

"It's okay." She offered him a brief smile. "I'm glad we're talking about it now because I just realized something. I really enjoy event planning. Those days didn't feel like work to me. Maybe I could find a job in that industry."

"Seems like a much better fit for you. I think you'd be a fantastic event coordinator," he said.

"Thank you." She sat up a little taller as their waiter reappeared.

"Are we ready for dessert?" Gabriel asked.

"I believe they are," Lisa said, standing. "Thank you, Jack, and Mrs. Brody for listening. Again, I'm so sorry for the interruption." She put on her hat, scarf and gloves, something she rarely did in Denver for fear they would mess up her hair.

Jack frowned. "How did you get here without a car?"

"I walked."

"It's starting to come down out there," Michael said, and everyone looked out the window.

Jack couldn't have Lisa wandering around in freezing cold temperatures. "You're not walking. Come on. Sit down. Have something to eat, and then I'll take you wherever you need to go."

"I've intruded on you and your family too much already."

"My shift is over in fifteen minutes," Gabriel said. "I'll be happy to help you folks out. I can give you a ride." He set his gaze on Lisa.

"Thank you, but—" She glanced at the waiter and did a double take. Disappointment seemed to drain from her face as she couldn't stop staring at the good-looking guy. "What's your name?"

"Gabriel."

"Thank you, Gabriel." Her eyes seemed much brighter. "I'm Lisa, and I'll take you up on your offer."

"Great." Gabriel flashed her an impressive grin and Jack wondered if the sudden spark between them was related to the Scrooge Legend. "Are you staying in town?"

"Yes. At Mrs. Richardson's out on Evergreen Lane."

"*I* live on Evergreen Lane."

"What?" Lisa let out a little laugh. "This is a happy coincidence."

"It sure is." Gabriel moved closer to her, forgetting the rest of the party at the table. "You're going to love Mrs. Richardson. I've known her since I was five years old. She'll pamper you so much, you're not going to want to leave."

"I'm really starting to like St. Nicholas." Lisa beamed, tucking her chin down in a flirtatious way.

"I'm so glad to hear it," he said. "Now, let me get all of you a piece of our famous angel food cake. It's on me."

"That's very sweet of you. Thank you." She watched him go, then sat back down and opened her handbag, taking out her makeup pouch.

Jack and his parents were throwing glances at each other, not daring to speak, while Lisa was in her own world, fixing her face in the mirror of a tiny compact.

Bill, on the other hand, seemed to be the only one not fazed by what had just happened. "Did Mary tell you about the ripple effect?" he asked Jack.

"Ripple effect?" Jack gave him an exhausted look. Did he really want to know?

"As you've discovered, the Scrooge Legend doesn't only affect one person, it affects many. It has a ripple effect," Bill explained. "And this right here is the ripple effect in action." He laughed as he polished off the last bite of the turkey potpie.

"Here you go." Gabriel set down a huge piece of angel food cake covered with drizzled chocolate right in front of Lisa. "I brought five forks in case anyone else wants to try it."

"Thank you." Lisa smiled at Gabriel before he walked away, then took a small taste of the cake. "Delicious." She passed out the forks. "Dig in, everyone."

Bill picked up a fork and started at the opposite end while Jack and his parents only watched.

"This is so good." Lisa purred, slowly taking another bite. She closed her eyes for a moment, seeming to savor the flavor, then she fixed her gaze on Jack. "I'm sorry it didn't work out between us, but I truly hope you and Charley are happy together."

Bill cleared his throat and motioned to the front door. "I believe your work is done here, young man."

Jack picked up his keys and cell phone off the table, then hurried out the door.

Charley sat in the back of Tom and Rebecca's car, forcing herself to make idle chitchat even though her thoughts were far away. She wanted to believe that she and Jack would be okay, that he'd be able to finally get through to his ex, but she didn't know for sure. Lisa seemed so obsessed with Jack. Leaving him with her was difficult, but the thought of having her show up indefinitely was worse.

Before going back to the B&B, Tom and Rebecca stopped by Santa's mailbox to drop in a wish for their friend Dave, and then they posed for a few pictures in front of the Christmas tree in the town square. Charley took some great ones of them with the snow falling around them. It not only reminded her of her walk with Jack, but the couple was standing in the exact same spot where she and Jack had stood. The same spot where she'd been so incredibly happy only a few hours earlier. *How fast life changed.*

When they finally arrived back at the B&B, Tom and Rebecca went in the direction of a warm fire in the living room, while Charley started for the stairs.

Mary came bounding out of the kitchen and almost collided with her. "Oh, Charley, excuse me!"

Charley quickly cast her eyes to the ground, but it was too late. Mary could immediately tell something was wrong.

"What happened?" she asked, her voice full of concern.

"His ex happened."

"Oh," Mary said on a sigh. "The requirement."

Charley frowned. "This has nothing to do with—" She froze, took a breath. She started to replay the conversation she'd had with Lisa over in her head. And then she saw it. "She's the Scrooge." Her voice was breathy. "Mary, I think she's the Scrooge!" Charley grabbed her hand. "Please, tell me she is."

"What did you give her?" she asked calmly.

"I… I gave her what is most dear to me." Charley's eyes riveted to hers. "I gave her time with Jack."

Mary smiled, nodding. "And how do you feel right now?"

Charley put her hand to her chest, trying to slow her racing heart. She had passed through anger, through betrayal, through fear. She'd taken a chance on love again, let it go, and it had come back to her stronger than ever. She hoped Jack would finally get through to Lisa because she wanted her to be happy. She wanted their issues to be resolved so they could all enjoy a life filled with love. "I feel hopeful that it will all be okay. That everything will work out because we're truly meant to be."

"Well done, Charley, well done."

She threw her arms around Mary and gave her a big hug. "I've got to find Jack. Is he here? Did he come back?"

"I don't know, dear. Did you check his room?"

Charley took the stairs two at a time. She flew down the hallway to the very last room on the left and banged on the door. "Jack! Jack!" She waited a second, then two. She banged again when she heard an alert come in on her phone. Thinking it was from Jack, she withdrew her phone and discovered that Reality Check had left a comment on her blog. She quickly opened it.

My Dear Sweet One,
This thread is done, and it's the last that I'll be sending. True love awaits, don't hesitate, go find your happy ending.

Charley smiled, and then her eyes shot up, hearing commotion coming from downstairs. A moment later, Jack appeared, out of breath, at the top of the stairs. He came to a dead stop when he saw Charley standing by his door.

Their gazes locked on to each other, and all the things she wanted to say to him rushed through her head. She wanted to tell him how much she loved him and how much she missed him the second she left. She wanted to tell him that she would move anywhere, at any time, to be with him. She had so much to say, but she didn't know where to begin.

"Fun fact," she finally managed through a voice breaking with emotion. "The holidays are when couples break up the most." She took a step toward him.

"You consider that a fun fact?" Jack took a step toward her.

"People don't call me The Cold Hard Facts Queen for no reason." She took another step.

"Here's a real fun fact: the most streamed song last year was 'All I Want for Christmas is You.'"

Her chin trembled as she slowly nodded. "One point to Jack Brody. That's a good fun fact."

"Yeah, it is," he said, smiling. "Because it's true."

She ran into his arms. He held her tight before he picked her up and twirled her.

"I love you, Charlotte," he whispered, staring into her eyes. "I love you so much."

"Oh, Jack, I love you, too, with all of my heart."

Jack found her mouth and tenderly kissed her. When he at last pulled back, Charley searched his eyes. She saw so much love, devotion, and trust. She saw someone to laugh with and cry with. Jack kissed her again on her lips before he kissed her on one cheek, and then the other, and then on her forehead. He covered her face with little kisses until she couldn't stop laughing. He then put his arm around her as they walked down the hallway, and she snuggled into him knowing that wherever she was, as long as she was with Jack, she would always be home.

Epilogue

Two days later, Mary sat relaxing in the living room, reading on her iPad, when Joe came in with a tray of milk and cookies.

"You are such a dear," she said as he set the tray down on the coffee table and sat next to her.

"You worked so hard on this one, Mrs. Carroll."

"So did you, Mr. Carroll." She took a cookie off the plate.

Joe glanced at her iPad. "What are you reading?"

"Charley's blog. She announced her new recommendation post called 'Great Places in The States.' Want to take a guess which town is first on her list?" She handed her iPad to Joe.

"Oh, boy," he said, skimming the article. "We're going to be bombarded with visitors."

"Nothing we can't handle." She took a drink of milk. "Besides, everyone needs a breather and a *reality check* once in a while." She winked at Joe.

"Yes, R.C., they do." He took a cookie for himself. "I never knew my wife was such an amazing poet."

"I have a wonderful muse," she said, curling up next to him.

He put his arm around her, enjoying a little peace and quiet.

A moment later they heard *ting, ting, ting, ting.* It was the familiar sound of metal bouncing off the bricks inside the fireplace, and out dropped an ornate silver-and-gold metallic tube.

Joe sighed. "I just sat down."

"Don't I know it." Mary got up and went over to the fireplace. After setting the fire screen to one side, she picked up the tube, opened one of the ends, and pulled out a scroll. "Oh, my." Her eyes flew over the elaborate cursive writing, reading as fast as she could. "It looks like Santa's sending us another Scrooge. And this one is going to be a doozy."

* * * * *

Acknowledgments

Even though this is my sixth novel, *Colorado Christmas Magic* is my first with Harlequin's Carina Press imprint and their amazing publishing team. I am so grateful in particular to my fantastic editor, Deborah Nemeth, for believing in *Colorado Christmas Magic* from the beginning, and whose keen eye and wonderful suggestions have made my story a stronger one. I'd also like to give a heartfelt thank-you to my acquiring editor, Stephanie Doig, who brought me into the wonderful Harlequin family.

A big thank-you to my early-on editors—Caroline Tolley for showing me the path forward, and Barbara Bettis for her great insight.

I wouldn't be able to be an author if it weren't for my support team. I am blessed to have such a sweet and caring husband who takes it upon himself to do all the errands and bring home dinner so I can keep working. Thank you, honey. And a tremendous thank-you to my sister who goes above and beyond, reading every version of every scene. She can recite this book in her sleep.

Thank you so much to my dear friends Kerry Gutierrez, Luisa Leschin, Lucy Lin, and Frank Sharp who have read these pages at all hours of the night, and thank you to Danielle Leigh Reads, Danica Sorber, and Barb Barkley for their added support.

Many thanks to all of my readers out there—may the magic of the holiday season bring you love, joy, and laughter that will last throughout the year.

About the Author

Ever since she can remember, Caitlin McKenna has always loved a good story. Whether it was in the form of a long-winded joke told by her dad around the dinner table, or an outlandish story of alien abduction and missing homework imagined by one of her classmates, she loved to hear every one of them. Naturally, her love of a good story landed her in Hollywood where she embarked on an acting and screenwriting career.

While in the theatre, she had the opportunity to play complex characters like Anne Boleyn in *Anne of the Thousand Days*, and Eliza Doolittle in *Pygmalion,* which has helped her tremendously as a writer when fleshing out her own characters. Even though Caitlin saw her stories as movies in her head, she felt the need to have more control over them, so she switched her focus from screenplays to novels.

Now she enjoys writing any story where love drives the narrative. Her previously published novels include *No Such Luck, My Big Fake Irish Life, Super Natalie, Manifesting Mr. Right,* and her dystopian thriller, *Logging Off.* When not writing, she can be found at one of the major studios working as a voice-over actress and voice-casting director for an upcoming movie or television show.

Caitlin lives with her husband and two spoiled dachshunds in Southern California, and is working on her next novel.

Website: CaitlinMcKenna.com

Twitter: Twitter.com/CaitMcKenna

Instagram: Instagram.com/AuthorCaitlinMcKenna/

Facebook: Facebook.com/AuthorCaitlinMcKenna/

Email: AuthorCaitlinMcKenna@gmail.com

Events coordinator Violet won't allow the Grinch-y heir to Peach Grove's finest mansion to back out of the annual Christmas tour, even if it means helping him…and risking her heart. Brady's in town only to sell the ancestral home before returning to his Atlanta law firm, not to host a Tinsel Tour for an annoying elf. But Violet is all about making holiday magic happen…

Keep reading for an excerpt from
Christmas on Peach Tree Lane *by Jules Bennett!*

Chapter One

Don't get your tinsel in a tangle.
** Violet Calhoun*

"You get a headband, you get a headband. Everybody gets a headband."

Violet Calhoun tossed reindeer antler headbands to her best friends, Simone and Robin. Robin put her festive accessory in place between her bangs and ponytail while Simone twirled hers between her fingertips and glared.

"Why do we have to do this every year? It's not even Halloween, yet," Simone complained.

Robin laughed. "Dates are irrelevant with Violet and we do this because we love her…tacky headbands and all."

While they were all the very best of friends, and had been since they were forced into a group science project in first grade, Simone didn't embrace the holidays quite the same way Violet did. Violet figured Robin just appeased her to keep the peace.

Actually, Violet didn't know anyone who embraced this season in her enthusiastic way. Obviously that's why she'd been deemed the best candidate to spearhead the Tinsel Tour every December here in Peach Grove, Georgia.

Decorating historic Southern mansions in a million

twinkle lights, garland, gold and red ribbons, and anything else she could find for that wow factor was seriously what she lived for. Each home had a theme and each one was magical in its own, charming way. Twelve months out of the year she was seeking inspiration and new décor.

"Don't you think it's a bit early to start wearing these?" Simone asked.

Violet adjusted hers and fluffed her long curls around her shoulders. "I'm going as a human Christmas stocking to the town carnival."

Robin shrugged. "I like it. Creative."

"Creative?" Simone laughed. "She's something Christmasy every year. Although the human snow globe was pretty cool. Creative would be if she went as a Playboy Bunny or even a typical witch."

Violet gasped. "You'll never see me in either of those costumes, thank you very much. And the event is for the community with families, not a tasteless bachelorette party."

"Well, I'm going as a Greek goddess," Robin declared. "It's comfortable and pretty, which are two components I want in my Halloween costume."

"What about you?" Violet asked Simone. "Wait. Let me guess. You're doing the Playboy Bunny?"

Simone pursed her lips. "Funny, but no. I opted for Jasmine from *Aladdin*."

Violet gasped. "Ooh, you'll look sexy. I like it."

"Thank you. I haven't been working out these past six months to hide this new body." Simone gave a mock bow. "So, where's Mama Lori?"

Violet's mother was always with them. Growing up, the three girls were always together and usually at Violet's house where Lori was always treating each of them as her own. When they were teens, Robin's mother passed away suddenly and then after graduation, Simone's mother took off with her free-spirited boyfriend and they barely visited Peach Grove. So, the three adopted Lori as their group mother and often included her in their GNO.

"Mom isn't going to make it," she told her friends. "She's out with Porter again."

"Whoa," Robin exclaimed. "Weren't they just out last night?"

Violet nodded. "They've been seeing each other for about four months now. I'm really happy for her."

Her parents had divorced when Violet was fifteen, but they'd parted on good terms. They hadn't been in love for years and had just stayed together for her. When her father remarried, Violet and her mother went to the ceremony. Violet loved how her parents remained not only supportive of everything she did, but also friends with each other. Sometimes people could love each other and just not be meant for each other—her parents were proof of that.

And now her mother was giddy like a teenager with a new crush and Violet couldn't be happier. Lori Calhoun had dated over the years, but nobody had captured her attention like city mayor Porter Crosby.

"Good for her," Simone chimed in. "I'm glad someone has come into her life that pulls her away from us. She deserves to date and find love."

"I don't know that she's looking for long term," Violet said. "She's been independent for so long, but I agree. I'm glad she's found someone to go out with."

"I hope you didn't make her wear a damn headband," Simone mumbled.

"I mean, really, like I'd do that."

Violet wasn't about to mention that she had taken her

mother a festive headband with a small light-up Christmas tree earlier in the day.

Sipping on her pinot, Violet glanced across to her two friends. "So, while I have you guys here—"

"Please don't say it," Simone demanded.

Violet merely smiled. They truly did have that special bond where she rarely had to say what she was thinking. Some friendships were stronger than any blood relation. They had their own unique sisterhood.

"I thought we were having a relaxing girls' night in." Simone set the headband on the sofa beside her and reached for her wineglass on the side table. "I can't relax wearing that and I most definitely cannot relax if you have us helping you put up Christmas decorations the day before Halloween."

Violet slipped around the corner into the narrow hallway and carried in a tote, then she went back and forth until she'd pulled in the other six.

"Okay, we love you, but even I need to step in here." Robin came to her feet and glanced around. "You are aware you live in about a one thousand square foot space and you have enough decorations for more than double that size? And you don't even have the tree out yet, which will take up even more room."

"Trees," Violet corrected. "I've decided to put up three this year."

"We rest our case," Simone added.

Violet plucked the lid off one tote and squealed at her beloved white shimmery snowflakes, which she suspended from her arched doorways.

"No negativity, please," she told her friends as she started pulling out the décor. "You don't have to help if you don't want, but don't bash the most wonderful time of the year."

Simone straightened out her legs and sighed. "I'll just watch if it's all the same. You know I get twitchy if I put up anything before Thanksgiving, even if it's in someone else's house."

Violet shook her head. "I don't even know how we've remained friends."

"Because I ply you with raspberry macarons that make you weep."

Simone Adams owned Mad Batter, honestly the best bakery Violet had ever encountered. The place was slammed at any given time and to get a wedding cake from Simone would require getting on the list nearly a year in advance. After she won twenty thousand dollars on the popular TV show *Bring the Dough*, her business skyrocketed.

Robin shifted around to face Simone. "Did you bring macarons?"

"'Fraid not. But I am working on a new flavor for the holidays. I'm thinking one with an espresso, caramel blend and a spin on my vanilla bean with a little champagne in the filling. I promise to let you two be my tasters."

Robin lifted her glass in a mock cheers. "Sign me up for that."

Violet popped the lids off all of the totes because she had to find her garland first. The main rule of decorating was to layer and always start at the bottom or the base. She needed her window and fireplace garland. Not that she had a real fireplace, she only had a faux façade she'd purchased at an estate sale a couple years ago. She'd promptly put it in the space between her two windows overlooking the alley behind her shop.

One day, she vowed, she'd have a big traditional Southern home with multiple fireplaces and a curved banister leading to the second story. There would be lots of porch space on both levels of the home, and her children and husband would help her decorate and bake cookies. She thought she'd be in that position by now, considering she was thirty-three, but it was good to have goals. Family life wasn't for everyone, and she appreciated that her friends actually didn't want that familial lifestyle… but Violet dreamed of the future.

"She's doing it again."

Violet nestled a swag of greenery onto her window ledge and laughed at Robin's whispered statement. "I can still hear you and I was only daydreaming a little."

"Are we ready for these next two months?" Simone asked. "I'm afraid this will be our last girls' night until after the new year."

"Business is booming." Robin curled her feet beneath her on the sofa. "The Tinsel Tour alone is keeping me busy with all the fresh wreaths you requested."

Robin Foster owned Boulevard Bouquet, only the best florist in the entire state. Well, maybe not the entire state, but at least the tri-county area. She was the go-to for all things horticulture and outdoorsy. She could whip up an arrangement worthy of a royal wedding and never chip her signature pink polish.

"You know I appreciate how hard you work behind the scenes for me." Violet reached for her wineglass from the end table. "And, don't shoot me, but I need to add twenty more evergreen garlands." She cringed and shut her eyes, ready for the backlash.

"Already done," Robin laughed. "You think I order conservatively when it comes to you and Christmas? I actually have thirty more bundles coming in and I knew if you didn't ask for them, you'd still find a way to use every bit."

Violet relaxed and focused on her friend. "You know me so well."

Robin adjusted her headband and shifted on the sofa. "How's the chocolate walk menu looking, Simone?"

"Overwhelming at the moment, but nothing a ton of extra hours can't make up for. You know I do my best work last minute and my team is used to me." Simone groaned and dropped her head back. "Ugh. I just remembered the newspaper asked for an exclusive on Monday morning. I don't know how that slipped my mind."

"That's wonderful," Violet exclaimed. "I'm sure it will be front page, which will only help push those ticket sales for the events this season."

Not to mention help aid in a little surprise she hadn't told them about yet. Violet was so eager to tell them the exciting news, but she wanted to let the news naturally fall into the conversation.

Peach Grove was about to become a bit more popular, and Violet knew her friends would be thrilled...once they got over the shocking announcement.

In the not so distant past, their quaint area had become almost a ghost town. Businesses had closed, families had moved to larger cities to restart their lives. But Violet, Simone, and Robin grew up here, they loved this place, and slowly but surely they were breathing new life back by using their individual talents.

They'd each taken affordable, run-down buildings and started their businesses and saved money by living in the lofts above. Little by little, with word of mouth and the power of social media, plus Simone's television debut, their shops grew bigger than any of them expected. Weddings were the leading draw and the ladies realized they all complemented each other in that market. They often did cross-promoting and planned marketing strategies together to pull in even more brides.

Three years ago, Violet brought back the Tinsel Tour, a festive, fun tour of the old town mansions that was founded by William Jackson fifty years ago. So this year was a major milestone and she intended to go all out… even more than usual.

Violet had always loved the annual event when she'd been a kid, wondering what it would be like to grow up and actually call one of those places her own. But now, she got to decorate them and set the stage to launch Peach Grove's Christmas season.

Her seasonal Christmas shop, Yule Sleigh Me, was the perfect opportunity to use her creative skills and assist others in making their homes beautiful or finding that perfect gift.

"Make sure to talk up the tickets for the tour and the walk since the proceeds will go back to the city for that new park for the kids," Violet reminded her. "Oh, and if you could name-drop William Jackson, that would be great. His passing is a huge void to the community, but his home will still be on the tour."

She hoped. She'd yet to speak to William's grandson, who was now the new owner. Granted the man would have to actually come to town for Violet to speak to him because her phone calls had gone ignored, as had her emails and the save-the-date cards she'd mailed.

"I haven't seen Brady Jackson in years," Simone said, picking up her headband and twirling it enough to make the little bells jingle. "Not since our third and final date when we realized we had nothing in common and he seemed offended that I was a vegetarian."

Violet nearly snorted wine out of her nose. "You didn't tell him on the first two dates?"

"It never came up." Simone defended herself with a defensive huff. "The first date was a charity event we met at and the second was a movie so I had popcorn and Milk Duds. The third, he picked me up and we went to a steakhouse. I nearly ended things right there, but I decided to go in. When I got a salad and a side of fries he wasn't impressed. Which was fine, I wasn't impressed with how much he talked about his work, spreadsheets, and all the hours he spent in the office. Honestly, I'm surprised we made it three dates."

"There must've been one redeeming quality," Robin suggested.

Simone shrugged. "He was a pretty good kisser, but we didn't do anything beyond that."

"Well, I'm not looking to kiss him or anything else." Violet swirled the final drink and tossed it back. "I just need to know when I can get in to decorate and if he'll be around for the tour or if I can get a key."

Really, this was cutting it close. As the date closed in, Violet found herself growing quite twitchy. Hadn't he received the save the date back in August? Seriously. This was not a surprise she was springing on him. His grandfather started this entire thing, for pity's sake. You'd think the grandson of the town's equivalent of a patriarch would want to participate.

"Good luck." Simone snickered. "If he's anything like he used to be, I'm sure he'll send his assistant to handle the house and talk with you. And I wouldn't hold my breath on getting that key."

Violet didn't care at this point who she dealt with or who let her inside, so long as the Jackson mansion remained the last stop on the tour. Between William's passing just a few months ago and the fiftieth anniversary, this home was more important than any other.

Every estate had its own character and charm, but there was something about William's that had always tugged at Violet. Maybe it was the history, maybe it was the second-story balcony that stretched the length of the home and matched the grand porch. The tree-lined drive that provided a canopy of shade from the century-old oaks only added to the magnetism.

"We've lost her again," Simone whispered.

"Is she ever really here?" Robin laughed. "Nobody daydreams like Violet."

Violet rolled her eyes. "I can hear you guys, you know? I'm excellent at multitasking."

She turned to face all of the open totes and grabbed a bundle of gold flowers she always used to decorate her tiny breakfast table. She plucked one flower from the bundle and crossed the space to shove it behind Simone's ear.

"If you won't wear the headband, at least do something festive," Violet complained. "You're sucking the fun out of my apartment."

Simone laughed and tapped the flower. "I'll take this over that headband any day."

With her friends plied with their first glass of wine and all in good moods, Violet couldn't hold in the news anymore.

Waving a pair of gold candlesticks in the air, Violet cleared her throat. "Okay, so I have a major announcement. It might add to the stress of the season. We will have to all pitch in and do extra work, maybe even pull in some others to make everything flawless, but I think it's spectacular and I hope you guys—"

"What is it?" Simone yelled.

Robin laughed and held up her hands. "Why do I always have to play referee with you two. Simone, just let her ramble, she'll get around to it. Violet, spit it out before Simone explodes."

Violet bounced on her feet and clutched the candlesticks close to her chest as if she could hold on to this magical moment. An announcement of this magnitude couldn't be given while seated.

"Oh, this must be good." Robin's smile widened. "You're getting extra dramatic."

"You mean there's a time she's calm?" Simone asked.

Violet crossed her tiny living area and came to stand in front of the window. "Okay, so I got a call today that had me a little nervous at first, but the more I think about this idea, the more excited I'm getting."

"And the call was from?" Simone asked, motioning for Violet to get on with it.

"You're not going to believe this." Violet couldn't believe it herself, but she was over-the-moon excited…and a little terrified. "*Simply Southern Magazine*."

Robin's eyes widened. "What for?"

Violet squealed and Simone groaned. "Oh, no," her friend said. "No, no, no."

With a nod, Violet went on. "Oh, yes. They want to do a feature article about Peach Grove and our holiday events. And…"

Simone narrowed her eyes. "And what? Don't make me stab you with that reindeer headband."

Violet twisted her mouth and muttered, "They might

want to interview each of us about our roles and our businesses."

Robin's laughter filled the living area and Simone simply fell back against the couch with her eyes closed. Her friends' reactions were exactly what Violet had expected, so at least she was somewhat mentally prepared.

Simone held up her hands. "Wait. How much time do we have to prepare for this? Because I have a couple of weddings coming up before I can start work on the chocolate walk menu."

Violet paced in her living area. "Well, they would like to come in two weeks so they can get the magazine to publication in time, but I told them we couldn't possibly have things set up by then."

"Well, that's something," Simone stated. "What did they say?"

Violet paused and cringed. "That they're coming anyway and plan on documenting the process."

Simone and Robin stared at each other, then back to Violet. From their wide eyes and gaping mouths, she had to assume that's the exact look she had when first presented the idea.

"This will be fun," she assured them. "Trust me."

Don't miss Christmas on Peach Tree Lane *by Jules Bennett, available now wherever ebooks are sold.*

www.CarinaPress.com